PRAISE FOR *GIRLS OUR AGE*

"Nostalgic, aching, and sharply observed, *Girls Our Age* is a story about the friendships that shape us, the lives we think everyone else is living, and the quiet heartbreak of realizing we only ever see the polished version. With tender precision, Phoebe Thompson reminds us that girlhood never really leaves us and that the people who knew us then often know us best now."

—Alissa DeRogatis, author of *Call It What You Want*

"*Girls Our Age* is full of heart, tenderness, and characters who are so lifelike they might as well be my own friend group, with all the struggles, doubts, and aches of twentysomething adulthood. Thompson's empathetic and riveting debut pulls on the heartstrings, will make you text your friends just to tell them how much you love them, and announces an exciting new voice in fiction."

—Isabel Banta, author of *Honey*

"I see myself and my closest friends in the characters of *Girls Our Age*, an honest and gripping coming-of-age story about the ways that friendships bend and waver in your twenties, only to grow back stronger. I devoured this book, and I didn't want to say goodbye to Lily, Margot, and Ana!"

—Morgan Pager, author of *The Art of Vanishing*

GIRLS OUR AGE

GIRLS OUR AGE

A NOVEL

Phoebe Thompson

Published by Lake Union Publishing, Seattle

www.apub.com

EU product safety contact:
Amazon Media EU S. à r.l.
38, avenue John F. Kennedy, L-1855 Luxembourg
amazonpublishing-gpsr@amazon.com

ISBN-13: 9781662539213 (hardcover)
ISBN-13: 9781662534324 (paperback)
ISBN-13: 9781662534317 (digital)

Cover design by Tree Abraham
Cover image: © Lindsey Cherek Waller; © Rawpixel.com, © kumachenkova/Shutterstock

Printed in the United States of America

First edition

For Charlotte and Sophie

PROLOGUE

It's Friday. The fourth floor of Acadia Hall is buzzing, the lacrosse guys are throwing a party, Avicii and Rihanna are playing over each other in the hallway. No one is thinking about learning or growing up or global warming.

"Can I wear that top I like?"

"Duh." Lily tosses Ana a mess of fabric.

Margot pulls on a dress, asks Lily to zip it. She looks good in red, will stand out tonight in a sea of black tops and jeans. "Too much?" She turns to the mirror to examine herself.

"No!" Ana says, smoothing a flyaway. "It's perfect."

Margot nods, swipes mascara over Ana's dark lashes. Ana strips, tries on something else. Lily hands her a necklace. "Wear this. Don't lose it."

Ana nods, clasps the necklace behind her neck, puts the first outfit back on.

"Let's play a game," Margot says, pulling three cans of beer from their minifridge. The room is messy: three beds, two microwaves, clothes and books strewn everywhere. Their shared two hundred square feet.

"Like what?" Lily asks, threading a belt through her jeans.

"Truth or dare?" Ana asks.

"Boring," Margot says. "Text or shot?"

Lily rolls her eyes. "Fine." She unlocks her phone and places it face up on the table. Margot and Ana follow.

"I'll go first." Ana grabs a bottle of marshmallow Smirnoff from its hiding place in her dresser, sets out three shot glasses, fills them to the top.

"Okay, truth," Ana says. "Sometimes I worry that no one will ever want to marry me?"

"Ana," Lily says, "that's both completely impossible and literally the wrong game!"

"Yeah," Margot says, nodding. "Drink. And I also get to send a text." She leans over, plucks Ana's phone from the table. "So I'm texting Drew, as in lacrosse captain Drew. I'm writing: 'Hey, super excited for tonight, wanted to mention that I'm hosting a bake sale to raise money to buy new UGGs and I would love if you could spread the word.' And, sent."

Ana shrieks. "I literally hate you." She throws back a shot. Lily and Margot take theirs, too.

Lily stands, clips her dark bob back to show off her pretty new nose, glances in the mirror. "Do you honestly think about getting married?" She sits back down to join them. "Kind of a surprise."

"Wait, yeah," Margot says, pointing a finger in Ana's direction. "Don't you think the entire institution of marriage is, like, totally antiquated? Sort of an affront to feminism as we know it?"

Lily props her bare feet on the coffee table. Her toes are hot pink. "That's so cynical, Margot. Tradition can *be* a good thing. I more just meant, obviously *I* think about it. I just didn't know Ana did. You know." Lily waves a hand at a pile of clothes and paper on the desk that also serves as Ana's dresser. "She's not exactly a planner?"

"Ignoring that," Ana says.

Margot reaches over to the minifridge and hands out beers. "The thing about marriage," she says, cracking hers open, "is something shifts. Friend-wise. Anyway, I just think it's fucked up that we act like a woman's greatest accomplishment is landing a husband and planning a wedding. Like, when my cousin Megan got married, everyone was freaking out, telling her congratulations and stuff, when she's literally an astrophysicist. I was like, you guys, Megan discovered black holes, and you think it's impressive that she's marrying Dustin? He's not even that hot."

"Not to totally undermine your point, Margot, but I think black holes were actually discovered by a man," Lily says, "like, a while ago. And I don't think our friendships *have* to shift, right?"

"No, I know," Margot says. "Karl Something. But the point is, Megan has a PhD. And I think that's way doper than being married to some dude. But regardless, she stood up there and told everyone he was her best friend, and I just literally cannot imagine. You guys," Margot says in a whine, elbowing them, "I don't want to lose you to some rando dudes. Can we just live in a house together instead? Why would you want to live with a man when it could just be the way it is now, forever?"

"We have a million years until then," Lily says, rolling her eyes. "Let's just get drunk."

"I guess you're right," Margot says. "It's just depressing."

"Cheers," Lily says, raising her glass and winking. "To our future weddings."

"Ew, Lily," Margot says, laughing. "To our future friendship."

"To Hawthorne Res Life," Ana says. "For bringing us together."

They clink bottles, drink, giggle, turn up the music, zip up their coats.

"Seriously," Ana says as Margot locks the door behind them, "we're, like, so lucky to know each other."

PART ONE

One: Ana

Ana was glad to be home. It had been a long day: She'd hopped on the wrong bus that morning and ended up ten blocks from Horizon Academy, with only twelve minutes until she was supposed to introduce her fourth graders to their new unit on marsupials. Teaching was always exhausting, but today she'd stayed late to grade papers. Now, at seven in the evening, she was starving—and she and Silas still hadn't bought a single grocery since moving into their brand-new apartment together four days ago.

She walked through her building's lobby and pushed open the door to the package room, then breathed out a heavy sigh. She scanned the room, first for anything addressed to Silas, who'd ordered a host of kitchen accoutrements for their new place; he'd decided it was high time to upgrade his knives. *Their* knives, she supposed. She stooped to collect three bubble-wrapped packages with his name on them, shoved them into her bag, paused for a second before reaching down to read the label of an espresso machine–size box addressed to her.

She'd been expecting the box. Knew about its contents, had been tracking its two-day journey from Boston—here's a tracking number just in case, you know what this is about, xxx, Lily had texted just one day before. Ana hoisted the package onto her hip, pushed her way out of the package room, stepped into the elevator. Felt the heft of the box where it stuck into her side as the elevator whirred up to the building's top floor.

She unlocked the front door of their apartment and dropped her bag and the box onto the floor, next to all the other boxes that were all over the floor: her entire life, plus Silas's entire life. They'd get around to unpacking eventually.

It was hard to believe she really lived here: their 1,200 square feet of San Francisco. The marble counters, a big wooden table waiting patiently for chairs. A coat closet by the door, so she'd never have to see coats strewn everywhere ever again; big cabinets that reached the ceiling; and a fridge that faded into surrounding cabinetry, with a freezer that pulled out like a drawer.

She took in the sunset, visible over the water from their wall of floor-to-ceiling windows. It was kind of egregious, really. She went to the window and pressed her forehead into the cold glass, let her breath fog up the pane.

Obviously, Ana knew that a gorgeous apartment and marble countertops couldn't magically undo the knot between her shoulder blades that had been tightening ever since she started at Horizon. But still, the sharp angles and unpopcorned ceilings didn't hurt. She'd pictured the apartment all day long, like a talisman, every time she needed to shrug off any one of the millions of atrocities that came with teaching fourth grade. First, Harry's mom's sly comment that morning—"Ana, we were so *worried* about you," she'd clucked from the child-size chair she'd set herself down in. Ana had been only four minutes late, and plus, Ana's across-the-hall colleague Bryn was there; it wasn't like the kids were unsupervised.

I live in a luxury high-rise.

Then Cooper threw a paper plane at Hadley during social studies; Hadley unfolded it, read a message inside, and promptly tore it up, leaving Ana with little recourse other than to send Cooper into the hallway for five minutes, which he chose to interpret as a reward rather than a punishment.

I have access to a complimentary gym.

Then Piper's mom dropped in around noon to bring gluten-free brownies in the shape of kangaroos—"to celebrate the new unit!"—and then the kids were hyped up for the rest of the afternoon, which made teaching a lesson on numerators versus denominators nearly impossible.

Garbage disposal. Dishwasher. In-unit washer-fucking-dryer!

Normally, all this rote parental involvement and child-induced frenzy would render Ana tight with resentment and badly in need of a glass of wine from somewhere her students' parents would never set foot. Not that she didn't love her job and her students—she absolutely did—but she was human, and it was March, and the accumulation of seven months of school was starting to catch up to everyone. The kids were too comfortable with her now, knew how to push her buttons. A few had started developing body odor. Her classroom was smelly and chaotic, and all of them were in urgent need of spring break.

But now she could simply let her mind drift back to their apartment. To the reading nook she'd set up in a corner once their new lounge chair came in, where she'd hang the Gauguin print Silas had bought her last Christmas. To the walk-in closet she had all to herself, where the modest crop of teacher clothes she'd unpacked so far looked a little drab, as if maybe the closet was expecting linen and cashmere and wool. But all that space! All those drawers, the way they slowed to a close when you pushed on them. All those hardwood floors, pale as bread and smooth as glass.

It was true that she and Silas had forty-odd boxes to tackle and Ana pretty much hated everything in her wardrobe and her checking account was one pack of marsupial stickers away from overdrawn, but still, she thought to herself as she turned in a slow circle, took in the bay and gleaming marble countertops and the bay again—all things considered, life was pretty good.

Two: Margot

Margot braced against the Chicago wind as she emerged from the train at Merch Mart. Three blocks to Lake Street, scan in, press four. She could do it in her sleep.

"Hi, you."

"Morning, Amelia," Margot said, adjusting her bag on her shoulder as the elevator opened to the Astroturf-walled reception area. It was supposed to be a metaphor: like, "ideas grow here" or something. There had been a time not so long ago when Margot had found it inspiring.

"Package for you." Amelia patted a box.

"Fuck—I told Lily to send that to my apartment. Thanks, girl."

Of course she knew what was inside—the box, like pretty much Lily's entire upcoming bachelorette party—had been planned mostly by Margot.

"Margot Peterson. Walk with me, chica." Jenny, Margot's manager, typically arrived around 9:45 a.m., iced coffee in hand. Jenny had explained during Margot's first week at McQueen O'Doul that she was responsible for school drop-off, that Margot shouldn't expect her before ten o'clock, that it was a wonderful company benefit that Margot would very much appreciate one day, too.

"Oh, I don't want kids," Margot had said.

"Really?" Jenny asked, furrowing her brows. "Don't you think that will change when you meet the right person?"

Margot just shrugged. So far, she *hadn't* met the right person—her dating history had been a series of bored-ish romps with guys who were good enough until they weren't. And even if she *did* meet a guy who could hold her attention past a couple of weeks, she didn't really understand how that would lead to kids: You liked a guy, and suddenly, you felt like waking up in the middle of the night to breastfeed a stinky, squirming worm? Margot would rather stick with creative proposals and martinis and spending all her money on herself.

She checked her watch: 8:55. "You're here early."

"Yeah, no drop-off today," Jenny said. "School holiday. Jesus. What did you order?" Jenny nodded at the box, still on Amelia's desk.

"Oh, I didn't. Not important." Margot adjusted her bag on her shoulder, matched Jenny's pace as they walked past the office bar that lined the front entryway. "What's up?"

"So the German guys are in. Totally last minute, obviously." Potential clients: four of them, looking for an agency to help launch a zero-waste hotel chain they were tentatively calling Infinity. Their budget was enormous, and if they chose McQueen, they wanted Margot to manage their account. It would be an ahead-of-schedule promotion, and Margot could practically taste it.

"Shit!" Margot said. "I mean, *good* shit, but shit!" She'd have to move some things: a one-to-one with a particularly difficult copywriter, no problem; a kickoff with their influencer agency, which was a little more time-sensitive, but they were in California, so she could see if they were available tonight—

"They were in Chicago anyway for Ogilvy. So they just hopped over. Told me, like, ten minutes ago."

They rounded the corner, past shelves of tequila from the CEO's distillery—his second business, he called it, although everyone knew that really it was his first.

"Well, the guys are obviously very smitten with your proposal," Jenny went on. "I mean, they kept talking about you. Like, Margot this and Margot that. Sounds like they're leaning toward telling Ogilvy no."

"Smart of them," Margot said, avoiding the compliment. It had been the news of the month: "Magic Margot," she'd heard, over and over again, after the agency's CMO reached out to Jenny with loads of praise she'd received from the German guys for Margot's concept. *This is really well done, you guys got us in a way none of the other agencies we RFP'd seemed to, we're thinking it over, more soon.* Margot had been getting feedback like this since she could remember.

"So obviously we need to be totally ready for them."

"Duh!" Margot said. "I have a follow-up deck ready to go."

"When do you find the time?" They crossed the carpet, stopped at Margot's desk.

Margot shrugged. She hadn't been able to sleep last night—as soon as she closed her eyes, she'd been struck with an idea for a campaign, so she'd grabbed her laptop from under her bed, mocked up a few ideas in Photoshop, and then it was four in the morning and she had an entire proposal ready to go. "I've been feeling energized." A half-truth.

"So they're in around eleven. I know it's, like, two seconds away. Can you handle lunch?"

A flicker of something in her belly. "Sure, of course. I can present my deck, get something catered in the Big Room. Do you want to see it first? The deck, I mean. Not the room. You know what the room looks like. Oh!" She waved her hands. "What if we did a creative brainstorm? I could totally whip up some conversation cards, lay them out—I could fold them into the napkins like a menu, a nod to that gorgeous tablescape we loved from their Paris hotel—"

Jenny put up a hand. "Margot, you know I love your enthusiasm." Her watch pinged and she flashed it toward her face. "Fuck," she murmured. "Okay, I have to go deal with—" She waved her hand in the air frenetically. "Let's just keep it simple. Social. Relationship building, not pitching. Just someplace good for talking. Italian, nice, but not *nice* nice. Hard to get into, showy, good bread, whatever. Call ahead and remind them about the walnut thing," Jenny said, turning on her heel, click-clacking to one of the glass conference rooms.

"Claire?" Margot called out as she settled in. Claire was newish, fresh out of college and eager to please.

She swiveled her chair to face Margot.

"Good morning!" Margot said. "Two things for you. Ready?"

"Ready," Claire said, notebook in hand.

"The hotelier guys are in today, so let people know. No strewn paper, no lewd comments, and absolutely no single-use plastic. If people need to hide their Dasani in their desks or whatever, they should do that."

"No single-use plastic," Claire said, nodding.

"And can you make sure to get out a pitcher of water before they get here? Glasses and stuff, in the conference room. They're mainly here for lunch, but just to show them we prepared. You know."

Claire nodded vigorously.

"Then we need a reservation. Let me think. That place in the Loop with the sourdough could work, or maybe see about Avec—or that Greek place on Wabash Jenny likes, but only if they have the good table."

"Got it," Claire said. "No trash, no lewd comments, water in a pitcher, good table."

"Thanks, Claire," Margot said. "You're killing it. I'll be prepping for them, so just let me know if you need anything."

Margot could practically taste it: an interview with *Ad Age*, *Boutique Agency McQueen O'Doul's Rising Star*, thirty under thirty. The whole nine yards.

She turned back to her desk, saw the box from Lily waiting, still on Amelia's desk. She'd get to it later. She just felt so far away from that world. And so deep in this one.

Three: Lily

Two days prior. Lily was first to the post office—she wanted to beat the lines so she could handstamp the boxes, and plus, the last thing she wanted was to lounge in bed with an entire day ahead of her. Better to get started, set her body in motion. So she called an Uber, rolled her eyes when the driver didn't offer to help her load the boxes into the trunk, rolled her eyes again when he didn't offer to unload them, either, schlepped the boxes into the post office herself.

"You want to do what?" the lady behind the desk scoffed.

"Handstamp the boxes," Lily said, handing over a credit card. There were seven total, one for each of her bridesmaids: Ana and Margot, obviously; Liza, Zoe, and Emily, her second-tier Hawthorne friends; Eileen, whom Lily had known since they were eight-year-olds at Whispering Pines; and Jack's sister, Cameron, who was way too busy with a toddler to come to Miami but would get a box anyway in the name of social inclusion. The girls (with the exception of Cameron) had all long ago confirmed they were in for the bachelorette trip. The boxes were just a formality—Lily wasn't going to ask her friends to take time off from work and book flights to Miami without at least six months' notice—but still, she wanted the boxes to feel special.

The woman slapped labels onto the boxes and slid them back across the counter.

"Your stamp." She handed it to Lily. "Here's the ink."

"Perfect," Lily said. She stamped, paid, thanked. It was only a few minutes after eight, which meant she could still catch Jack before he left for class.

She walked the three blocks back home, took in the fresh early-spring air. A woman in a long jacket pushed an UPPAbaby stroller across Boylston, her hands in thick fleecy gloves attached to its handle. A couple strolled, hand in hand, sipping from steaming cups of coffee. Everyone wore shapeless behemoths of winterwear. Car horns honked and the sun tried its best to peek through gray clouds and pedestrians obeyed traffic lights. Lily pulled her coat tighter around herself and dashed through a crosswalk.

She entered her building, smiled at the doorman, rode the elevator upstairs.

"Lil!" Jack said as she pushed open the door.

"Hi, baby," she said, went to him, kissed him on the cheek, kicked off her shoes. "You heading out? How was last night?" He'd crawled into bed late, kissed her on the forehead, told her that it had been impossible to get a ride home from the Seaport but he was back now—was she in the mood for anything? She'd murmured something to him and reached for his arm, willing him to stop talking so she could drift back into a dream in which her entire wedding went perfectly.

"Good, fun," he said. "Lolita was packed. Pete had this great idea—he wants to do Airbnb, but like, for winter coats, right? So you rent the coat for the month or whatever. The efficiencies are insane. Same products year-round, alternating hemispheres."

"I think that exists, babe. Rent the Runway? And how is that anything like Airbnb?"

He grabbed her shoulders, pulled her to him. "Hemispheres!"

She looked up at him, smiled. "I think Rent the Runway is familiar with seasonality, babe. But I appreciate your willingness to explore the world of women's fashion. I got the boxes out to the girls, by the way. What time is the cake thing, again?" She and Jack and Lily's mom, Gina, had tasted cakes the week prior, but none of the frostings had been quite right, according to Gina. The baker, Stephan, was an old friend of hers, so of course she'd planned another trip from New York for a second round of tasting. "You know I love you more than life, Steph," Gina had said, "but I can't have *vanilla* frosting at my only daughter's wedding. Can't we do something fresher? Citrus-y? Floral?"

"Your mom texted us," Jack said. "She pushed it to Friday. You didn't see?"

"Oh," Lily said, reaching for her phone. "Hmm, I guess I forgot. But fine, I have florists to call anyway. And I need to finalize some Miami stuff. Margot tried to get us dinner at Gianni's, but they said they're booked, which I don't believe . . ." She trailed off.

He opened the fridge, shut it. "Yeah? And any interviews or anything today?"

She bit her lip. The truth was, there weren't, and it was her own goddamn fault. She should have known that the publishing jobs that existed in Boston had nothing to do with publishing at all: They were content jobs at sports-betting start-ups or social media manager jobs at places that self-identified as "content conglomerates." The only job currently hiring at Simon & Schuster in Concord was for a project manager in children's publishing.

So, Lily, despite her track record of excellence and a once-revered perfect score on the language section of the SAT—despite working her way up from editorial assistant to senior mother-effing editor—was now unemployed and unemployable, at least as far as this second-rate city was concerned.

Which was entirely fine! It wasn't like money was a concern. Nor boredom: Lily wasn't sure how anyone planned a wedding on top of a full-time job.

"Speaking of your mom," Jack said.

"Oh god. What now?" Gina had been a bit of a nightmare ever since they'd started planning the wedding six months ago. Probably it stemmed from some kind of profound love for Lily, or maybe a deep-seated boredom that could only be quelched by weeks-long back-and-forths with the planner and the band and the videographer, which Lily let Gina handle, not because it was helpful, but because she didn't have the heart to tell her mom that she'd given strict instructions to all the vendors to pretty much just ignore her mom's requests.

So the wedding was doubly hard to plan: There was Gina's planning, and then there was Lily's unplanning and replanning. And then there was the convincing of Gina that what Gina was contributing was helpful, even though it actually wasn't helpful at all.

It harkened eerily back to a long-since-fired therapist's parting words to Lily: "Making things harder for yourself because you think it's kinder to those around you is not a very honest way to live."

Like, duh. But also: If we all put honesty first, then what would become of any of us?

"So, I wasn't going to say anything. But your mom called me the other day, ostensibly to get my thoughts on the frosting—"

"Jack, you can tell her you're busy if you need to—"

"I like talking to her, actually," Jack said. He took another sip of his coffee. "I mostly tried to talk her out of it. But—what would—well—you like talking to your therapist, right?"

"I don't *like* it, but it's *help*ful, if that's what you're asking." Every Monday at two, Jack evacuated the apartment so she could have privacy for her weekly Zoom meeting with Barri. Lily had been working with Barri since high school, except for a brief pause during her sophomore year at Hawthorne when everything was going so well that she'd decided to try life without Barri for a bit. She'd considered switching to someone local upon moving to Boston some six months ago, but everyone had wait-lists or wore gauzy scarves in earth tones or both, so she'd given up. And anyway, Barri knew everything about Lily's life: her upcoming wedding and all that was going into planning it, her loving but way-too-involved mother back in New York, her history with anorexia and all the effort that had gone into placing it behind her. Starting over didn't seem worth it. "Is my mom thinking about trying therapy? I can definitely get Barri to recommend someone. Therapy would do the woman a world of good."

"Well, I agree with you, for what it's worth, but no. It's nothing bad, Lil," he said, leaning back against the counter.

"I didn't think it was until you said it wasn't."

"I meant to bring this up earlier, it's just—" He blew out a huff of air. "Your mom thinks we should do a prewedding counseling session. I think she meant it as a premarital gift or something, but now that I say it out loud . . ."

She felt her chest go hot and staticky. "Wait." Now she saw her mom's face in her head, red-hot and ugly, and suddenly she wanted to get pregnant with her grandchild and move to the West Coast and never talk to her again. "My mom thinks *we* need therapy? What the fuck?"

"I know. You're right. She made it seem like something you'd be excited about—'You know Lily, she loves her therapy appointments!'—and I just kind of let her run with it."

"That is *so* deeply not her place."

"Obviously I'm on your side, Lil. But what was I supposed to say? 'Lily and I don't really want to take any kind of marital advice at all from you, Gina, my dear future mother-in-law, because you haven't been married for many years and went through the craziest divorce in history, no offense, and by the way, I can't wait to marry your daughter, gotta go, bye?'" He raised his eyebrows and his forehead went wrinkly. "To her credit, you *are* all about therapy."

"Of course I am, Jack. I spent three *months* in *inpatient* treatment." She almost never threw it around like that. "This isn't about me and therapy. This—it's obviously about my *mom*, and—she can't just—I mean, you know I love my mom, but this is *our* marriage, Jack." She felt her face go hot. "If there's something wrong between us, then you should tell *me*." A familiar tightness in her chest that felt like the world was turning and she was stuck still.

"Lil, no—" He opened the fridge again, closed it again. "It's not like that at all. If you want me to go back and tell her we're not interested, I will, of course. I told her how solid we are, and she said she knows. I'll tell her it's a no. Or we can not go and say we did. She just . . . made it sound so normal when she brought it up." A pause. "Maybe it could be fine? You know, Cameron and Bill did that premarital counseling thing and they liked it enough."

"Right, because Bill is *Catholic*, Jack. The Cameron and Bill thing is a literal *requirement* of the church. Can you stop with the fridge?" Her heart was beating faster now, her breathing more shallow. She pictured Barri: "Feel the floor, breathe in for three, hold for three, out for three. You are in control, Lily. Can you name the feeling?"

He put a hand on her waist. "I think she's just worried about you. You know how she gets. I think this is her way of telling you she cares? And also, maybe she's just kind of bored?"

She pictured Jack on the phone with her mom on the streets of Boston or in a conference room or somewhere else where Lily wouldn't overhear. Gina reminding Jack that Lily was his responsibility now. That she was a ticking time bomb capable of relapse at the drop of a hat, that Lily was used to a certain standard of living and it wasn't like Lily would go back to work after they got married and had kids, ha ha, right, Jack? That they should make sure they're on the same page about all this.

It was infantilizing, it was unfair, it was rude, it was meddling.

He glanced at his wrist. "Shit. I'm late—but I really don't want you to worry about this, okay? I can totally cancel it if you want me to."

"Who's it with? And when?"

He grimaced. "It's this afternoon. With one of my mom's therapist friends. Someone in Newton."

"So everyone's involved in the preemptive demise of our marriage? Jesus Christ."

He picked up his backpack and slung it over his shoulder, took the distance to the front entryway in two steps. "It's weird. I know. I think they meant it as a bonding thing between them? We can totally say no. I'll text you the address, think about it, and I'm totally down to play hooky. Ball's in your court, okay? Love you."

She closed her eyes. How dare he let her mom meddle? How dare he judge her mom for meddling? And plus, she was way too busy to get to Newton last minute on a Tuesday afternoon. She had plans; she couldn't fit this in.

But it wasn't true: The days had been stretching out in front of her since she'd left her job six months prior.

Lily sucked in a sharp breath of air, rapped her knuckles lightly on the counter. "Love you, too," she said to the empty apartment.

Jack and Lily had met five years prior, at a party to celebrate the recent cohabitation of a pair of mutual friends. A cranky neighbor had knocked, complained about the noise when it was still only nine-ish, so the group had meandered over to someplace someone liked, dark and throbbing with youth, and Lily had ended up perched on a barstool to Jack's left. He was talking animatedly to the guy to his right, and because he was left-handed, he kept bumping Lily with his elbow. By the fourth or fifth time, it had become a joke, and by the fifth or sixth drink, the friend to Jack's right had disappeared, and Jack whispered in Lily's ear that he wanted to take her out sometime, if she'd let him, and she'd wanted to turn and kiss him in the pulsing bar, which was completely unlike her.

Instead, she'd unlocked her phone and placed it face up on the bar, and he'd tapped in his number, named himself Jack Lefthanded.

A few nights later, they met at a wine bar, Lily in a jean jacket over a silk slip, Jack in chinos and a button-down, rumpled from the day's work.

"Lily," Jack said as he pulled out her chair for her, "I'm going to cut to the chase: I am totally enthralled by you."

"Oh, please," she said, waving him away. But it was true, she could tell—the way he hung on her every word, told her about his family.

Falling in love with Jack had been quick and painless, with none of the heartbreak or misunderstanding that had plagued so many of Lily's early relationships. Before Jack, there'd been the guy at Hawthorne who wanted to keep it "casual," which meant he only wanted to eat meals with her if they were in a group, then the guy postcollege who took her to meet his family and then broke up with her three days later because he "wasn't feeling it."

With Jack, it was easy. One day, they were flirty acquaintances, and then some months later, they were wordlessly together, probably forever.

And a year later, they were living together, spending weekends with each other's friends, or with each other's families in New York (hers) or in Princeton (his), or alone, just the two of them, enjoying each other's company and basking in the solidity of their union. There was no one who made Lily feel more like herself.

Getting married. Barreling confidently in the direction of their lives.

A therapy session for the express purpose of pleasing their moms couldn't possibly derail that.

Fine. They'd go. They'd tell their moms they went. They'd forget about it. Everyone would feel happy and chummy and ready to get on with the wedding.

Four: Ana

"Hey," Silas said, dropping his backpack on the floor in a heap. "How was your day?"

"Hi!" Ana said, turning self-consciously from the window as if Silas had walked in on something. *I live here,* she reminded herself. *I'm allowed to take in the view from my own apartment.* "Good, fine. We started our Australian marsupial unit. The kids are really not grasping the whole platypus-as-marsupial-edge-case thing." She had put on the sweater he liked, white and blue with delicate stitching at the neck that was more itchy than cozy. "You?"

"Good board meeting, synergies galore." He rolled his eyes. He'd been promoted recently—VP, a big deal, Ana knew—and had become at once freer and more serious with his disdain for the French tech company toward which he devoted eighty hours a week. "Dinner? I wanted to go out. Italian?"

"Sure, yeah," she said. "Let me just—" She gestured to the package. "From Lily. For Miami, you know. Some stuff came for you, by the way. Any idea where the scissors might be? Maybe we unpack a little before dinner?"

Silas had hired a moving company, which had felt like an incredible luxury before Ana had realized it meant someone else would be in charge of categorizing and labeling every single one of her worldly possessions.

"No clue," he said. "I'm *so* hungry. Can we eat, and deal with all this tomorrow?"

"Sure," she said, shrugging and reaching for her purse, then Silas's hand.

It wasn't like Ana wanted to be the type of woman who dropped everything just because her boyfriend was hungry. It was just that she didn't mind when his needs trumped hers. She liked it, even. *I'm hungry, let's eat, you can wait.*

His confidence made her feel safe, like there was always a right answer, and all she had to do to know it was listen.

Ana and Silas had met an entire decade ago. She had been naive to enroll in Intro to Economics—it was an *intro* class, she'd figured at the time, not realizing that most of her classmates had graduated from private high schools named after majestic animals or rich old men where they'd completed much of the curriculum already. They were always trading names they knew in common, even though these private schools were scattered across the country. And these schools had prepared their graduates for Intro to Econ in a way that Mr. Eagle at her small high school twenty-five miles from Madison, Wisconsin, had absolutely not.

She'd been utterly overwhelmed in those first few weeks, not just because the material was confusing, but also because confronting the fact that material could be confusing was a threat to her entire identity. She'd learned to read early! The lowest grade she'd ever gotten was an A- in gym one year, because she'd complained about cramps, which was a lie, but only a lie for the purpose of getting to spend the class period in her school library reading! The gym teacher had called her bluff, but you couldn't really give a kid a bad grade for liking books more than dodgeball, could you?

Ana went into office hours one day, at Lily's suggestion (office hours, Lily had explained, was for asking questions and getting extra help, and the professors were happy to do it, really—she'd been going to office hours at Dalton for years), and much to her embarrassment, she'd burst into tears almost immediately. Professor Feldman had been surprisingly kind, even if awkward, handing her a tissue and assuring her that this kind of thing happened all the time. "Ana," he'd said, "you've got to understand that every single student here is used to being at the top of their class. And it's okay to struggle." Ana hiccupped, and he handed her another tissue. "You can come talk to me as much as you'd like," he said, "and I'll help you. You're capable of the material." She felt her bottom lip quiver at this, and had had to curl her toes and clench her entire body to keep from exploding into uncontrollable sobs. "But I find that peer tutoring is even more helpful. I'd love to pair you up with one of the students who's really grasping the material, if that's okay with you." She nodded—any help was welcome, and plus, nodding was all she could do to avoid melting down even more.

That evening, Professor Feldman introduced Ana to Silas via email. Silas had responded enthusiastically and almost immediately, asking Ana if she was free to meet up in the Union that night, to which she'd had no choice but to say yes, of course she was free, thank you, looking forward!

"Oh!" Lily had said, clapping her hand to her mouth when Ana had read the email out loud. "I think our moms are friends from Exeter? I'm supposed to say hi. Is he cute?"

"I don't know," Ana said. "I have no idea who he is."

When they met, Ana had to do a double take. Silas was tall and solid, had the easy smile of a man who was used to getting everything he wanted. How had she not noticed Silas in class before? She must have been too overwhelmed with the full-time task of worrying that she was stupid.

Their first meetup had been largely inconsequential.

"So I figure we can start with supply and demand, unless you're good on that?" Silas asked.

"Let's—I mean, I have an idea about it, but can you just show me?" Ana squeaked out, embarrassed.

He drew a diagram, then explained his diagram patiently and without a hint of condescension, and Ana found her eyes drifting toward his biceps, which were veiny and reminded her of penises, not that she'd seen a penis before, because she hadn't, except in pictures, and not that she looked at pictures of penises very often, because she didn't.

But still.

She returned to Acadia Hall, and Lily pulled out her earbuds and cocked her head. Margot was at a Campus Democrats meeting and wouldn't be home for a while longer.

"It was helpful," Ana said, trying to sound casual.

"He's that cute, huh?" Lily asked, swiveling her desk chair to face Ana. "Spill."

"No, it's nothing—I mean, he's my tutor, right?" she asked. "So—wait—how do you know him again?"

Lily squealed, helped Ana compose a thank-you text to Silas, called her mom. "My mom says he's, like, amazing," Lily said, pulling her phone away from her ear. "Hold on, Mom? I'm putting you on speaker. Tell Ana."

"Ana, sweetie," Lily's mom said. "Do you like this boy? Lillian! Oh, Lillian! Ana would practically be your sister-in-law!"

"Mom, oh my god," Lily said. "Ana, I am so sorry. Ignore her. She's crazy."

But it had been an honor to be folded into the fabric of Lily's family so readily. For her status as roommate to automatically qualify her as relevant.

By Ana and Silas's third meetup, she'd stopped apologizing when she didn't know an answer, and also, she knew more of the answers the first time she attempted the worksheets. Silas was exorbitantly competent, not just at this, but at everything that boys his age sucked at: He opened doors for her, not with awkward deference, but with practiced masculinity. He brought her study snacks without even asking what she wanted—gummy bears one day, crackers another. He always arrived early, and sometimes Ana would find him barking into a phone like he had a job (which she knew he didn't), and despite the performative aspect of the whole thing, something in Ana's ancient biology was drawn toward this capable future father to her children. It was just that simple.

"Are all private-school guys like this?" she asked Lily, four or five weeks into her tutoring sessions. They were lying on their beds, face up. They were used to spending their evenings together while Margot rushed between clubs and practice and volunteer work.

"God, no," Lily said, smacking a stick of gum and extending the pack in Ana's direction. "Most fucking suck."

"Mm," Ana said, smiling to herself. She felt lucky to have been paired with Silas, but more than that, she felt lucky to have been paired with Lily, lucky to have become instant best friends with a girl who was not only gorgeous and glamorous, but who also seemed to take Ana seriously for a million reasons that had nothing to do with her inability to put together an outfit or talk to a boy.

It was life-affirming, to be liked by someone like Lily. It made high school, which had ended only five months earlier, feel like nothing more than a blip.

It had been pouring rain one day, so the student union where they usually met up was packed, and Silas invited her over to study instead. "Welcome," he said, greeting her at the front door and walking her up the two flights of stairs to the room he shared with exactly nobody. Ana would learn the ways of the rich at Hawthorne: finding loopholes that afforded them single-occupancy rooms, even when roommates were an "essential" part of the first-year experience; filling dorm rooms with cast-off furniture from their parents' remodels.

They spread their books on a gorgeous wooden table that was absolutely not standard-issue Hawthorne furniture, and Ana found herself tracing the whorls of wood with her finger and wondering how much this table cost in relation to her scholarship. She looked up to find Silas watching her, with a lilt to his lips that could only be interpreted as desire.

She held his eyes for a moment, and he leaned in just halfway, then paused to touch his thumb to her chin, tucked a lock of hair behind her ear, pulled away.

It had left her buzzing, understanding for the first time in her life what attraction really felt like, and all she could think of for the rest of the study period and the entire week until she saw him next was what it would feel like for his lips to fall squarely on hers, to kiss urgently in his room or in public on the quad.

It was six weekly tutoring sessions and two econ quizzes (she got a B+, then an A) until they finally kissed. She'd almost given up on anything happening, chalked up his flirtation to just how he was.

"You know what's cute about you?" he asked, handing her a Bud Light. She took it, pretended she always sipped Bud Lights on Wednesday afternoons while studying.

"Uh, no?" she said tentatively.

"Exactly," Silas said. "You have no idea how cute you are. That's what's so cute." He leaned in, a hand on the back of her neck, held her gaze for a second, smiled, let her breathe in his air. She couldn't lose her virginity fast enough.

And now here they were, ten years later, on their way to Italian food. Their relationship had become a quiet constant, not just between them but in the architecture of their adult lives. Ana had learned how to navigate his family vacations: Use the family's bar tab but send a nice thank-you note afterward. Don't try to join them for tennis, because when they said they played for fun and she should totally join, they didn't actually mean it. She'd learned to live as an adult without him, and he without her—Ana with roommates, Silas solo. They'd fought and almost broken up, once over Ana's insistence that Silas could be condescending toward her mom, and another time when Silas offhandedly suggested that his parents' donations to Hawthorne might have paid for Ana's scholarship.

But now they'd reached a state of consistency in their relationship, and that was huge, but they'd also reached a state of consistency in their lives. Ana was seven months in to teaching fourth grade at the prestigious Horizon Academy, where Silas had gone from kindergarten through twelfth, and where his mom served on the board, and the independence she'd held on to so dearly since moving to San Francisco no longer felt like a necessary lifeline. She felt good about taking the next step with Si. She felt good about letting go of her need to fend for herself, about letting him in completely. They practically never fought. Their frontal lobes were fully developed, and they were thinking about getting a dog.

—

When Silas had first floated the idea that she apply for a position at Horizon, she'd brushed him off. First of all, they weren't hiring—she knew, because she guiltily checked the listings at most of the private schools in the Bay at least once a month, just to be aware of her options—and second, because they hired teachers with master's degrees or higher.

"Oh, don't worry," Silas said. "You know my mom's on the board, right?" Ana had not known that, and anyway, she didn't believe that her boyfriend's mom's trustee status would be relevant enough to land her a job that she wasn't qualified for. But she'd had him pass along her résumé just in case, and lo and behold, they wanted to interview her, and then they wanted to have her back in to meet some of the parents, and then they wanted to hire her.

"Look, Ana, I'd take it, too, if I had the offer," another Oakbrook teacher had said.

And most days, she was glad that she'd made the switch. She loved her students, and she had the entire summer off to look forward to—the first summer she'd have off, since they all pitched in to teach summer school at Oakbrook. Plus, working at Horizon had won her a nod of approval from Silas and his mom, and she didn't want to admit how important that had been, but the truth was, it had felt good. If nothing else, working at Horizon was part and parcel to the life she was now living.

It was cold out, and even though she'd lived in San Francisco for six whole years, Ana was still always forgetting to put on a jacket when they went outside at night. The need for one felt at odds with her long-standing view of California weather.

"How's the marsupial unit going?" Silas asked, opening the door to their favorite Italian place and holding it for her. It was a sliver of a restaurant, wedged between an upscale candle shop and a glass-front building that was either a massage parlor or a Reiki studio. Ana still didn't really know the difference.

Silas stuck out his hand in a peace sign to the hostess—two, please, was what he didn't say—and she escorted them to the booth in the corner they liked.

"Fine, yeah," she said. "Gemma freaked out because her dad told her about the koalas that burned in Australia, and I was like—well, that *did* happen. And then she was all sulky for the whole day, and it was super disruptive. But she has a point. It's fucking depressing." The waiter came over and took their order. "I have parent-teacher conferences tomorrow, by the way. Are you working from home tomorrow? Because I need you to stay out of the living room, please." Horizon had done conferences virtually last year, back when it had been a necessity instead of a convenience, due to the pandemic. And now the parents were sold. They didn't want to leave their offices downtown to drive to Horizon to spend just thirty minutes with their kid's teacher. They didn't want to come in from Sea Cliff or Mill Valley, paying for a sitter just so they could learn that their ten-year-old was falling slightly behind in reading, or that he was disruptive in class. They didn't even want to skip an important meeting to learn that their kid was doing great, that she was sensitive and passionate about the future of our planet and kind to everyone, even the weirdos.

Their pizza came, and they both reached for a slice.

"They want me at HQ in June, by the way," Silas said.

"In Paris?" Ana asked.

He nodded, took another bite. "I was thinking you could come with?"

Ana put down her slice of pizza. "Oh!" she said.

She pictured it: Silas, laughing as he tore a baguette in two. Both of them, fucking sweatily in a hotel room, talking about the rest of their lives.

"Probably first week in June. Work will pay, obviously. And I'll pay for the rest. Just—I don't want you to worry about any of that. I was thinking we could celebrate living together, your first year at Horizon. And plus, you've never been to Europe."

"You let me go on and on about marsupials!"

She'd text Margot as soon as she got home: Silas! Paris!!! Margot would respond right away: OMFG he's proposing Ana you know that right??

He shrugged. "I like hearing you talk about marsupials. It's cute."

She'd ask Lily for Paris recommendations, obviously. Lily would know where to eat, to shop, to browse engagement rings.

He smiled, reached out to touch her. "So you want to go?"

"Obviously!" she said. "Of course!" It was like that first kiss all over again. If she could re-lose her virginity right now, she would.

He could still make her melt.

Five: Margot

The day passed in a blur. By the time she was done with the deck and her meetings and everything else, it was ten, which was late, even for Margot's standards. Jenny had left hours ago—"I'll jump back on when I'm home," she'd said, "after the kids are asleep." It had been a hollow promise, but no matter: Margot didn't want Jenny's virtual interference anyway. She worked better alone.

Her phone pinged with a text from Lily. Made some changes to our wedding website, have a sec to look?

It was a rule of Margot's to save personal tasks for home. But it was late, and no one was here, and she'd signed up to help Lily with anything she needed, planning-wise.

Margot clicked the link.

The margins were a little tight, and the colors were too saturated, but overall, not bad.

Looks sooo good! She texted back. Really exciting Lil!

Lily texted back right away. You sure you don't want a +1??? Or maybe you like one of the groomsmen? A link to the wedding-party page.

She scrolled through them. These men would probably brag about having rowed crew in college or rowing crew on the club team of whatever university they were getting their MBA at, if that was even a thing, not that they'd use the actual university's name when they talked about it, as if everyone on earth knew about Wharton or HBS or GSB.

She sent an eye-roll emoji back to Lily.

"Who are they?" she heard. A hand on the back of Margot's chair.

"Amelia!" she said, slamming her laptop shut. "Jesus. I didn't see you." Amelia had been manning the front desk at McQueen for upward of two years now, but Margot knew that her real dream was to make it as an art director. She was always staying late, usually working on her portfolio after she'd finished restocking the snack cabinets.

"Margot Peterson distracted at work? This is a first."

"God, no—I mean—it's work, sort of," Margot lied. "I was asked to give feedback on this website."

"Margot, first of all, it's ten at night, and there are three of us in this entire godforsaken office. Second of all, I watched an entire episode of *Desperate Housewives* on my work laptop yesterday while nodding along on a video call. Let me see." She pulled a chair next to Margot, flipped her laptop back open. "Who are they?" she repeated.

"No one. I mean, my friend's boyfriend's groomsmen. Fiancé. Whatever. She asked me to take a look at her website. She's the one I've been planning the Miami bachelorette for?"

"Right. That'll be fun." Amelia scooted closer. "Not in love with the colors."

"Right," Margot said. "And the margins are obviously way too tight."

"It's well executed, though. Clearly by a professional. And as a professional, I'd like to well execute any one of these men."

"I can't tell if you want to murder or fuck them," Margot said.

"To clarify, I want to fuck them."

Margot laughed. "I seriously need to get back to work," she said.

It wasn't that she thought Amelia would judge her for getting sidetracked by strange men on the job. It was just that power was nebulous in a place like this, and Margot had fought hard to set herself apart from everyone who half-assed their jobs while waiting around for their lives to start. Maintaining an image was full-time work. And plus, these random dudes were just that: random.

"Send me that link so I can masturbate to these guys later," Amelia said.

"Gross, no."

"Fuck! I totally forgot. I'm supposed to meet some guy from Tinder. We're getting a drink in Streeterville."

"At ten?" Margot asked.

"It's not that late, Margot. We're still young, remember?" She stood, grabbed her bag, left Margot prickling at their three-year age difference.

"Bye, girly!" Amelia called out as she bounded toward the elevator.

Margot turned back to her laptop.

Margot didn't need a guy, let alone a guy who was rich. She didn't even need a guy who was self-actualized. She didn't need to be taken care of, and she certainly didn't need to be on the receiving end of lectures about Ivy League crew teams or work accomplishments that hadn't even been earned.

Six: Lily

Lily paced her apartment, her feet bare and her coffee sloshing in its mug. She turned on the TV—she liked to listen to something while home alone—and considered the therapy situation.

She actually wasn't opposed to a premarital counseling session, was the thing. It was something she'd considered, and even wondered if she should float it to Jack herself, not because she had any marital concerns, but because it was never a bad idea to talk through things with the humble guidance of a professional. She liked the idea of paying someone to ask them the kinds of questions they might not think to ask each other or themselves. And she knew he'd be open to it.

It was just that she would have wanted it to be on their terms. She didn't want to sit in a musty room with someone selected by both her mom and his. And anyway, they were so busy with everything, and this—talking through whatever people talk through at this juncture of life—was something that could potentially be pushed to after the chaos of wedding planning. It didn't need to happen now. What was the difference, really? They'd been living together for years. Nothing tangible was going to change when they signed a ketubah.

But also: If she called her mom to tell her what the fuck, then her mom would come back at Lily with a million questions about why *not,* Lily, and just the idea of talking Gina down—or worse, convincing her that no, Lily wasn't mad, just very slightly annoyed, but it was totally okay, seriously, don't feel bad, Mom—made Lily feel heavy as the contents of a coal mine.

She didn't want to argue.

She didn't want to take for granted how much her mom cared, even if sometimes it felt a little misplaced.

If this was important to her mom—and to Jack's mom, for that matter—she'd make it happen.

After a Pilates class and a quick solo lunch at Tatte, Lily went to the closet and pulled out dress pants and a sweater, tried them on, examined herself in the mirror. She looked professional and put together, but maybe it was too much. She swapped the dress pants for jeans, the sweater for a blazer. Now she looked severe and unwilling, which was not the impression she wanted to give to a therapist who'd probably break HIPAA to report back on their appointment to *both* of their moms.

She settled on a plaid skirt and tights with a simple black sweater—girlish but sophisticated—and applied just enough mascara to look effortlessly pretty, before wiping it off in case she cried, then reapplying it and promising herself she wouldn't.

It was only nine months ago that Jack had gotten into Harvard Law—late, in June, off the wait-list. By then, he'd already put down a deposit at NYU and re-signed their lease in the West Village. He was hesitant to accept at first: They'd be uprooting their lives. They loved their apartment and their routine.

"Continuity is important for you, Lil," he said. "Your routines."

"Yes, but Boston's not so far. And you got into *Harvard*, Jack. If you want to go, I'll move with you," she'd said. "And honestly, I wouldn't mind some space from my mom." Gina had gotten into the habit of stopping by Lily and Jack's apartment unannounced, complaining about her wrinkles and then complaining some more when Lily didn't interject to say her mom wasn't wrinkly, asking Lily over and over again when she and Jack were getting married, when she could have grandbabies, how much longer she had to wait.

"Anyway, it's only two years. Not forever." It was a sacrifice, but Lily knew it was what Jack wanted, and it would be a greater sacrifice to live with the knowledge that she'd kept him from that.

So they found an apartment.

She loved her job in New York—she'd just edited an autobiography by a prominent printmaker she'd respected since her work had come up in a graphic design class back at Hawthorne—but no matter: They'd be back in New York eventually. And now was the perfect opportunity to take a step back and reevaluate. She'd been there for six years, and most days she loved the work, but sometimes it was starting to feel a little stale.

Perhaps it was time to level up, to network and apply to jobs and plan her wedding, to practice self-care and self-improvement, to meditate and go to yoga and get a job at some direct-to-consumer publishing company or an art gallery instead.

Sure, she'd be leaving behind everything she knew and everyone who'd formed her. Her parents were there, even if separated by a chasm of hatred and Central Park. She had friends there, and not just friends she liked meeting up with once in a while, but actual, real friends she'd grown up with, known forever. And sure, New York was home. It was where Lily had gotten her first period (at the Serafina near the park) and where she'd had her first kiss (on the tiny balcony of her mom's apartment on Eighty-Sixth—at the embarrassingly geriatric age of sixteen). It was where her parents had announced they were getting a divorce (why they chose to share that information during a family walk across the Brooklyn Bridge, Lily still didn't know), where she'd been when she learned Hawthorne had accepted her, and where she'd rebuilt her life from scratch after it was demolished by an eating disorder. Barri was there. Her favorite pottery studio was there—a steamy, cramped room under a coffee shop, where she blasted music and learned to accept feelings of shame.

But she could spend two years just one state away from the place where she felt most like herself so the love of her life could get one step closer to practicing environmental law, because of course she wanted to support that.

Lily approached a woman behind sliding glass. "Jack—and, well, Lily and Jack, but my mom, Gina—made the appointment?"

The woman was even stouter than the building where she worked. "All checked in," she said, grinning.

"Thanks," Lily said. She tried to hedge, hoping her soft smile conveyed that she and Jack were fine and just doing a little tune-up before the wedding, which they were only doing because Lily's mom was projecting her *own* fears about divorce onto her daughter, which was *entirely* unnecessary, because if Lily was good at one thing, it was not repeating her mother's mistakes.

Gina's own husband—Lily's dad, technically, although she hadn't called him that in years—had long ago climbed the ranks at Goldman, then skipped Lily's fifteenth birthday for a "guys' trip" in Costa Rica, only to come home with an apology gift for Lily (an age-inappropriate teddy bear) and a new girlfriend who was only eight years Lily's senior.

Meanwhile, Jack hated the beach (too sandy), disliked unnecessary international travel (too pollutant-y), and agreed with Lily that each of their future kids would have a maximum of three stuffed animals, and any more was unnecessary clutter that had no place in their future home.

Lily sat in a chair upholstered in geometric shapes in primary colors and waited for Jack to arrive. She hearted a reel about club outfits from 2012 that Ana had sent in their group text with Margot.

She heard Jack enter. "Hi, Lil," he said.

"Jack," she said. "Hi."

He sat down next to her and kissed her on the cheek. "Sorry I'm late."

Another door opened. "Lily? Jack?" asked a woman with a folder clutched to her chest. "I'm Barb. So nice to meet you. Come on back, you two."

They followed her through a dark hallway, into a bland room.

"You can sit anywhere," Barb said, closing the door. There were a few chairs, positioned separately—those must be for the cheaters. Or the couples on the cusp of divorce. Clearly, the right place to sit was on the couch, hands on each other's knees in willing deference to Barb's expertise.

"Tell me what's going on."

"We're here because my mom thought it would be a good idea," Lily said by way of introduction.

"That's great," Barb said.

"It's true," Jack said. "I mean, I don't know what her mom—our moms—told you."

"I'm interested in hearing what you two have to tell me, actually," Barb said. "Tell me about yourselves. Who are"—she paused, looked down at her paper—"Lily and Jack, individually"—she looked up at each of them—"and then also, together?"

"We're getting married soon. We both come from divorce. My mom wants to make sure I'm asking the questions she didn't ask. But of course I've done that! Jack is flawless. I'm not worried. That's pretty much it," Lily said.

"Wonderful!" Barb said. "Gina did mention you're getting married. What a good time for a tune-up."

Lily bristled. "It's not really a tune-up," she said. "We're really good, overall."

"Sure," Barb said. "And have either of you been in therapy before?"

"Oh, I have," Lily said. "I still am. I was struggling with—I was, or had, anorexia. The therapy was very helpful. Lots of great interventions, routine, the usual. I'm fine now, but I keep up with it."

Barb nodded.

Lily watched Barb size her up, taking in her legs, her stomach, her arms. Making sure she wasn't anorexic still. Maybe wondering if she ever was for real.

"And you, Jack?"

"No, but Lily has told me all about her experience."

Barb wrote something down. "Alright, good. So this will be your first experience, then." She raised her eyebrows at Jack. "This will be fun!"

Lily wondered how many times she'd said that. She probably had a worksheet: *Ten ways to get straight males who have never been to therapy to open up in therapy.*

"We can do this one of a few ways: If there's anything either of you would like to talk about, we can start there. Otherwise, I have this bowl." She reached across herself to grab something ceramic and misshapen and filled with laminated cards. "My kid made it, if you're wondering about the shape. It's full of thought-provoking questions. Or TPQs, as I like to call them." She paused, rubbed the bowl like she loved it. "So, do you have a preference? Open-ended or TPQs?"

Lily tapped her knee against Jack's. They'd make fun of Barb after: for the rhombus pattern on her sweater, for taking ownership of an acronym. "*I* like to call them TPQs," Lily would say to Jack in the car ride home. She could hear his laugh already.

"Why don't we start with a TPQ," Jack said.

So he was on Barb's side now.

Barb smiled, pushed the bowl across the coffee table. "Please," she said.

Jack pulled one out, read it: "What does an ideal life together look like in five, ten, and twenty years—and where do your visions diverge? You want to go first, Lily?"

"Uh, kids by five years, for sure. Probably two. You're a lawyer, obviously, and I'm probably on pause from work still?" She said it like a question.

Barb nodded. "Jack?"

"Sure, or Lily could be running her own publishing company if she wants."

"Is that what you want, Lily?" Barb asked.

"That's not, like, something you can just *do*," Lily said.

"Why not?" Jack asked. "I mean, if you want to. Or you could do something else. We could hire a sitter. Only if you want."

"It seems like it's important to you that Lily works, Jack. Lily? Is it important to you? Have you two discussed much about the financial implications of only one parent working?"

A beat. Lily felt her breath quickening.

She was pretty sure they'd talked about it, or if nothing else, they'd certainly talked around it: They'd done the whole financial planning thing, and they didn't *need* her to work. Certainly if they had, she would have chosen a different career. But there was money. A trust she'd gained access to at twenty-five, and he was getting his next year, at thirty. There were millions.

"I liked my job, a lot. But . . ." But what?

"You know I'm fine with you staying home, Lily," Jack cut in. "And I think it's good you're taking some time to decide what's next, plan our wedding. I just—Lil, don't take this the wrong way. You just seem more at ease when you're working. I just know that staying busy is important to your ongoing recovery."

He paused, and Lily froze. She felt her legs disappear under her and the walls contract around her. *Breathe, Lily,* she thought.

"I'm at ease," Lily said. "I couldn't be more at ease."

"Jack?" Barb said. "It seems like you're worried about Lily. Can you elaborate?"

"I'm not worried, per se," Jack said. "It's just—" He turned to face her. "Remember how excited you were when you finished the last version of that woman's book, the printmaker lady? I haven't seen you that energetic in a while, is all."

"Jack," she said, looking up at the ceiling. She wouldn't cry. She was good at swallowing tears. "I'm busy. I'm so busy. I've been networking. I'm figuring out what's next. I'm applying to jobs, not that there are any that are even worth anything in Boston, and I moved to Boston for you, remember. Which I'm happy about! I'm so happy you're pursuing what you want to pursue, and I don't want our kids to get raised by a nanny, and we've talked about this."

"No, Lily, I know. I know you're—busy. But you do so well with a packed schedule, you know? Back in New York, when you were always out late with coworkers and accomplishing shit, and you were so good at your job? I don't care that you're not working, Lil. I just don't want you to . . ." He trailed off.

She prickled. Felt the need to jump to her own defense.

"If you didn't want me to quit my job, we shouldn't have moved to Boston," she said. "And anyway, it hasn't even been that long. I'm healthy. I'm fine. I'm seeing Barri. I'm planning an entire wedding. I'm taking prenatal vitamins, just in case. You don't think I'm an expert in my own mental health by now? You're overthinking it, Jack."

"I'm sorry, Lil," Jack said. "You're brilliant. And it's up to you how you want to use that. Seriously. I'm not trying to pressure you to go back to work. I just want you to know that you don't have to stay home for our future hypothetical kids on my account. I want you to know that I think you can excel at anything you want. Motherhood. Starting a company. Seriously."

"I get it," Lily said, softening. "I hear you."

"Great communication skills, you two!" Barb said, clapping her hands together. "Would you care to pull another TPQ?"

Lily blinked, swallowed, grabbed another one, read it out loud, answered how she was supposed to.

—

"That wasn't terrible, right?" Jack said, pulling out his keys as they left together.

"You could have just brought up the whole working thing with me privately," Lily said as she slid into the passenger seat.

"I know," Jack said. He placed an arm on the back of Lily's seat and reversed the car. "I meant to. I'm sorry. I should have. You're—okay, Lil, right? Can you just promise to tell me if you're not? Or if you *become* not okay? Do you want to maybe find a pottery studio in Boston?"

"I'm fine, Jack," she said. "Can you stop asking? You're freaking me out."

And she *was* fine: taking informational interviews and networking calls and meeting friends of friends for coffee and rooting both of them in a brand-new life and planning a wedding was all very engaging, and also an assload of work. And that was coming from someone who'd worked really hard, actually: coming home late when her boss needed more from her, going to happy hours with coworkers, and sucking up to her boss by answering emails when she was technically off the clock because she knew full well that being "off the clock" wasn't really a thing. She would get there when she got there. The right job would materialize, and if that job was motherhood, then so be it. It wasn't a crime to need a break. It wasn't a crime to not care about her publishing job as much as she cared about herself and their future.

They were so good, so happy together, so communicative, so not in need of saving emotional conversations for ugly rooms with poor ventilation. Maybe she had been wrong to take their relationship for granted, to assume since they'd met that it was enough that they had so much in common: that they'd both grown up in or around Manhattan, that their lives centered around the friends they'd made in college, that they turned instinctively toward the other, eyebrows raised in mock disbelief, when someone mentioned Disneyland or Chili's or democratic socialism.

She felt a twinge in her chest that felt like it could bloom into sobs.

She'd never set out to be a perfectionist. She hadn't woken up one day at eight years old and decided that she'd never miss a homework assignment. Maybe it was an oldest-daughter thing, or an oldest daughter of a dad who'd go on to leave his family for a Costa Rican twenty-three-year-old thing: Someone in this family had to be the responsible adult, and Lily had sensed that, even as a young girl. It was like she knew there was a countdown toward a moment when her family would combust, and even as an eight-year-old, she'd been holding everything together as best she could, as if she had any control over anything at all.

All she had to do, she had realized, was absolutely everything to the absolute nth degree.

It wasn't like, in seventh grade, she'd wanted to go on a diet, which was what everyone at school had thought. It was just that she hadn't realized that there were numbers associated with every single food, and once she did, she couldn't unlearn it. There were the super-unsafe numbers, like 320, which was the number of calories in one serving of the chocolate chip cookie dough ice cream that was a consistent fixture of her childhood freezer, which she'd realized when her brother had asked, offhandedly, what a *calorie* was when they were eating their Sunday sundaes. There were the extremely unsafe numbers, which weren't numbers at all, but guesstimates at best: How could one possibly know how many calories were in her mom's salmon and mashed potatoes, or her grandpa's chicken casserole? Then there were the safe, certain numbers, like the hundred-calorie packs of Chips Ahoy. One hundred was clean and easy to remember. Square. Ten was okay, too, but much harder to find. Two sticks of gum was good. Two cups of coffee was okay, but she hated the taste.

She'd start the morning with peppermint tea, which her mom protested at first—"You need brain food, Lily"—but her argument was weak: Her mom had been replacing meals with tea since Lily could remember.

At first, Lily would allow a splash of cream, which then turned to milk, and eventually to nothing. It had seemed safer to avoid the milk, because the exact amount couldn't be controlled, and it didn't even really affect the taste enough to be worth measuring out, and plus, she felt sophisticated sipping murky water and running her hand over her shrinking arm. At school, she'd eat half of whatever was served in the lunchroom, and then as she got more and more accustomed to that, she worked her way down to a quarter, slicing square pieces of pizza into even smaller squares, and pushing the discarded squares of crust and cheese and tomato sauce around her plate until they were mangled enough that no one could blame her for not eating them. "This lunch is kind of gross for a private school, don't you think?" she'd said, which wasn't true, but was the kind of thing that the girls who'd grown up even wealthier and more sophisticated than Lily were always saying.

The weight fell off her quickly. She was young and had a fast metabolism, and she was still growing, too. In weeks, the corduroy pants that hugged her waist tightly were falling to her hips, their cuffs dragging on the ground. "It's just a growth spurt," her mom had said. But Lily, even then, could tell that her mom wasn't completely convinced.

By the time spring break rolled around, which always meant a trip to Boca to visit Lily's Grandma Linda, Lily's body had changed enough that spending time in a bathing suit in front of her family was no longer a viable option. In clothes, she looked almost regular. But in a bathing suit, even she could tell that her body was drastically thinner. Her hips were like paddles that she could grab with her hand, palm almost flat against bone. Her shoulders, too, had become satisfyingly slim, and her thumb and forefinger overlapped when she wrapped them around her wrist, which she did multiple times daily.

Sure, there were moments when she'd glance in the mirror and see the gap between her legs or the hollows in the cheeks of her reflection, and she'd realize, with gratitude and shock, that the reflection was *hers*. But she spent most of her time criticizing her body: wondering how she could eat so little and still have pads on her fingers and toes, a bit of extra flesh under the wings of her scapulas, a slight jiggle to her upper arm. The thinner she got, the more critical of her body she became.

Finger pads. Toe pads. They refused to disappear, twenty tiny reminders that she could never overcome the facts of biology, that no matter how careful she was to count and add and track, that she'd still menstruate and grow older and have to decide if she wanted to be a lawyer or a dancer or a businesswoman or a mom, and she could always risk fucking everything up.

She didn't share this information with anyone because she wasn't yet in possession of the words, or even the ability to step outside herself and realize that her experience wasn't universal. Instead, she watched from a safe distance as people worried about her: Her mom suggested deviations from what had previously been a strict regimen of scheduled meals—salmon with pesto pasta, sushi from the place nearby, meat lasagna and salad, short ribs and broccoli, make-your-own tacos, spaghetti and meatballs, pizza from Mariella. She'd listened as her parents whispered, then shouted behind the closed doors of their bedroom, arguing about Lily without involving her. She watched her teachers' brows furrow deeper and deeper when she walked into class. Her younger brother was the only one who didn't seem to notice that anything was out of the ordinary, probably because he wasn't old enough to consider that bodies could be changed, or that anyone might want to change them on purpose. Not that it was about her body. It wasn't.

But also, it was.

Even at fourteen, Lily was aware that looking good—great, even—wasn't worth the sacrifices she was making. Maybe if she had wanted to be in the limelight, which she didn't, she'd be willing to cut out all her favorite foods and all the people she ate them with in order to be, ostensibly, beautiful. But the truth was, Lily hadn't wanted to be noticed. She'd wanted to blend in and feel safe in a world that made her brain hurt with its hugeness. She'd wanted to whip out a huge piece of paper and write down every fact and scenario and thing that she'd ever thought of, like a map of her brain, done up in gel pen and charts and graphs and order. How could she ever remember all the things she'd learned? How could she ever be aware of the possibilities that she was avoiding, or ruling out, or shutting off as options to her just by nature of being?

"How many different lives could I even *have*?" she'd asked her dad once while avoiding a muffin.

"Are you asking me about string theory?" he'd asked, cocking his head in the way he did whenever his kids surprised him.

"What's that?" she asked.

"You just described it," he said, and her brain whirred and her stomach hurt, just like when she used to have bad dreams about numbers expanding and expanding until the universe couldn't contain them. That was the first time she got up from the table to puke.

Two days later, the backs of her thighs were sticking to the plasticky cushions of chairs that were maybe supposed to feel inviting, but were clearly hospital chairs, which made sense, because she was in a hospital, despite everyone's reticence to use that word in front of her. A woman in scrubs that were tailored to look less like scrubs started to hand Lily a clipboard, then furrowed her brows and gave the clipboard to Lily's mom instead. "We'll just have mom fill in this information," she said, looking Lily up and down, probably, in retrospect, because she was trying to assess her age, but at the time, it felt like she was judging Lily for being too fat to be there. Which obviously wasn't true.

Lily and her mom sat in silence as her mom scratched checkboxes into the form with a nubby pencil. Lily glanced over her mom's shoulder, trying to see what she thought about Lily, as if the forms were qualitative questions about Lily's moral value: *Is your daughter ever going to amount to anything, in your opinion? If you could change five things about your daughter, what would they be? You don't actually think your daughter is thin enough to be here, do you?*

"Lil, you can look if you want," her mom had said, and handed her the clipboard, which asked if Lily had allergies, or a family history of cancer or diabetes, which she didn't think was particularly relevant to eating disorder treatment, which was what she was there for. Unless eating disorders caused cancer? She clapped her palms to her ears and counted down in tens from one hundred, then replayed everything she'd eaten that day: Black tea, round up to one hundred calories. One carrot, round up to one hundred calories. A slice of her brother's apple, round up to one hundred calories. Two rice cakes, round up to two hundred calories to be safe. Five hundred calories. Good. That was okay. As long as they didn't make her eat lunch here.

Her mom had squeezed her shoulder then, which hurt more than it should have, then walked up to the window and handed the clipboard to the scrubs lady. She whispered something to her, and Lily strained to hear it. Her mom's body was soft and embarrassing, her hips straining against the thin fabric of her jeans. If Lily's body ever looked like her mom's, she'd cry. But also, she loved her mom. Everything about her. The way she made Lily open up without trying to. Even the way she clearly favored Lily's brother. It was familiar, and she didn't want to be separated from her. But she knew, even though no one had expressly told her, that she would be. That was why she was here. To be separated from her family so she could be force fed until she was fat. Normal. Her stomach heaved.

She cared so much then: about every single solitary detail, including but not exclusive to her body—measurements down to the eighth inch, and the way her stomach increased her waist measurement by almost a half inch when she'd had too much water to drink, which was unfortunate, because lots of water was the surest way to squelch her appetite. About the numbers that whirred through her head: multiples of one hundred, which was embarrassing in and of itself, because if she'd been smarter, maybe she'd count numbers that weren't so friendly—multiples of seventeen, maybe, or 131. About her math tests, which she always did well on, but hyperventilated throughout nonetheless, especially if the teacher started them late—for some reason, she thought that starting after the first seven minutes of class would make her brain go totally blank. About which of the girls in her class thought she was relevant, a word whose absence had the power to ricochet through her, rendering her entire being worthless, just because Annabelle or Vera or one of the other girls who walked through the world like they owned it had said it. About the girls in her class who looked over her shoulder at her paper but never straight at her, unless they were whispering about her, which she thought would feel better than no attention at all, but didn't. It felt worse. It made her want to disappear. And, it turned out, she was good at that: at creating routines for herself that felt like a shelter but ultimately turned around to bite her. Skip breakfast, apple for lunch, knock knuckles to wood if someone looked at her as if they thought she was failing, repeat. It helped until it didn't.

After eight weeks of inpatient treatment, then twelve weeks of intensive outpatient treatment, then a couple of years of twice-weekly therapy with Barri and some critical mass of antidepressants that slowed her thoughts to an almost comfortable crawl, she stopped caring so much.

By the time she reached senior year of high school, she'd put on some forty-five pounds since that initial admission and gifted thirty-eight not-so-impressive ceramic mugs to everyone she knew. She'd become intimately familiar with the cramped patio behind the ceramic studio she frequented after school, where she'd regularly share a glass of wine with whoever was willing to buy her alcohol. She bought clothes that fit, and felt some empowerment in that: She was just slightly chubbier than her friends, whose weight had never fluctuated—you could tell—but it was *because* she'd been so much thinner and more careful than they'd ever been, and she made a whole thing of letting them know she was in *recovery*.

When she started at Hawthorne, she made a point of telling her new roommates about it all. She showed Ana and Margot her before pictures, and they gasped: She'd been so thin then, like a bird, and she told them not to be shy if she stopped eating again. They should shake her, call her out, call her mom, here was her number, by the way. And she felt important knowing that these girls who were becoming her best friends were worried about her. She loved the way they'd glance over at her plate in the dining hall, trying not to make a show out of checking out what she was eating, as if one day they'd look to her dinner plate and see just a single leaf of lettuce or one grape, cut lengthwise.

—

For the most part, she was normal now. Patient, at least compared to how she'd always been. Getting married. Eating regularly, most of the time.

She'd be fine. She and Jack were fine. Everything was going to be fine. She knocked her fingers against the window of the car for good measure, counted to ten, then back down to zero. Again. Again.

She could handle Boston. There was plenty she liked about Boston, even: walking through the Commons, spending afternoons reading on a bench at the Isabella Stewart Gardner Museum and privately pretending she lived there. Watching all the students, boisterous and horny and yelling in the streets and reminding Lily that it was good, actually, not to be nineteen years old anymore.

But Boston wasn't home.

She didn't expect Jack to understand.

Jack's upbringing had given him the mental fortitude to thrive anywhere. He'd grown up safe and happy, playing soccer with the same group of boys for the duration of his precollege schooling. He'd gone through all the milestones that set a boy up to be an altogether well-adjusted man: His first crush had been on a babysitter, and his first kiss was at a classmate's bar mitzvah. His mom picked him up from school every day—even though she was a full-time lawyer—handed him a Ziploc of something homemade and nutritionally balanced, grilled him on the goings-on of his day before dropping him off at soccer or guitar lessons and heading back to work.

Jack was solid. And Jack was solid everywhere, not just where he was comfortable. And plus, he was busy, taking classes and studying and staying out late with his new friends. That was what she wanted for him. That was why she'd nudged him toward Harvard in the first place.

All she wanted was for Jack—for everyone she loved—to be happy.

Seven: Ana

The walk home from dinner was freezing cold, but Ana almost didn't mind: Now there was Paris to look forward to, and a potential diamond ring.

By the time they got to the apartment, she wanted to bundle up with a tattered blanket on the sofa and make a packing list for her trip to Paris. Or read a book, curled up against Silas and sipping chamomile tea. But something about all those white countertops and white walls and huge windows and silent climate control felt a little antithetical to tea and a cozy night on the couch. It was almost like dipping a toe into a hot tub only to realize the water was only room temperature. For a second, it made her think about the house she'd grown up in, the disdain she'd brought home during that first spring break. She'd said something terrible to her mom, like: "You know that couch looks like a homeless person lives on it, right?" Her mom had looked wounded, said it had been her dad's favorite piece of furniture in their house, and it still felt good to curl up on it and pretend he was there. Ana had rolled her eyes. The last thing she wanted was to become a vet tech with a dead husband and a parasocial romance with a couch. "Suit yourself, mom," she'd said, and gone up to her room.

She and Silas had a Restoration Hardware Cloud Sofa, delivered just yesterday. It was pristine. But it made Ana a little nervous: What if she had schmutz on her jeans? She actually hadn't sat on it yet.

"We should hang some art," she said, looking around.

"I don't know," Silas said, his voice trailing behind him as he walked to the bathroom to brush his teeth. "I kind of like the blank walls. They remind me of possibility. You gonna open that box, by the way? From Lily?"

Ana had almost forgotten.

She went to it, cut it open to find another box inside. TO ANA, WILL YOU JOIN ME IN MIAMI? She flipped it over to find the details of the weekend: club, beach, shopping, massages, repeat.

"Jesus. This is a packed schedule."

"Yeah?" Silas said, emerging from the bathroom. "I mean, it's a bachelorette party, not a sweet sixteen."

"My sweet sixteen was a taco bar at my friend's house."

Silas rolled his eyes. "That's Wisconsin, though."

"I guess."

"Remember my sister's bachelorette? That was so insane. She did, like, thirty things. Plus the shower or whatever. Girls, right?" He disappeared back into the bathroom. She heard him brush his teeth and spit in the sink.

Ana didn't remember, because Harper hadn't asked Ana to be a bridesmaid at her wedding. "It's not that she doesn't like you," Silas had said, and Ana understood that it had been bigger than that: Harper hadn't fully believed that Ana would be a permanent fixture in her family. Well, now she would be.

She grabbed at another layer of tissue paper. A bottle of champagne, a pair of flip-flops, a tote bag with Ana's name on it, a face mask, a tube of Supergoop!, a pastel-colored bikini.

"Ana, baby," Silas said, holding his arms out to her. "Put down the bikini or put the bikini on."

She let it drop to the floor. Knowing Lily, she'd selected bikinis in different colors for each one of the girls, matched them to tissue paper, spent an inordinate amount of time making sure everything was curated exactly right. It was overdone, a little wasteful, made Ana think for a second about her mom and what she'd say about an invitation whose value was at least $200.

She wouldn't have understood it ten years ago, but now she did: This wasn't about the money, which was inconsequential to Lily. It was about the intention, and the arbitrary monetary floor people like Lily and Silas placed on what counted as meaningful. Silas had explained it to her some years ago: "My mom always said that a thoughtful gift should cost at least a hundred dollars." He'd shrugged. "You can't really find anything worth giving for less than that." At the time, Ana had thought he was joking.

The box was extravagant in a way that made Ana feel a little funny, but it was sincere, and Ana knew Lily well enough to understand that her heart was in the right place. No part of her had assembled the box and thought, wow, this will definitely be the most expensive bikini that Ana has ever owned, and it'll probably stir up some kind of buried class resentment—that a bikini meant as a party invite costs more than pretty much anything she buys for herself. But Ana felt it anyway. That old ache, back again.

"Do you think I'll do something like this?" Ana asked Silas. She hadn't meant to say it—she had to remind herself that the fantasy of their post-Paris wedding existed in her mind only. "I mean, in forever. Or, like, whatever."

"You know what's crazy to me?" he asked. "You still have no idea how beautiful you are. You know that?"

She batted her eyes. A nonresponse. It was corny, but she was a little drunk.

He reached for her hand, pulled her toward the bedroom.

Eight: Margot

It was ten thirty by the time Margot shut her laptop. She needed a martini, stat.

There was a place, not far from the office: Blind Barber, dark and moody, perfect for not thinking about work and staying a little, for giving her roommate, Sabrina, time to fall asleep before Margot got home. That way, she wouldn't be there waiting for Margot at the entrance to her bedroom. "How was work? What's in that box? What are you up to this weekend?"

She grabbed her work bag and the box from Lily and walked around the corner, settled into a barstool, ordered something stiff, took a sip.

It wasn't an ideal situation, living with a roommate who wanted much more to do with Margot than Margot wanted to do with her, but it was just one in a line of many sacrifices she was making in order to have the life she wanted.

It had been a lesson her parents had ground into Margot's bones from the moment she'd become a semiautonomous being: Your choices now pave the way for your future. Her parents were always like this: pragmatic, repetitive, even a bit puritanical, with their sensible sneakers and hatred of excess.

Her upbringing in the Chicago suburbs had been pretty much idealistic: She and her brother had grown up in a house that was big enough for them to run around in. They didn't have gardeners, but they could have. Their dad coached both of their basketball teams, their mom belonged to the PTA, and every Christmas, they'd drive past the house from *Home Alone*, take in the lights, and express their gratitude for each other in a way that had seemed cringey at the time but, in retrospect, was kind of nice.

Margot had always known she'd go to college—her parents both had master's degrees in applied linguistics from the University of Illinois, where they'd met. It wasn't like she'd been trying to escape the Midwest by applying to and then choosing a college up the coast of Maine, which was farther than either of her parents had wanted her to go. But they'd imbued in her a certain relentlessness that she understood, now, to be a slightly problematic, pick-yourself-up-by-the-bootstraps type of rhetoric. Her parents had grown up Catholic and traded religion for academia—but not necessarily open-mindedness. They corrected her grammar over dinner and rolled their eyes when Ellen DeGeneres married Portia de Rossi. Her dad once joked—awkwardly, she now realized—that it was a good thing she was a tomboy and not "actually gay." That was really all you needed to know.

Margot had applied to Hawthorne because her high school English teacher had graduated from there, and that teacher was the smartest person she knew, always gallivanting in front of the class, sharing insights about characters and the world that almost knocked Margot off her feet.

"Margot," Ms. Hawkins had said during a required one-on-one—she was the only teacher who'd worked that into her curriculum, "you have a real skill with language. Are you considering attending a liberal arts school?"

Margot hadn't—she had her eyes on Rhode Island School of Design, actually, because her favorite class was photography (New Trier High had a state-of-the-art darkroom, which had been a big deal when it was constructed Margot's sophomore year), and because the pictures of students on campus made her wonder who she might be if she had the confidence to dress in all black and smoke cigarettes.

She blinked at her teacher and told her that attending a liberal arts college was actually her goal, even though she hadn't considered it until this moment, and did Ms. Hawkins have any suggestions?

"I think you'd be a really great candidate for Hawthorne," Ms. Hawkins said. "I think you might like a different perspective on the world. You have—" Ms. Hawkins had searched the ceiling, looking for the words, and Margot had sat, her stomach fluttering and her feet tip-tapping on the linoleum floor. "I think it's a certain capacity for insight. I think you have a sense for inquiry, and I think rooting that in some serious English classes—you wouldn't believe what you'd get out of Medieval English, for example—would do you a world of good." It had felt like an insult: Here Margot had let Ms. Hawkins butter her up, only to turn around and tell Margot there was something more she needed. She was only seventeen—of course she knew there was much more she needed to learn and be—but still, it stung.

"I'd be happy to write you a letter of recommendation," Ms. Hawkins continued, and the stingy feeling had melted into liquid molten cake, from Margot's chest and all the way down.

"Thank you," Margot had squeaked, and felt a little flustered from where she sat in Ms. Hawkins's teeny-tiny, magazine clipping–plastered office.

And now look at her. Margot had married the best of whatever remnants of Catholic Social Teaching had been wrapped around her by her parents in a tight, chaste, very productive little bow with the expansive creativity she'd learned at Hawthorne. She'd been notorious at Hawthorne for doing everything: She'd majored in economics, and double-minored in English and studio art, and plus she'd been the president of Campus Democrats and the star of the oldest a cappella group and the captain of the club lacrosse team and so many other things that weren't even worth getting into.

And now, she was so close. To the promotion she wanted, which would place her squarely in a leadership position, which would earn her two weeks of paid sabbatical and a raise that would equip her to buy her very own apartment. She'd done everything right: finding a deal on a slightly shitty apartment with a slightly shitty roommate so she could save plenty of money toward her eventual down payment. Landing a job at McQueen, and bringing to it all the attitude of a personality hire, then also killing it at her actual job. She was individually responsible for $750,000 worth of new business this past year alone. All that, and she was this close to finalizing a seven-figure deal with Infinity. All that, and Warner from Infinity—arguably the most important future client in McQueen's current rotation—trusted her more than he seemed to trust Jenny, which he made clear. All that, and she ran three times a week and went to spin class on the other days and had drinks or coffee or dinner with some combination of women she'd met in Chicago—not best friends or even super close friends, but people she liked enough.

The bachelorette weekend and all the planning she'd taken on for the group was an inconvenience, she thought as she took a long sip from her glass. It wasn't great timing: She had so much left to focus on to make sure the Infinity deal landed, and she'd prefer to focus on it from Chicago. She was this close to the denouement that would make her parents and Ms. Hawkins and everyone else proud. She was moments away from landing Infinity and getting her raise and buying her apartment and watching her life take off, and she loved Lily to death, but there really couldn't have been a worse time to get out of her flow and spend a weekend popping champagne in the great state of Florida.

Margot was interrupted from her thoughts. "That good?"

She looked up: a woman, short-cropped blond hair, around her age, maybe a couple of years older, with a boyish confidence.

"Yeah, my favorite in Chicago."

"Alix," said the woman, offering a nod instead of a handshake. "I think I've seen you here before, to be honest. Not to be weird."

Margot laughed. "It would only be weird if you were some creepy dude. Margot." She extended a hand. "I work around the corner. Come here a lot, actually. Which I guess you know. Since you've seen me. Or, noticed me. Or—whatever." It was weird: for Margot to trip over her own words. "You?"

"Same. Google. Over there." Alix jerked her head toward the street. "What do you do? I can totally leave you alone, by the way. If you just need your martini in peace. You probably get approached a lot. Wouldn't take it personally." She smiled, and Margot watched the way her freckles shifted. Was she flirting?

"No!" Margot said. "Not at all. Actually, I always hear that I seem intimidating? Which I think is so weird, because I'm really friendly? I actually like being approached!"

Alix chuckled and leaned back, slinging one ankle over her knee. Something dormant in Margot stirred.

It wasn't like Margot had never considered that she could be gay. Obviously, something was up if she pretty much never liked guys back. But when she'd floated the idea—first to her high school best friend, Greta, and later, to Ana and Lily—she'd been met with a nose wrinkle and a "Are you sure? I really don't get that from you." So she'd shrugged it off and let it go.

She would be fine with it, if she was gay. She wasn't, like, deeply ashamed or in the closet or anything. It was just that her sexuality hadn't really taken precedence in her life thus far. She'd been so busy, so involved, so striving for so, *so* long, and of all the things that had kept her various suitors over the years from achieving romantic intimacy with Margot, gender was pretty low on the totem pole.

Over the next hour, Alix told Margot about a guy at work who refused to wear both shoes and socks, and Margot told Alix about the copywriter who insisted that ads had "souls."

"It's embarrassing for him, don't you think? Like, if you want to be an artist, just be an artist."

Alix laughed, took a sip of her beer. "You're really interesting, Margot," Alix said.

"I'm completely average," Margot said, surprising herself with the admission of such a deeply held fear.

"You're not," Alix said, brushing some hair out of her eyes. "There's an intensity to you that's, like, super approachable. And appealing. And you have gorgeous eyes."

Margot bit her lip. "Thank you," she said. "Do you—I mean, would you want—"

"I would like to get your number, and take you on a date."

"Oh, I meant—"

"Fuck, you're straight, aren't you? I totally misread the situation." Alix laughed, but without a hint of embarrassment. "Well, I'd still love to hang, honestly."

Margot considered correcting Alix: *Actually, I thought I was straight, but now I'm wondering. Well, I guess I've always wondered, but it's been a background wondering, and suddenly it feels like a foreground wondering. I've always sort of wondered if the time I kissed my friend in middle school was more than just "practice"? Or if I went to Ms. Hawkins's office all the time because I was actually passionate about high school English? And, like, I enjoy sex* enough *with guys, but sometimes it feels like a trip to the gym: I feel good after, but during, I'm kind of waiting for it to end. And I just thought that was sort of how it is? And maybe that's not what it's supposed to feel like?*

"No pressure," Alix said, and Margot realized it had been too many beats of silence.

"I'd love that!" Margot said, taking Alix's phone, ignoring Alix's question about her sexuality. Whatever. Two people could hang. It didn't need to be so clearly defined from the get-go.

"I'm always looking for new friends!" Margot added, then immediately regretted relegating Alix to that corner.

It was late when she got home. She'd checked her phone no less than four times for a text from Alix, even though she'd left the bar only eighteen minutes ago. She still had that godforsaken box tucked under her arm, and the radiators were rumbling.

Margot reminded herself that soon enough, she'd have central air. She'd live in one of those nice condos that had a rooftop pool. Her entire life would be climate controlled, as insulated from the unpredictability of weather as her future would be from anything besides upward mobility.

She stood up to strip off her dark jeans and silk top, then lay back down, clad in only her underwear.

A knock. "Hi," said Sabrina, pushing the door slightly open and leaning into its jamb. "Oh, sorry—I didn't realize—" Margot watched Sabrina's eyes linger on her bare body.

"Oh, it's fine," Margot said. "Anyway, hi."

"I heard you come in, so I just wanted to say hey. Ooh, what's that?" Sabrina gestured toward the box.

"Yeah," Margot said. "It's from my college friend. Lily, you know? Her wedding is soon—it's a bachelorette-party giftbox thing." She wanted to be alone, to find Alix on LinkedIn and then Instagram. This was so unlike her.

"Wow, fun!" Sabrina said, lingering. "By the way, I'm making Hamburger Helper with ketchup, like my mom does. I know it's almost midnight? But I had a craving. Do you want any? I won't even charge you for it or anything."

"That's really nice," Margot said. "I'm good, though, thank you."

It had been Ana's idea for Margot to turn to Craigslist for roommates. "You get along with *everyone*," Ana had said, and she was right. Margot got along with Sabrina, who was kind and inoffensive. Sabrina worked for an event planning company, hated her boss, and loved the Hallmark Channel. She spent her weekends curled up on the couch she'd inherited from her older sister, watching movies about holidays that were still eight months away, and scoffing when the characters had sex. She believed fetuses were babies, that alcohol should be avoided, and that the highlights in her hair weren't egregiously streaky.

Margot's phone pinged. Alix. She couldn't swipe it open fast enough.

But it was Jenny: Ran your new deck by leadership. They're good with it. They say, and I quote: "Margot has serious balls and we love it." Good to send, thanks for everything!

She fell back onto her pillow and waited for the wave of elation to flow through her. To feel too big for her apartment. To see a vision of her future *Ad Age* interview that she'd frame and send to her dad.

But she didn't feel much. It was too early to celebrate, to be fair. "Put in the work and the result will follow." She could practically hear her dad's voice and the squeak of shoes on the basketball court. She looked around at her tiny, neat room: the holes in the wall from the previous tenants, the postcards in TJ Maxx frames posing as art. She wanted to remember it all, so that when she had a brownstone in Wicker Park and the kind of art on the walls that would make her think, she would recall that she was solely responsible for bringing in the kind of money McQueen hadn't dreamed of up until this point, that she'd done it with humility and grace. That she'd been young and free and suffering, and that she'd earned every bit of what she'd gotten.

Warner, team, hi! She wrote. Please find the scope proposal attached. It was so lovely to see you, even if briefly, in the office today. Please also find attached some preliminary creative concepts—would have loved to show them in person, but this will have to suffice! Any questions, text or call anytime. You know that!

Warner responded right away. Looks good, you never miss, M, he wrote, and signed it with a single *W*.

Margot smiled. She snapped a selfie, sent it to her parents, told them big things were coming, said she loved them, checked again for anything from Alix. No, but whatever.

It was happening.

She pulled on some sweats. "Hey, Sabrina?" Margot shouted, bounding out of her room. It felt too small to contain her potential. "Do you wanna take a shot?"

"Um, of alcohol?" Sabrina asked, as she pushed meat around a pan. "Isn't it a Thursday? At, like, midnight?"

"Yeah," said Margot, pouring them each an ounce of tequila.

"I guess so," said Sabrina. "Margot, you are the craziest person I've ever met!"

Nine: Lily

Jack dropped Lily off at their apartment, then drove away—he had a seminar, then dinner with some classmates—and she didn't want to be alone at home, and they needed groceries, so she started the eight-block walk to Whole Foods. Her phone rang. "Mom, hi."

"Lily," her mom said, "I just had coffee with Cindy, and she said she's doing two bands at Gretchen's wedding and asked me how many we're doing. I had to tell her that we're only doing one. How is the job stuff going? Why don't you push that to after the wedding? Do you really want to start a job right when you're busy with all this? I'm heading to Boston in three days. That tasting is at four, on Friday. Where are you? It's loud."

"Walking to the store. It's just the street noises."

Her mom had a million opinions—historically, she'd done anything in her power to keep Lily from the outcome of feeling potentially disappointed—but Lily didn't mind: She found it kind of endearing, actually, how excited her mom was about all the little details. And anyway, Lily knew that getting married was an opportunity to include everyone who was important to her. It was one of the things she liked best about the planning: having an excuse to fold her mom back into her world. To make her mom feel relevant, needed, helpful.

"Lillian, you're cooking? Since when do you know how to cook? Come home soon. We can order takeout and watch a movie. Or I can make you that lasagna you love."

She was overdue, and sometimes the thought of her mom alone in her apartment petting the dog and watching Instagram reels was enough to break Lily. "You know I'm actually not a bad cook. But yes, I will come home for a weekend soon."

"Good. How was that florist?" A friend of a friend. Another of Lily's mom's suggestions.

"Oh, fine. But they don't usually do peonies, they said."

"Really? The florist Julia likes? They don't do peonies? That doesn't make any sense. You told them Julia sent you? They're still not willing to? Let me text Julia. We're cutting it a bit close on the timing, let me tell you."

"Okay, Mom," Lily said as she entered the grocery store. She would have actually been fine with *any* flowers, but it was a bone she could throw, and it would satiate her mom for at least a couple of days.

"You sound stressed. Are you stressed? Give me tasks. I have nothing but time. Is that mother of Jack's helping? I know she has a big important job—"

"Don't worry, Mom, seriously. I'm really having fun with all of it. And Jack's mom is retired, by the way. You know that."

"Don't say that word, *retired*. It makes us sound old. She's helping, though? What are you having her help with that I can't do?"

"Just little things. Gift bags," Lily said. She tried to sound upbeat and present, but really, she was distracted.

"You don't want your forehead to wrinkle before your wedding. Don't exert yourself. You know stress causes weight gain. Sorry. I didn't mean to say that. Wrinkles, though. If you need more money, I'll give you more money. Did you get those boxes out, by the way? It was such a shame we didn't include those little box sets from Ladurée. That's where Gretchen and Cindy went. When is that bachelorette? Two weeks from now? You would hate me if I showed up, right? I'm kidding, obviously."

It was loud, she needed to focus on choosing the best head of kale from the others, and she suddenly wanted to be alone with the strangers around her. "Mom, is it okay if I focus on shopping? It's a zoo in here."

"I love you, Lil. Call me tonight. I'll see you in, what—three days for the frosting? I'm so glad everything is going so well for you, okay?"

"Love you, too, Mom." The line went dead, and for a brief moment, she considered calling back and unloading: that Jack was worried she was unemployed! That maybe Lily was worried Lily was unemployed! But there was no need to turn it into something it wasn't. It would only make her mom worry, too.

Ten: Ana

Silas had been up early for a run. He'd left a bagel sandwich and a coffee on the counter for Ana, and then he'd gone off to work. She savored both: the rare treat of working from home, and the small gesture that made it feel even more special.

She was on a Zoom meeting with Beth, Horizon's principal; her colleague Bryn; and Cooper's parents—Bryn had just finished delivering the news to Cooper's parents that he "was not where we need him to be" in math. Not that they gave out grades at Horizon Day School—they'd swapped letters for qualitative assessments a decade ago—but a parent who'd shelled out a couple of grand for a climate-controlled fish tank to support a unit on the life cycle of salmon felt the same about a report card flush with rows of *Needs improvement* as they did about F's.

"We're here, of course, for anything," said Beth.

"Any time of day," Bryn said. Ana would have to punch Bryn for that later: They were trying to train the parents not to treat them like around-the-clock assistants. She watched Bryn wince in recognition of what she'd said. "Is there anything else we can help you with immediately? Advice, resources, tutoring?"

"Actually," Cooper's mom said, "Cooper mentioned to Scott and me that he's been having some issues in Combined Reading."

Combined Reading was Bryn and Ana's answer to their postlunch drop in energy, which unfortunately coincided with their students' postrecess hyperactivity. When they were both in the room, the kids seemed to behave, and having them read in pairs gave Ana and Bryn a solid fifteen minutes to gossip or look at pictures of ugly dogs on Reddit.

"What's going on in Combined Reading?" Beth asked, furrowing her brows at her laptop's camera.

"It's come to our attention that a student has been copying our son's answers," Cooper's dad said.

In Ana's class? She felt her face go hot, not necessarily with the accusation, but with its absurdity. It wasn't like she graded the kids on the answers to their Combined Reading worksheets. It was an exercise. It was about fostering a love of reading and keeping the kids busy for a moment so Bryn and Ana could have a second to decompress.

It was dim enough in her living room that the redness didn't translate from her cheeks to the screen.

"Which student?" Beth asked, shaking her head from side to side like a nervous bird. "Academic integrity is absolutely core to our values here at Horizon, and this isn't the kind of thing we tolerate in our classrooms."

"Hadley, right, Scott?" Cooper's mom said. "We're not trying to throw a little girl under the bus. It's just that Cooper has been upset about it, and we figured it was better to bring it up."

Ana watched her own brows, in the square of her face on her screen, knit together in confusion. Hadley was Ana's best student: shy and a little bit awkward, but entirely brilliant. She was obsessed with red foxes, ballet, and space travel, and she wanted to be an astronaut or a chemist. She'd finished fourth-grade math in second grade, so she left Ana's classroom during math to join the sixth graders down the hall. She had one friend, who was a second grader, and on good days, the other kids ignored her; on bad days, they whispered under their breath and pointed at her or whined when they were paired with her for partner activities. Ana did her best to dampen the blow of social exclusion for Hadley, but Hadley, for her part, seemed relatively unaffected: She played happily on the playground with her younger friend; she was kind and polite and thoughtful; her parents had reported that they sent her to play therapy and the therapist had "exactly zero concerns." Ana knew that Hadley would go somewhere, eventually: The kid was genuinely exceptional, and not just because her brain was advancing at twice the rate of her peers'. She was squarely herself, a little manipulative (Ana had caught her claiming period pain during gym class so she could go to the library—the girl still had the body of an eight-year-old, but Ana, of course, appreciated the ruse: a page out of her very own book), and shockingly funny. Every few weeks, she'd drop off a strip from a comic series she was working on, about a girl who was friends with a balloon, and her insights were always witty, were spelled correctly, and demonstrated a knowledge of humanity that would have impressed Ana had it come from someone her own age.

"No, that was absolutely the right thing to do," said Beth, nodding vigorously. "It's best that we get ahead of these things, whether or not they are true. Hadley, though," Beth said, tapping her pointer finger to her chin, clucking her tongue. "Ana, what's your awareness on this? Anything you've observed?"

Ana loved Hadley, plain and simple. And Ana knew she shouldn't disparage Cooper—he was just a kid—but the kid was an idiot, and Hadley was a peach. There was just no way she was cheating off him. "The reading reports are totally low stakes," she said. "Just some answers on an index card, turned in and not graded."

Beth cut her off. "But of course it's the principle, and if Cooper is feeling uncomfortable, that's something we want to be aware of," she said. "Horizon is a safe space for learning, and as you both know—you were the winners of the chair at the auction last year, right? The one the kids painted in the theme of academic integrity?" They nodded. "I thought so, yes. Great chair! Anyway, you both understand the importance of our school's values, of course. Your family has been with us for so many years! How is Julien, by the way? He's at Amherst?" Cooper's brother was quite a bit older; Cooper was probably an accident, and maybe that was why they babied him so much. "Anyway, rest assured, Ana and I will take this offline and get back to you."

They nodded slowly, apparently calmed enough by Beth's recognition of their tenure and contribution to the scholarship fund that was a direct result of their purchase of that heinous chair. "Thank you so much for your time, Mr. and Mrs. Searle. Always so good to see you both."

"Thanks so much," Cooper's mom said, smiling. "And we're not trying to villainize the child, of course. We're not like that." She smiled, fingered the diamonds at her neck.

"No, of course!" Beth said. "We're so grateful you brought it up."

"Thanks so much, you two," Ana said, even though she didn't feel thankful at all.

"Cooper's doing great," Beth said, winking, as if it were true, as if she spent any relevant amount of time in Ana's classroom. "Ana, can you stay on for a moment?"

Hadley had been one of Ana's students at her first and only teaching job prior to Horizon, a charter school called Oakbrook, where she'd taught third grade. Hadley had been a standout in Ana's class the year prior, and as soon as Ana'd gotten the job at Horizon and learned there was a scholarship available to a student with a track record of academic promise, she'd mentioned the opportunity to Hadley's parents. It was crazy: that a kid with two parents with good full-time jobs would be eligible for a scholarship. But Hadley's parents were both high school teachers, and if Ana's salary was any relevant marker, then together, they were hardly making enough to get by. That was San Francisco for you.

Everyone had been hyper welcoming of Hadley at Horizon, even if Ana got the sense there'd been some hope that the scholarship would have gone to someone whose face, on the school brochure, might make Horizon seem like they were doing a better job with diversity than they were. It was the question mark in the eyes of the parents when they met the new kid, when her name was Hadley. "Hadley just isn't exactly the type of name I expected from a student like that," Ana had overheard at Welcome Night. "Well," the other mom had responded, "the city's getting more expensive," and she'd shrugged, raised her eyebrows as if to say, *That's irrelevant to us.*

Of course Ana wanted Horizon to be more inclusive, more affordable, to cater to a wider racial profile of children throughout the Bay Area. But at the same time, she couldn't help but wonder if it was a little cruel to the handful of children at the school who were both on scholarship and of color, who often sat together even though they weren't in the same grade. It must be exhausting for them.

She felt bad for thinking it, but in a lot of ways, Hadley's whiteness maybe made her transition to Horizon easier. Her classmates had included her automatically.

But then things had started to shift. Maybe it had nothing to do with the fact that Hadley's family lived far in the Outer Sunset, while all the other kids lived right near school or in Mill Valley. Perhaps it had nothing to do with the fact that lots of the parents came across each other outside Horizon: They worked together, or one was the other's attorney, or they went to the same gym or tennis club or Pilates class, or their kids were friends because it was so much more convenient to send your kid across the street than it was to have to pick them up all the way across the city.

What Ana loved about fourth grade was the combination of self-sufficiency and relative innocence. But what she hated about fourth grade was when their relative innocence was refracted as a certain parroting of whatever their parents had said. "Don't you live, like, really far away?" one of the kids had asked Hadley over lunch, as if the city wasn't forty square miles in its entirety. "Um, I don't think so," Hadley had said.

And it was worse at Horizon than it had been at Oakbrook, maybe because Ana preferred the source of the things that were parroted in the classroom back at Oakbrook. Or maybe because the Horizon parents were oh-so involved: In so many of the families, only one parent worked, or both parents worked, but their jobs were important enough that they could pop out whenever they wanted. They could delegate everything that needed to be done and handle the thinking part of their job while simultaneously handing out speared olives to kids at Peace in the Middle East day.

Ultimately, it was good for the kids to have involved parents, probably. Ultimately, Ana was happy for the kids who had a stay-at-home mom and a nanny and clarinet lessons and soccer camp and French lessons and swim team and all the things that they'd one day look back on and realize were the foundation of their approach to the world. Ana knew that the right way to feel about this was happy for them. It was just that sometimes it was way too much: the way the parents would email Ana with edits to her curriculum, packaged in eloquent prose littered with smiley faces and a stated awareness that they were overstepping—"I'm not trying to be that parent, Ana, and I appreciate you so much—it's just an idea, and Pete would be glad to come in to help, of course, if you do decide that you would like to teach math with this sort of spin. As you may or may not know, he has his PhD in applied math from MIT—not that you'd guess it from what he's doing now! :)" Ana wouldn't have guessed it, because she had no idea what Pete did, only that he wore black turtlenecks as if he were Steve Jobs, and anyway, she was pretty sure applied math had almost nothing to do with multiplication.

Cooper's parents had every right to stand up for their son if they thought someone was copying his work. And if the accusation had been toward anyone else—Oliver or Nate or Cecily—then Ana might have given it some weight. They were kids, they were taught to collaborate, and sometimes they didn't know where that started and where that ended. It was totally fine.

But Hadley was *so* not the problem here, or anywhere, or at all. Even if she'd wanted to get close enough to copy another kid's answers, they'd probably scooch away, make some kind of scowling noise, make it clear that she wasn't welcome in their circle of personal space. It was enough to break Ana's heart.

The problem was that San Francisco was eroded by tech money. The solution was not blaming a nine-year-old girl.

"Ana. Thanks for hanging on here with me," Beth said.

"Of course," Ana said to Beth's square on the screen.

"Look, why don't you talk to Hadley, okay? I know this whole thing is a little absurd. I know that Hadley's—" Beth looked to the ceiling, blinked rapidly. "She's a good kid, and I'm not concerned about her *cheating*. They're kids, right? This isn't that kind of a thing. But I also know that we put a lot on kids here at Horizon, and that Hadley is still relatively new."

"It's really not an assignment they can't work together on," Ana said.

"Like I said," Beth replied, "I'm not concerned that she cheated on a collaborative time filler." She waved her hands. "No offense, Ana. You know I'm supportive of child-led learning. I'm just saying, Cooper's parents are missing the point. Don't repeat that. But it's still, well—I don't think that Hadley is the issue, but I do want you to check in on her. But do you think it's possible she's not getting the support she needs, either at school or at home?"

"It's possible," Ana said. Had she not been there for Hadley? It could be wearing on the kid, all that exclusion.

"You know, Ana, this is always a risk with students from"—she paused—"less affluent backgrounds. Sometimes the pressure is just too much."

Ana blinked. Hadley certainly hadn't grown up with the level of privilege that most of her classmates had, but it wasn't like she had it all that hard, either. She had two parents with good jobs and health insurance. She was well fed and well dressed and had been to Tahoe.

Beth breathed out a huff. "It's a learning curve, the culture here at Horizon, and Hadley might still be picking it up. You know, at a lot of schools, they take a more punitive approach. Not every student is ready for the type of leeway we give them here at Horizon. How long did it take you, Ana? You know, of course, that many of our teachers attended Horizon themselves. And you've done a beautiful job of living our values, but remember: Hadley is only nine. It would be entirely understandable if she needed a little more time to get it."

"Oh," Ana managed, stiffening. "Right."

"Like I said. I'm not worried about cheating. But maybe Cooper's parents are onto something with regard to Hadley's well-being, right? I'm late for another meeting, but we'll be in touch, okay?" She bowed her head, and then her square on Ana's screen went dark.

Eleven: Lily

Three days later, Gina arrived at South Station. The train had been delayed, so there was no time for a prefrosting lunch. They agreed to meet at the pastry shop in Back Bay at four.

Lily sent a voice memo to Ana and Margot from the back seat of an Uber: *Frosting tasting with my mom today, which reminds me: Send me your dresses, I don't think you have yet?*

She blew out a breath of air—five, four, three, two, one—then got out of the car and headed for the front door of Stephan's shop.

Gina was waiting outside, dressed in a sleek, gray wool skirt and a black cardigan over a sheer turtleneck, her hair loose around her shoulders. "Lily!" Gina clapped her hands together in prayer, then extended an arm out to Lily's shoulder. "When was the last time I saw you? Don't look too closely at my skin. I just got a laser peel, it's healing. The derm said it would take ten years off me."

"Hi, Mom," Lily said, going in for the hug. "I think it was two weeks ago."

"Well, it feels like forever. I hope Barb was fine—was she? I didn't mean to spring it on you, but it just felt like a why not. Jack said everything went really well. I texted him this morning."

"Oh, yeah," Lily said. She let the TPQs and the job thing and the future pregnancy rumble around in her stomach, then sucked them back in. "It was fine."

She followed her mom through the glass front door and to a small table set up with plates and empty coffee mugs. Gina turned toward the kitchen. "Steph, we're here! Lattes, if you would?"

He emerged from a swinging door, a tray of ramekins balanced on one hand.

"Lillian, so good to see you," he said. "I am so excited about this buttercream." He extended the tray in her direction.

"It smells great!" Lily said, plucking a tiny spoon from a tray in the middle of the table.

"Is that lavender? You're a visionary," Gina said, raising a spoon to her mouth.

He winked. "Good nose."

Lily fiddled with her engagement ring, smiled up at Stephan.

"Oh, Lily," Gina said, reaching for Lily's hand, "don't touch that. You'll smudge it. It's so pretty, that cut and clarity is to die for. Here, I think I have jewelry cleaner in my purse." She reached down to rummage in her bag.

"Take a spoonful, like this," Stephan said, demonstrating. "I want you to experience it. Don't just taste it, okay? Be the frosting. Let the frosting be you. Let it soak into your veins, do you understand?"

Lily didn't, but she plunged her spoon into it anyway, raised it to her lips.

"It's incredible," Gina said, smacking her lips. "Stephan, you're paying for my extra personal training session this week."

Two hundred, she heard, glanced left and right.

It took her a second to register: It had been a while since she'd heard that voice. *Two hundred,* she heard again. *Two hundred empty calories, a moment on the lips forever on the hips, two hundred.*

She shook her head a little, looked around to see if anyone else had heard the voice, too, even though she knew that of course they hadn't. Lily felt her stomach churn. "Do you have a restroom?" she asked.

"Right back there," Stephan said.

Lily smiled apologetically, grabbed her purse, went to the bathroom, sat down on the toilet's closed lid.

Breathe in. Breathe out. I am in control. I measure myself in strength, not pounds. God, she hated that last one; it didn't even make sense. How could she measure her objective strength? It was so much easier to step on a scale and just know, for sure—no. She didn't need that.

She pulled out her phone, typed out a text to Margot and Ana:

Feeling so excited for the bachelorette party but my mom is kind of getting on my nerves?

No, she deleted it.

Do you remember that voice in my head I told you about a long time ago?

No, she was overreacting. It came back occasionally. It was frustrating, but hiccups were just part of the ongoing process of recovery.

So excited to see you in seven short days omg! There. Send.

Ana liked it immediately. Me too! She responded. This dress good? A screenshot of something blue and silky.

Yup!

Breathe in, breathe out. She stood up, did twenty jumping jacks, returned to the table.

"Everything okay, doll? You look a little red."

"A tiny bit of a headache. Probably just dehydrated. I'm fine." She smiled.

"I think this citrus lavender option is just perfect," Gina said. "Lily, it's up to you, of course. But I think we can sign, seal, and deliver."

"The citrus lavender is complex, classy, understated. Just like you," Stephan said.

Lily looked up to flash him a gracious smile, only to realize he was looking at Gina.

"It's great," Lily said, smiling, returning her hardly eaten ramekin of frosting to his plate. "Let's do it."

"Oh, wonderful!" Gina said. "You certainly saved us some calories, Stephan! Lily, this is so exciting."

Relief washed through her, followed by red-hot shame.

Twelve: Ana

The Hadley thing was really nagging at her. She hadn't been able to focus during her other meetings with parents. She'd texted Lily about it, but Lily hadn't responded, then she felt bad about putting her work stuff on Lily when she knew it was Lily's frosting day, and wasn't there some kind of rule about not putting your work stress on your bride friend when she was tasting frosting with her mom?

She went for a walk, picked up a nice bottle of wine, baked her frustration into meatballs. By the time Si got home, there were two heaping plates of spaghetti and two glasses of wine (hers half finished) on the table.

"It smells amazing," he said, opening the door and kicking off his shoes. He leaned in to kiss her. "How was your day?"

"Terrible," Ana said. "We had conferences, you know? And apparently Cooper's parents think Hadley is cheating off him, which is totally unfounded? Like, Hadley just wouldn't cheat at all. I feel like Horizon has this vendetta against her because her parents aren't in tech."

"Maybe," he said, shrugging. The dishwasher hummed in the background. "Ooh, meatballs. Oh, wait. Cooper? Isn't that Scott's kid? You wanna eat now? I'm starving, actually."

They sat.

"You know Scott?"

"He's at Andreessen, right? He was a big part of our most recent round."

Silas seemed to know everyone who was involved with Horizon, and usually it wasn't even because he'd gone there. It was just that San Francisco seemed to circle around a few midpoints, and most of them were in tech, but when you dug deeper, there were concentric circles around these midpoints that intersected around a few key things and places, and Horizon was one of them. If you were successful at Salesforce or Google, your kids went to Horizon. If you'd gone to Horizon and moved back (after leaving for college back East), then you were now successful at Salesforce or Google.

It was a whole language: one Ana didn't even know how to speak before she'd moved to San Francisco.

"You know his whole expertise is trust and safety in tech? Like, his whole thing is integrity. He led the Series A for this start-up that's working on integrity in AI."

"That's ironic," Ana scoffed.

"What? No," Silas said. "I meant that he's probably drilled that into his kid."

Ana stiffened.

"I mean, I have no idea." He stabbed at his spaghetti. "This looks great, by the way. But Scott is a really good guy. Hey, is there any way you could grab my shirts at the dry cleaner tomorrow? I'm gonna meet the guys for a run, and I don't know when we'll be done."

"Just because he's a good guy, doesn't mean his kid isn't a liar, Si."

He rubbed his temples. "Okay, fine, whatever."

It felt like she'd been kicked in the stomach. "Not whatever," she said.

"Okay, not whatever." He shrugged. "I didn't realize it was such a big deal. But can you? The dry cleaning?"

"It *is* a big deal," Ana said, ignoring the shirts. "It's like—this is the problem, you know? Nepotism? This is the thing that *kills* me sometimes about that place. They're all so spoiled, and they have to pick on a kid like Hadley?"

"Ana, I mean, it's fourth grade, right? Isn't it supposed to be fun?"

The *point* was that teaching was Ana's calling. The *point* was that each time a kid grasped something Ana taught them, she felt like her place in the world made sense. "Actually, that's *not* the point, Si. It's a serious job, you know? It's not just fun and games."

"Sorry! If you're so stressed about—I don't know—like, you know I make enough money that you don't have to do this job if you don't want, right?"

It was like a gunshot. He was generally supportive of her career. And sometimes she couldn't tell if it was just in her head: Did he brush her off, or was she just too sensitive, too unappreciative of the fact that she got to spend her days discussing koalas and teaching reading, which was objectively more fun than whatever it was that he did all day, which she still didn't completely understand? It was something to potentially get into before they got married, if a proposal was actually coming as soon as Ana thought it might be.

"I'm going for a walk," she said. "You're really bothering me."

It was confusing. It also wasn't the first time they'd run into conflict like this: From the beginning, the severity of the chasm between their worlds was obvious, and for the most part, they'd worked through it.

This felt different, though, and Ana couldn't place her finger on why.

It was the kind of thing Lily could talk her down from, had a million times over the past decade. She could almost hear the advice now: "He loves you so much. He means well. Give him a break, but be honest with him, too. Would you consider talking to him about how that bothered you?" Subtle, kind, true.

In one week, she'd be in Miami, drinking cocktails and wading into the lukewarm ocean. Lily would set Ana at ease, just like she used to, from their neighboring twin beds.

It was hard to wrap her head around the fact that Lily was really getting married. Of how much had transpired since that first day when

Lily had arrived at Hawthorne, some hours after both Margot and Ana, who'd already claimed parallel twin beds and wondered out loud about whoever would be their assigned third in the bed perpendicular to both of them.

Ana and Margot had bonded instantly because they were both from the Midwest, which Ana hadn't expected to be such a big deal. After all, plenty of kids on their floor were from California, which was a lot farther away. But it *had* been a big deal: "Wait, you're both from the middle of nowhere?" some kid had asked, and Ana tried to explain that Margot was from New Trier, which wasn't the middle of nowhere at all, and Ana was from only twenty minutes outside Madison, and Madison was a much bigger city than this one, where they all were now.

Eventually Ana had learned to stop trying to explain. That the California kids and the New York kids were just in a different league. They knew the same people from before, which didn't make any sense—why would a kid from LA go to summer camp all the way in Maine?—but it wasn't worth getting bent out of shape over, or even trying to understand.

Their friendship with Lily had unfurled more slowly. Lily was quiet, which they'd interpreted as snobbish, although it later came out that she just felt excluded, worried that those few hours Ana and Margot spent before she arrived had meant something. That she'd never catch up.

But of course she had. And Ana learned she'd been wrong about Lily. Or maybe half right, but too quick to paint with the broad strokes she'd relied on back in high school. Lily was just a normal girl who was insecure in all the wrong ways, just like she was, and Ana had been biased because her understanding of New York came from all six seasons of *Gossip Girl*. And because she'd been a little intimidated by Lily, with her keratin-treated hair and her makeup that came from a department store and the real diamonds that she wore in her ears, on her neck, on her wrist.

Then, little by little, Lily unfolded in front of them. She was generous with her clothing and her knowledge: Soon they were all three dressing in

Lily's sophisticated frocks and marching up to the doors of whatever upperclassman boys Lily vaguely knew from high school. But she also turned out to be surprisingly generous with her vulnerability. One night, when they were all lying in bed, she told them all the details of her stay at Hope House, admitted that she still sometimes worried that people had liked her more when she was sick. They enveloped her in a hug. Lily came home the next day with cellophane-wrapped bags of gummy hands, one for each of them, as a thank-you for being such good roommates, and it had been so childish, so kind in exactly the wrong way, that they started laughing, and shoving their mouths full of gummies. That was when Ana understood that Lily felt just as left out of the world as she did. That no one had a monopoly on feeling excluded. That rich people could be generous and kind and deeply insecure.

Ana had spent years believing that no one in the world could possibly understand the unique loneliness of the world's capacity to misunderstand her. She'd spent years thinking people like Lily were selfish and one-dimensional. And here was this beautiful roommate of hers: thoughtful and generous and a little bit sad.

They'd all melded, through some kind of osmosis that was maybe unavoidable when so many bodies were crammed into so few square feet: Lily became weirder, or at least more public with her weirdness, and Margot and Ana learned to wear neutrals instead of colorful fringed mesh, to invest in "basics," as Lily called them, and to let texts from boys "breathe" awhile before responding. She was experienced, not just sexually, but emotionally, too: She had a practiced detachment that, once she'd stopped using it against Ana and Margot, they learned to imitate. And it had served them.

Soon, Margot was pulled in a million directions: club lacrosse practice and a cappella and biweekly Campus Democrats meetings, and Ana and Lily found themselves alone most of the time, together. Ana had come to appreciate Lily's bluntness, how she punctuated the evening with questions or exclamations or lessons. "You know, Ana, boys like it when you use *both* hands," she'd say, or "Getting an internship is more about connections than experience." Both of these were facts that Ana actually hadn't known. "I actually didn't know that," Ana would say, again and again, surprising herself: All her life, she'd pretended to know things she hadn't, and suddenly, she didn't need to. "Yeah, well, now you do," Lily would say, and it hadn't even been condescending.

It was just such a relief to be chosen as a best friend. She'd been so lonely for so long: in high school, where no one disliked Ana so much as tolerated her, shrugged their shoulders when asked about her, said that she was "nice, but I don't really know her that well." At home, where it was just Ana and her mom, it could be suffocating, sharing a roof with a woman who liked quilting and Folger's coffee and who hadn't read a book in years and who didn't understand why Ana felt so alone. All Ana had ever wanted was to be known, truly seen, and completely included, and finally, it had happened.

Thirteen: Margot

Another long day at work. Warner at Infinity wanted a few more details on their social media strategy proposal before he was willing to sign, plus confirmation that they'd limit the use of generative AI. "Too wasteful, too much water!" he'd barked into an impromptu Zoom call in which he said only that before logging off, claiming he was late for a red-light-therapy session.

Margot had wrapped up her day at a reasonable 6:00 p.m., run home and changed into Lycra, then made her way toward the lake.

Now she was running, settling into a good pace as the lake air whipped at her face. She loved to be outside in the dark, moving her body at the same pace as her mind.

She wanted to use the time to catch up with Ana about some of their plans for Lily's bachelorette. She tapped Ana's name on her phone.

Ana picked up on the first ring. "Margot. Hi. What color bikini did you get?"

"Green. I'm running, by the way. If I'm out of breath. Lily texted me today. Did she send you the dress she's thinking about?"

"Yeah," Ana said, "it's really pretty. But she looks kind of skinny? It's probably just the angle. I'm crazy to worry about her, right?"

"You think?" Margot asked. "I think she looks the same. I just think the lace looks kind of cheap, which is so unlike her."

She kind of wanted to tell Ana about Alix. But maybe it wasn't really a crush. Maybe it was just a friend thing.

And anyway, she had called Ana to talk bachelorette planning. She needed to stay on track. "So, let's talk Miami. One-week countdown, I feel like we're in a good place? I have custom hats for the girls coming tomorrow, and then I'm getting some bedazzled claw clips with everyone's name, and I made reservations for Saturday dinner and Sunday brunch. I'm thinking we could do an activity? Do you think we should do a club? I was looking into renting a boat, too, but I don't know if it's a lot to ask people to pay for that, too. What do you think?"

"Hmm," Ana said. "We could do custom hats?"

"Right. Arriving tomorrow. I literally just said that. I was asking about a boat. You good?"

"Sorry. Boat. I'm distracted. Beth thinks Hadley is cheating, which is crazy. It's irrelevant. Yes to boat."

"That nerdy one who's obsessed with cats or something? Who you're obsessed with?" Margot's watch dinged at her first mile.

"Foxes, but yeah," Ana said.

"So talk to her? I mean, she probably didn't mean to, or maybe she's going through something tough at home, or, like, overwhelmed? I mean, you feel overwhelmed, right? And you're a grown woman?" She leaped over a curb, jogged in place at a stoplight. "Not that you *should* feel overwhelmed, 'cause you're a genius at your job." It wasn't that Margot thought her job was more important than Ana's, because she didn't. It was just that Ana sometimes made such a big deal out of the minutiae. "I think it's really great that you are totally in her court, don't get me wrong. But what's this really about, Ana? You don't usually get worked up over stuff with kids. Like, you love your job."

Ana sighed. "I don't know," she said. "I just feel like Silas immediately jumped to the other kid's side, like, he wanted me to be wrong—I'm probably overthinking it. He was trying to be nice, like, about me not needing to work. And he's stressed with work. And the move."

"Moving sucks," Margot said. "Why do you think I'm still living with Sabrina?" The light turned green and she crossed the street. "Wait, what do you mean not needing to work? Like, he wants you to be a stay-at-home girlfriend?"

Ana let out a sigh on the other end of the line. "Never mind. Sorry. It was nothing. He just mentioned that I didn't have to work if I didn't want to, I was complaining, and he was just, like, reminding me that he makes good money, as if I didn't know. He meant it in a nice way. I'm just being weird. I don't know why. I'm excited for Lily's next week. I think the boat is a good idea."

Margot considered pushing Ana on this, but decided to let her come to it in her own time. She would. "Okay, Ana. I'll book the boat, and then I'll look into towels for the beach—there's this cute place that does embroidery for cheap, I've used them for a shoot before. I want all the swag to feel cute and actually usable, not, like, the stuff that says Lily's name all over it, right? I'll send you pics. I have some intervals coming up, so I'm gonna get off, but text me if you want to talk more about Silas, obviously."

"I will," Ana said.

She turned up the music and let her stride open up. It was only at these kinds of speeds that her breath, paradoxically, felt slow. And then she could really think.

If it were any other weekend of the year, she'd be more excited about all the plans she had in place for Miami. She'd spend her run finalizing details in her head, sprinting and focusing and planning.

It was just that the timing of this trip was so bad.

She'd been working so hard for so long, and now she was this close to finalizing the Infinity account, and it was a mountain of extra tasks piled on top of everything she was already working on, and obviously she'd get it done, but she also knew that Warner would have a million last-minute questions and just as many urgent phone calls between now and the signature, and also, Alix hadn't texted her, and it was kind of bothering her, and it was bothering her that it was bothering her, and also, she was remembering that she used to have these dreams about kissing her friend Chloe, and she'd brushed them off as totally rogue, but now she was thinking about them again, and last night she'd dreamed about Alix pulling Margot's top over her head and circling her nipples with her tongue.

It was just that she wasn't used to being distracted by anyone who wasn't a client. It was just that she'd done it all, and she'd done it all alone.

Margot had moved to Chicago when everyone at Hawthorne was trickling toward Boston and New York and San Francisco. She'd landed her first job at a mid-tier performance marketing shop, and she'd excelled: In two years, she was promoted three times, which was practically unheard-of. After that, she set her sights on the city's top creative agencies. It all seemed so fun and glamorous: being independent, working on ads for products she loved, managing celebrity talent. She wanted, with her whole entire being, to work on the high-profile accounts at one of the most desirable shops.

"Maybe it's just not the right timing," Ana had offered unhelpfully when Margot called to vent after three months of rejections. "At least you have a decent job already, right?"

Lily was pushier: "Keep going, Margot," she said. "This is not an unreasonable dream."

When she finally got a call from a recruiter at McQueen, who said they wanted her to start "immediately" and that they were so excited to onboard her, she'd actually squealed.

"Sorry!" she said to the guy on the other side of the phone. "I've just been wanting this for so long!" And he laughed like he was used to this exact conversation, which he probably was: It was so glamorous to be glamorous, to have unlimited PTO and a corporate card and a desk in an open-concept office where there was cold brew on actual tap, and beer, too, because everyone was drinking all the time and having fun and making creative waves and changing the discourse of advertising as we know it!

That first day at McQueen had been so exciting. Margot had worn a cream cashmere sweater that exposed her collarbone, and a row of layered necklaces. She'd watched Jenny size her up, and felt thrilled to be working in a place where people looked at you.

The whole day had been all hustle and bustle: a headshot for the website, taken by their in-house photographer. A tour of the production studio. An invitation to eat all the dried mango and goji berries she wanted. A settling in: Do you want a standing desk? A sitting desk? A sit-to-stand desk? Two desks? Whatever you need for maximum productivity!

By the time she finally sat down, her phone had filled with missed calls and texts. "We never hear from you, Moo!" her parents were always saying when she finally picked up their calls, and Margot knew that they meant it as a compliment. She was becoming the woman they'd bred her to be: working hard and excelling and thriving and making the requisite sacrifices for down-the-line elation. A break would come soon, and she'd spend a weekend back home in the suburbs, or else they could come down to meet her for dinner in Streeterville, no problem, but things were just crazy right now, but they'd calm down soon, promise. "Busy girl," they'd said, and Margot had known that by that they meant "We love you." "I am!" Margot had said, and she'd known that they'd understood it to mean she loved them, too.

And then, one day after work, they'd all gone home, leaving their lunchboxes in the fridge and their running shoes under their desks, like always. And then they'd been urged to work from home for a few days. It was a nice change of pace, she didn't mind, and it would only be for a few days, max.

—

And then a week stretched into a month, working on laptops from kitchen tables, and a month into a year, and they'd set up desks in bedrooms, and people died, and they continued filming commercials for potato chips, outsourcing their production crews to places where there wasn't as much regulation.

Everyone had gotten more productive, according to the weekly memos that went out. Everyone had logged on for happy hours, pushing glasses of whatever alcohol they hadn't yet run out of into the cameras of their laptops, laughing defeated laughs and listening to so-called motivational spiels from the director. He was working from his second house in Sun Valley, until he got sick of the altitude and started taking calls from his third house in the Hamptons. They'd all pinned the rectangle of him big on their screens so that they could get a better look at whatever portion of his home was visible from his camera, and they all realized how fucking rich he was, that there were all the makings of prosperity in full view, and that was just what the camera could see: a casual Eames chair, a pair of designer dogs, a framed photo of his family with Taylor Swift.

It was frustrating, but Margot was good at staying focused, at channeling her disillusionment into online graphic design courses and setting big goals.

It had been sometime between Margot's grandmother dying alone in a cordoned-off hospital and her discovery that $80,000 a year was actually not that much money that she'd stopped caring quite so much, which is to say, she still cared a lot. But still, she'd started to see what she could get away with. It was little things at first: scrolling Instagram during a meeting, her phone face up on her desk where her laptop's camera couldn't see it. Turning her video off every now and again, citing poor internet connection but really just avoiding brushing her hair. Putting doctor's appointments on her calendar so she could take a walk during the day, then opting instead to take a nap. Using the time she saved not commuting to freelance for a competing agency, which was probably illegal—but the director of McQueen had an *airplane*! So what if she made an extra forty-five dollars an hour?

The return to the office postpandemic came with a renewed sense of urgency. It felt good to come back, to see her coworkers, to dress up for the day and get home late. Sure, it had been a little harder to wake up early and smile big at her clients, but she'd gotten back into the groove of things, and now she was better at her job than ever before.

And it was all leading up to this: the promotion, the move, the grin on her parents' faces when she finally accomplished something major. The rest of her life.

She finished her workout, ate a burrito bowl on the couch, and half watched *The Sopranos*.

A ping. She felt around on the couch for her phone.

Hey, it's Alix.

Her stomach flipped. She wanted to type it out: *I actually might be gay and I know you thought I wasn't but I had a sexy dream about you and like I've had sex with a bunch of guys but it always feels kind of hollow?*

Instead, she waited a moment, then wrote: Hey! Was nice chatting with you.

A couple friends and I are going to Soccer Mommy next weekend if you wanted to join?

For half of a split second, she considered skipping Lily's bachelorette trip.

I'll be in Miami! But want to do coffee when I'm back?

She waited for a response, didn't get one. Finished her burrito bowl, then must have accidentally dozed off, because it was midnight when her eyes fluttered open and she realized she'd fallen asleep with her phone in her hand.

Fourteen: Ana

The Monday after conferences, they were back at school, business per usual.

Ana and Bryn walked to a park where they liked to eat their packed lunch at a picnic table.

"Do you ever get frustrated?" Ana asked as she sat.

Bryn scoffed, pulled a Ziploc of grapes out of her bag and extended it to Ana. "With the parents? With the administration? With the disparity in education that I am implicitly furthering by teaching at Horizon instead of a public or charter school—both of which have plenty of issues, too? With the pretentious progressivism of the entire ethos of this place?"

"So, yes?" Ana said, and they both laughed a scornful sort of laugh.

"But seriously, yes. Of course. How could anyone not?"

"Yeah," Ana said.

"In a lot of ways, I love this job. The kids are great. It's wonderful to send out a newsletter to the parents requesting new markers and drawing paper and a box of glue sticks and receive all that plus three brand-new MacBooks and four copies of some unreleased graphic novel about immigration rights under Trump.

"It's good. Great, even. The kids are so well behaved, and so well taken care of." She thought for a second. "But if they didn't let me keep my aging mom on my health insurance, and if I didn't have student loans and a husband who barely made minimum wage, and if I didn't need to stay local to care for said aging mom who is way too stubborn to leave this egregiously expensive city, and if I had even a modicum of transferable experience to a field that wasn't education, then—well—would I be working at Horizon? I would not."

"You love it, though," Ana said, a little shocked at Bryn's crassness: Bryn seemed so passionate. She seemed, genuinely, to love the students, to throw herself into teaching, to care deeply about each and every one of them. She glanced around to make sure none of the parents were coincidentally nearby.

"Look, Ana," Bryn said, waving a potato chip in the air, "don't get me wrong. I love the kids. I am grateful for this job. But some of us don't really have—don't take this the wrong way—the freedom that you have. It's—I put on a face because it's, like, *survival* for me. It's okay if you don't get it."

Ana, flustered, took a long sip of lemonade. "I *do* get it. Of course I get it. Just because my mom has her own insurance—I mean, I'm sure she'll have health issues, eventually. And my friends—Lily has never had to worry about anything in her life. She has a trust fund and multiple vacation houses, and she's having this fancy wedding. Even *Margot* makes twice what I do. And that's in Chicago. I'm not like them." She considered citing Silas's wealth, too, but decided against it: Bryn might think Ana was bragging.

"Ana," Bryn said, "you're comparing yourself to some of the richest people in the country. From where I sit, you've got it pretty good."

Ana sighed, a little wounded by Bryn's willingness to draw a line in the sand between them. To push Ana away.

"It really doesn't feel that way," she said, considering the credit card bill she hadn't yet paid. The dress for Lily's wedding, plus her flight and the cast-iron pan she and Silas bought as a wedding gift, which were weighing heavily atop all the expenses of daily life in San Francisco.

Bryn shrugged. "Not to sound like a Pinterest bitch, but count your blessings, girl."

Ana rolled her eyes. "Can I tell you something crazy?"

"Of course," Bryn said. "Is it sexual? Are you and Silas getting into foursomes or something?"

"Ew," Ana said. "No. I had this thought today. I don't know why. But a tiny part of me kind of wants to go back to Oakbrook. Is that crazy?"

"You should," Bryn said. "Seriously. These Horizon kids are going to be fine no matter what. Like, no offense—you're a great teacher—but even if their teacher sucked, they're reading with their parents every night and going to French class and soccer and gymnastics after school and spending their summers at horse camp and shit. Like, these kids don't need you."

Ana had come to appreciate Bryn's honesty. The way she told her students to "stop acting like CEOs."

"Harsh." Ana smiled.

"You know it's true."

"I do."

They chewed in silence.

"What else is up?" Bryn asked. "Give me some gossip. Non-Horizon gossip. I am at my wit's end at this place. Does your classroom smell like ass too?"

"Oh god, yes," Ana said. "You'd think these parents could afford deodorant for their kids, right?"

"They're all afraid it's aluminum and toxic or something. I don't know. Okay. Gossip. Fun gossip. Please."

"Hmm," Ana said. "Um, Silas has a work trip in Paris, and—"

"He's taking you?"

"That's what he said."

"I see," Bryn said. "Is he proposing in Paris? You just moved in together. Is that what's next?"

"I mean, I don't know. With Lily getting married—"

Bryn nodded. "You thought you were a strong, independent woman who didn't define your relationship based on your friends' relationships, but now your friend is getting married and you're starting to get jealous?"

"No!" Ana said. "I'm not jealous! It has nothing to do with Lily. Why? Did *you* get married because your friends got married?"

Bryn shrugged. "In a way, yeah. Don't get me wrong: I love Max. It's not like I didn't want to get married. But it's also not a coincidence that our entire group got married in the span of basically a year, you know?"

Ana paused. "You don't think Hadley cheated, right?"

"Ana, she didn't cheat. You know this girl. I know this girl. She reads the encyclopedia in her spare time and once tapped me on the shoulder when I was supervising recess to say that she accidentally took a piece of the school's chalk home in her backpack, and then she handed it to me and said she was sorry, and I was like dude, oh my god, keep the chalk, you are way too good for this place. But how is that relevant to Silas?"

Ana smiled, avoided the question. "She's kind of a perfect child, right?"

"This place can be an elitist prick factory, but I do not think Hadley is one of the pricks." She twirled her hair in her fingers. "Ana, I mean this with all the love in the world—you don't have to marry him."

Ana blinked. "What do you mean? Of course I want to marry him! Not immediately, but when the time is right!" She took another grape from Bryn's Ziploc.

Bryn raised her eyebrows, crossed her arms. "Okay!" she said. "I believe you."

The next night, Ana and Silas were tipsy at a sushi bar on Chestnut. Ana ordered another glass of sake and wished she was dressed more like everyone else in here with their silk wrap dresses and chunky knits and heeled boots. They were dipping sashimi in soy sauce and touching knees under the table, and maybe Ana absolutely did belong here in this cashmere-and-silk type of city, with her cashmere-and-silk type of boyfriend. She made a mental note to ask Lily for some shopping recommendations.

"I don't know why I had this thought," Ana started, laughing to herself. "I told Bryn yesterday that I was kind of missing Oakbrook? But, like, that's so dumb."

"Yeah, what?" he said, laughing. "That was an objectively way worse job."

"I know." She leaned toward him, took another piece of sushi. "I guess I was just thinking about Hadley and the cheating thing and letting it get to me. Like, why is Beth turning it into a whole thing?"

"You're still thinking about that?" he asked, rubbing her arm.

"I know," she said. "I was, like, 'Bryn, maybe I should just go back to where the parents weren't such pricks,' and she was like, 'Yeah, you probably should.' It was so dumb." She bit her lip, waited for him to laugh.

"Look," he said, stirring wasabi into his dish of soy sauce, "I think it's great that you care about Hadley. But do you ever worry that you're ignoring the other kids? It's not as woke of you as you think it is to only care about one kid. Do you think maybe this is just your reproductive clock or whatever? Some motherly instinct kicking in?"

"Whoa," she said, stiffening, suddenly sober. "That's, like, kind of mean?"

"I'm just saying," he said, shrugging. "Cooper's dad is a good guy, Ana. And if you didn't want to work at Horizon, maybe you shouldn't have had me pull all those strings for you, you know?"

"It's not—" She swallowed. "Never mind. Let's just drop it."

They reached for edamame pods, popped the beans into their mouths, sat there chewing.

He wanted ice cream on the way home and Ana didn't. It was cold out, and dinner had been so strained, and Silas didn't protest when she suggested he go by himself and meet her at home with his pint.

The door creaked open. She hadn't realized until he was home that the anger in her chest from earlier had multiplied in his absence, and now she tingled. She felt her jaw stiffen. She wanted so badly to march toward Silas, to hurl the fragile globe of her rage at him in unrehearsed exclamations—*how dare you side with Scott, you always side with the Scotts*—to march out in a huff, to scream at him: He was supposed to find her sexy, and he was supposed to tell her that, and he was supposed to pick up his socks, and he was supposed to be as effusive with her as he was with the checkout lady at the grocery store or his cousin's new girlfriend, and maybe they were just two entirely different people who had met when they were way too young.

"You get your ice cream?" she said instead.

"Yup," he said. She heard a drawer open, the jangle of cutlery, the pointed lack of drawer close.

—

On Thursday, Ana's class cheered when she told them there wouldn't be homework over spring break. The building was already almost empty as she escorted her kids to the pickup lane—there would be no school on Friday, then the whole next week was off. A janitor mopped the hallway hurriedly. Kangaroos with labeled body parts hopped across the hallway bulletin boards.

Ana followed the kangaroos to the front entrance and supervised kids into cars driven by pretty moms, all of them old enough to have both a career and a nine-year-old, though their faces looked untouched by time, as if they'd managed neither.

She watched one of the moms kiss her kid on the head, and thought of her own mom, whom she spoke to often enough but hadn't actually seen in over three years. It was just too hard: listening to her mom explain in excruciating detail how they'd rearranged the grocery store, or that she was planning a dinner at Chili's next week with her group of friends. It was impossible to explain to this woman she hardly knew anymore what her life was like now, and anyway, her mom was always getting caught up in the details in a way that felt too grating to put up with. "I'm going to Miami with Lily for her bachelorette" would turn into a slow barrage of questions: "Can all the girls afford that? Is Lily paying for everyone? What kind of food do they eat in Miami?" Most days, it didn't seem worth the effort. But today, she kind of wanted to hear about her hometown grocery store.

It was a nice day. Ana would walk the two miles home and call her mom today.

She picked up on the first ring. "Ana!" she said. "I never hear from you on a weekday. Is everything okay?"

"Yes, hi, of course," she said, a trickle of shame washing through her as she walked past mansions tracked with ivy. Did she really never call her mom on a weekday? "Just saying hi. How are you?"

"Just out walking. First spring day out here, actually. It must be almost spring break, right, Ana? Are you unpacked?"

"Yes and no," Ana said, looking around as she walked: A cat thumped its tail against a trellised window.

"Well, you'll have some time for that next week, then, right? Unless you want to book a last-minute trip to come see your old mom."

Ana didn't. As much as she sometimes felt like a second fiddle here in San Francisco, there was something so much worse about being back home—where her mom, her Aunt Kate, and the moms of old friends she'd inevitably run into all looked at her like she thought she was better than they were, just because she'd left.

"Oh, Mom, I would, but I have Lily's bachelorette in Miami this weekend, and I'm leaving tomorrow morning."

"Of course. That will be fun! Hey, I wasn't going to tell you this until we talked on Sunday, but I guess you'll be in Miami, so now that I have you—I don't want you to worry. But I've had a few dizzy spells, and I went to the doctor today so they could run some tests. They're ruling some things out, but I should have more information in the next few days."

"Oh," Ana said, her feet stopping underneath her. "Is it serious? What kind of dizziness?"

"I didn't want to worry you. Don't worry, okay? How are you?"

"Okay," she said gingerly, started walking again. "They have no idea?"

"No need to jump to conclusions, okay? Let's not worry."

She was worried. But it would be kinder to brush it off anyway, to make it seem like nothing bad could ever happen. As an only child to an aging single parent, she often felt the need to stay upbeat, to absorb the fear so her mom wouldn't have to.

So she told her mom about work, about the kangaroo unit and the new computer lab and parent-teacher conferences and the fact that Silas had invited her to Paris.

It would be good, to spend a few days in the sun with her friends. To come back to herself within their orbit, her only effort flipping from one side to the other when she started to overheat. To drink Aperol spritzes and guffaw over shared details about their sex lives. To let Margot and Lily remind her that she was probably only feeling a little apprehensive about the potential proposal because she was about to get her period, that her mom would be fine, that the Hadley thing would blow over, that it wasn't the end of the world if she and Silas were going through a bit of weirdness as they transitioned to their life together.

She sat in the middle of an explosion of clothing, folding tiny tops and tiny shorts into her suitcase. She wedged her makeup bag between a rolled-up dress and four bikinis, and vowed to stay focused on the bachelorette party, on her friends, on Lily.

She dialed Margot.

"Hi," Margot said. "I'm at work."

"I'm bringing mostly casual stuff, but should I bring heels?"

"Obviously. Don't bring white, right?"

"Fuck," said Ana, plucking a mess of fabric from her bag. It was her favorite dress: light and silky, made her boobs look good and her skin look tan. She dropped it to the floor, let it pool. "Can I wear white jeans?"

"I wouldn't," Margot said.

"God," Ana said. "This whole thing is weird, right?"

"What? Not wearing white? I mean, it's a little outdated, but I get it, and it's not that hard to avoid."

"Not that. I mean, that, but—" *That my life is exactly on track, that I'm plenty old enough to commit to forever, and yet I still feel like a bumbling child inside, like the girl I was when Silas and I first met.* "Do you ever still feel, like, seventeen? Like, no one should trust us with anything, but we're old enough to commit to other people forever, you know?"

"Not really," Margot said. "You good?"

"Yes," Ana said, suddenly self-conscious. Why didn't she feel as rooted in adulthood as Margot did? "For sure. I just—"

"Because if you're not, just tell me! I'll come visit and we can fix whatever it is!"

"No, seriously," Ana said, "work is good, Silas is good. Nothing to fix. I'll see you so soon!"

Ana zipped up her suitcase and leaned back against the bed. Their bedroom was messy, and not just because Ana had torn through it packing. It was also filled with Silas's junk: a half-spilled box of baseball caps—he'd needed one the other day, and found it at the bottom; a stack of papers; a pair of pants with a hole in them, crumpled on the floor.

She fell asleep early, before Silas was home, then, in the morning, found him snoring next to her. She crawled out of bed, quietly so as not to wake him, grabbed a piece of paper, and scribbled a note: *Off to airport, love you, finish unpacking your boxes while I'm gone? xx.*

The *x*'s felt forced. She grabbed her stuff and left.

Fifteen: Lily

Wednesday.

Lily hadn't mentioned the voice from the frosting tasting to Jack. The whole impromptu therapy session and you-need-a-job thing still stung, and plus, they'd been so busy that there just wasn't time to sit down and talk—not about Jack's closeness with Lily's mother and how it made Lily feel both grateful and also like maybe her mom was using Jack as a back door to Lily's inner world. Not about their wedding's RSVP list (so far, they'd gotten only yeses, and that was going to be a problem), not about the rehearsal dinner (they needed to pick two signature cocktails and okay the menu and send place cards ahead of time), and certainly not about the way Lily's stretch marks in the mirror made her for a single second want to cancel the whole wedding altogether. It was irrational, and it wasn't worth getting into, and it was too hard to explain to a man who thought about his body a reported two to three times a year.

But mostly, there was just a lot to do, logistically.

"You're not going to believe this."

Lily looked up from where she was sitting on the couch they'd schlepped here from New York. A twenty-fifth birthday present from her mom. "I thought you had lunch plans with the guys," Lily said, a little self-conscious at being caught doing nothing in the middle of the day.

"I do," Jack said. "I'm heading out soon. But really quick, I just got this cryptic message from the Airbnb host—"

"About your bachelor party?"

He came and sat down next to her. "Apparently the whole house flooded. I told the owner that it wasn't a big deal, we don't care if it's in perfect shape, but he sent back pictures, and it's actually really fucked."

"That sucks," Lily said. "There must be other options, though, right? In the area?"

"You would think, but I guess this late, only the shitty places are left. Would it be crazy if we just pivoted to Miami?"

"This weekend? Like, with the girls?"

"Yeah, I mean, unless that's an issue. There's just tons of places there, and it could be fun to get the girls and guys together before the wedding. Maybe Margot and Alistair would hit it off?" He winked. "And it's so last minute, I don't really know what else to do."

"What about the flights?"

"There's a million to Miami," he said, shrugging. "All the guys have enough status to change their flights, anyway."

She smiled. "Hmm," she said, thought about what Margot would say: "This was supposed to be just for us girls." It wasn't Margot's weekend, though. "That could be fun."

Would it be, though? She loved her fiancé, obviously. She loved his friends, and for all their preference to talk stocks over feelings and software over their shared past, they *would* have a good time together.

But something about the idea felt prickly.

Truthfully, Lily wanted this weekend with her friends and her friends alone. The idea of Jack's friends' presence reminded her of college, when the three of them would have plans to prank the girls across the hall or paint each other's toenails, and then Ana would announce that Silas was coming over, and suddenly, something would be broken. Suddenly, Ana was all closed-mouth giggles and wearing a padded bra underneath her pajamas.

And then, of course, there was the problem of the voice in her head, which maybe she'd divulge at least to Ana or Margot if she was alone with them, but if all the guys were around, she'd have to stuff it down.

She *could* tell Jack about it: "Hey, Jack," she could say, "the weirdest thing happened when I was tasting those frostings with my mom. Remember the calorie-counter voice? It just—came back! Totally out of nowhere. So weird, but it did, and it's been back ever since, not all the time, not that night we had dinner in the South End with your law school friends, and not that morning you made me pancakes in bed. But a lot of the time. And I haven't told Ana or Margot, or you or even Barri, and it's freaking me out a little, not enough to really worry, but maybe I'm worried a little bit? And kind of suddenly nervous about a whole weekend of eating with every single one of your people?"

He'd probably wrap her up in a hug and tell her it was okay, that he was glad she told him, and perhaps it would make sense for her to go to New York for a few days, see Barri in person and spend a few days in her childhood bedroom.

"We can totally not do that if you don't want," Jack said now.

"No, Jack, of course you can. It makes logistical sense. And go to the lunch thing. I'll find something for you guys in Miami and I'll book it. You're eight, right?" See? Look how busy she was!

"You sure?"

"Super," Lily said. "Go. Seriously."

She wanted to be helpful. She wanted to be inclusive. And anyway, a little forced bonding ahead of the wedding couldn't hurt.

He kissed her on the mouth, grabbed his jacket, and reminded her that she could totally change her mind.

She flipped on the TV and scrolled through some options, made an executive decision that Jack should book a condo in the same complex that Margot had already booked for the girls. It would be easy. Fun. Maybe Margot would end up with Alistair balls deep inside her.

She felt restless, flopped onto the floor and kicked out a few bicycle crunches, eyes to ceiling. Her heart felt quick in her chest, like she'd overdone it on the coffee or run a seven-minute mile. She sat back on the sofa, focused on her breathing, turned off the TV and tried a guided meditation, but gave up after two breaths.

Fuck. Okay. She'd head out of the house, get her nails done. Walk the Commons. That always calmed her.

—

She was one coat of paint in, the smell of polish heavy in the air around her, when her phone buzzed. Probably Jack. She hated letting his calls go to voicemail. It felt at odds with the intimacy of a shared life.

She glanced apologetically at the manicurist, dried her soaking left hand on a towel. "Hi!" she said.

"Lillian!"

She pulled her phone away from her face. Jack's mom. "Annette?"

"What are you up to? I'm in town!"

"Oh! I'm just getting my nails done. Jack's at lunch with friends, maybe he didn't tell you? They have a whole afternoon planned, some symposium thing—"

"No, I know! He mentioned you're up to some R and R, so I made us an appointment at a bridal boutique my friend Judy owns out in Newton to scope out some rehearsal-dinner dresses. I thought I'd scoop you, if that's alright, but if you have plans, please tell me. I asked Jack, and he said you didn't have anything going on today, but I realize he doesn't know everything about you."

She felt her face go hot. This wasn't the plan. She had lots to do: packing and finalizing details for the weekend, getting ready and cleaning the apartment before they left. "Oh!" she said, trying not to show her frustration. And plus, she and her mom were going to shop for rehearsal-dinner dresses together. Lily had promised. "That's so nice of you, Annette. Really, I'd love to, the only thing is, my mom and I were going to look at rehearsal dresses next weekend, and—"

A squeal. "That's my girl!"

"Mom?"

"Darling. Lillian. I took the train in, and Annette picked me up at the station! Lillian, you know I wouldn't brave Boston shopping for anyone but you, so we'll just do a cursory search, a nice dinner if we can even *find* one."

"You guys are together?" First the appointment, now this? She supposed she should want her mom and her mother-in-law to connect, but it was starting to feel a little like collusion.

"Can you believe it?" said Gina. "Annette wants to take me to some earthy yoga class in Cambridge tomorrow. I told her I can't do *that.* So this was the compromise. Shopping. Common ground. Are you surprised we're here?"

Her breath quickened. "Definitely a surprise!" Lily managed.

"She's surprised. She sounds surprised, right? Oh, we're so good!" Gina said. "Okay. We'll be at your place in forty-five. This will be fun!"

Lily really, totally, absolutely loved her mom. She appreciated more and more with each passing year the depths of her mom's commitment to her grown children's well-being, the immense amount of energy she spent curating their childhoods: soccer practice and violin lessons and trips to Europe and lessons about empathy forged over homemade dinners, and all the ways this had panned out for Lily and her brother now that they were grown. Lily knew that when her mom eventually died, she would lose a piece of herself so significant that she'd spend the rest of her life trying her hardest to relearn who she was.

But right now, her mom was driving her crazy.

Lily emerged from a dressing room, her mom and Annette side by side on a velvet love seat, sipping champagne and lowering their glasses appraisingly.

"You don't like that, do you?" her mom asked.

"I kind of did, actually," Lily said. She'd tried on eighteen dresses so far, and she thought she looked good in at least a few of them.

"Oh, you look beautiful," Annette said, over and over again, and while her feedback was undiscerning and largely unhelpful, Lily found herself thinking with just a hint of jealousy that it must have been nice for Jack's sister, Cameron, to a grow up with a mom so generous with her praise.

"Lily, it's not flattering, that dress. You're wide in the shoulders, just like your dad. You need a V, or something different. I don't like this place, I don't think they're helpful."

"Mom," she said, glancing in the direction of the one woman who worked there, who was only ten feet away.

"Oh, Lily, shush. If she wants to be helpful, then she can help us."

"I think it's gorgeous, Gina," Annette said.

Lily's mom stood, went to a rack, picked up a dress. "Now this is a dress," she said. "It says it's a four. Lily, you're a four, right? Here."

Lily took the dress into the dressing room, wriggled out of the dress her mom didn't like, pulled the new one on over her head. The zipper was stuck—she could almost get it, but no—maybe she could work the fabric around so it wasn't covering her face, then she could glance in the three-way mirror and see where the zipper was caught.

Almost there, her eyes were free—

Oh!

The shock of it, the way the light caught on the stretch marks on the back of her thighs, the soft fleshy bit below her back ribs. The way her ass jutted outward, a note of a dip on the outside of her hips. Her shoulder blades were broad and expansive, enough shoulder for two women at least.

What had she been doing, gallivanting through life, assuming people loved her, planning a wedding and sampling frosting and getting her nails done and booking a facial as if extracting a few blackheads near her hairline could possibly fix a fraction of what she was dealing with?

"Lily? How is that cute dress? I didn't even look at the price, but it's your wedding, so of course it doesn't really matter—"

"It fits—" she lied, the dress still crumpled up around her neck.

"Come out and show us!"

"I think it has a stain, actually, ew, it's totally covered in something, I'm taking it off," she said.

"Oh, well, if you like it, I'm sure they have another in the back!"

She wriggled it up over her head, hung it back up, placed it behind the others, pulled her jeans back on.

"I'm getting a bit of a headache, actually. Let me just go home and lie down, we can reconvene for dinner. I'm sorry, it's my fault, I should have had more water to drink, it was the fumes at the nail salon—"

"I'm always telling you to drink more water, Lily. You know what I read in the *Times* the other day? If you're thirsty, it's already too late."

"I know," Lily said, emerging from the dressing room. She let her mom usher her outside, Annette in tow. Sometimes it was just easiest to do what she was told.

Gina pulled out her phone. "I made a dinner reservation at a place two blocks away. Do you need to go home? Or should we just go right there?"

"I guess I can just go if you want," Lily said. "We'll be early, but we can have a drink at the bar."

A pair of moms pushing strollers walked past. It brought Lily back to the TPQs. Was pushing a stroller and chatting with a mom friend from playgroup what she wanted?

They sat at a table by a window.

"Well, I'm sorry we didn't get you anything," Annette said.

"It was good that we ruled some things out, though, right? When you come to New York, we'll have a much more streamlined idea of where to start. What do you think about Rachel Comey for something? No, never mind. Too edgy. Bergdorf's is tried and true, it's just a little tired lately. I'll think about it, ask Julia what she did for her daughter."

"You feeling okay, Lily?" Annette asked.

"Yes!" she said, louder than intended.

Lily tried to skim the menu and not worry about her mom, whose world was Lily, who was probably grieving the end of an era in which she was the only formal mother figure in Lily's life. Lily wanted to tell her that Annette could never replace her, even if sometimes she did prefer Annette's energy: less frenetic, almost calming.

She counted down from five and reminded herself that it was okay to have a stressful day, that stress could coexist with fun, and that taking care of her mom wasn't her job. That she was grateful her mom and her mother-in-law-to-be were spending time together.

The waiter came over to take their orders.

"I'll have the Cobb salad with no bacon and dressing on the side," Gina said.

"Oh, that sounds wonderful," said Annette. "I was going to do the steak—but let's make it two of the Cobbs. Same with me, no bacon, dressing on the side."

Lily opened her mouth to order the salmon in brown butter, except that her lips instead formed around the words "Same for me," and the waiter nodded approvingly.

"Easy to remember," he said.

And then when it came, she ate one bite, and then couldn't bring herself to eat any more. She pushed her dinner around on her plate, sipped at her water. Took extra care to laugh loudly with her head thrown back when anyone made a joke, as if to say, "If there was something wrong with me, would I really be this happy?"

PART TWO

Sixteen: Lily

Lily and Jack's taxi pulled up to departures, and Lily wondered again if she should have warned her friends about the late addition of the boys. There was a part of her that knew they'd have wrinkled their noses and groaned *Whyyy*, but if she framed it as a last-minute surprise, then at least they would know it was too late for that.

Jack grazed her knee with his hand.

"You excited?" he asked. "And you sure it's cool that we're here? The guys?"

Lily watched a family pile out of a decrepit old van. Kids in polyester pajamas, tired mom, balding dad. "Mm," she murmured.

"What?"

"I just—I'm wondering if I should have told them ahead of time. About your friends." She let her head fall onto Jack's shoulder as the car slowed to a stop.

"I think it will be a fun surprise," Jack told her, shrugging. "Especially for everyone who's single." A hand on her knee. "You're so pretty. You know that, Lil?"

She napped during the flight, letting the whir of the engine hum her to sleep. She woke to Jack stroking her thigh, telling her they'd landed. A baby screamed, a pair of teenagers raced to the front before anyone else could get their bags. Lily and Jack grabbed their suitcases and waited to be picked up.

Seventeen: Ana

Ana watched four old episodes of *Girls* on the plane, then considered waiting for Margot at the airport so they could share an Uber, but decided she needed to get the plane smell off her and settle in.

She unlocked the front door, unpacked her stuff into a cramped closet, and watched TikToks in bed while she waited for the others to trickle in.

Margot was first, singing out as she pushed open the door.

"In here," Ana called to her, wrapped her in a hug.

It was good to have a few moments together before everyone else got there: They set up penis streamers in the kitchen and turned on a Taylor Swift album, set out the personalized hats and mini bottles of tequila.

Then Zoe and Liza and Emily arrived, all in from New York; then Lily's camp friend Eileen. The sun was starting to set by the time they all heard the door handle jingle with Lily's arrival.

"Lily's here!" Margot said.

Lily looked predictably elegant, even after a stuffy plane ride: loose jeans that hit right at her ankle, strappy sandals, and freshly painted toes. A drapey sweater, white linen collar peeking out from underneath. Her hair was blown out smooth, and her skin looked dewy and fresh. Ana waited her turn for a hug.

"So," Lily said, "slight update, which should be fun for some of us." She winked in Margot's direction. "Jack's Airbnb got, like, completely decimated, so Cabo was totally untenable."

"Do not tell me they're here," Margot said, scoffing. "Can you imagine? All those random former rowing guys fucking up our girls' weekend?"

Ana watched Lily's cheeks turn red. "Um," Lily said. "Well, it's not like we have to be tied at the hip to them, I was thinking just dinner and going out and maybe one beach day—"

"Oh my god, is the hot one here?" Zoe squealed.

"Not sure which is the hot one, but—yes?"

"Wait, Lil," Margot said. "The boat is capped at eight, and we have two reservations that I can't really change last minute without a big charge, and plus, we were supposed to do massages tomorrow."

"No, totally," Lily said. "And I'll cover the cost of anything that got fucked up. I just—thought it would be fun?"

"It will be fun!" Ana said, going to Lily, giving Margot a look. "That's great, and it will be fun to get to know them better before the wedding. Margot and I can totally figure out how to make some swaps."

Lily looked relieved. "Okay. Good. Yes. Thank you. Let me just go jump in the shower, then I was thinking we order in?"

It was late, and everyone wanted to conserve their energy for tomorrow, so they ordered Thai food delivery and sat on the floor in a circle, eating right out of the cartons.

Emily was blowing up a plastic doll with Jack's face on it, Eileen from camp was handing out Ring Pops, and Emily was hanging a banner that read "Lily's Last Ride."

"Should we play text or shot?" Ana asked, elbowing Margot. Then, lower: "If you're gonna be on your phone, we might as well have fun with it."

"God, I don't think we can," Margot said, shutting it off and slipping it into her back pocket. "We have bosses and stuff now."

"Well, we just won't text each other's bosses. Just, like, the most recent person you texted."

Margot reddened.

"What? Who are you texting?"

"Boring! Work stuff!" Margot said.

"Okay. What do *you* want to do? Lil? Eileen? Any camp games or something?"

"Honestly, I'm kinda tired," Lily said, and recrossed her legs.

They traded foil tins of Thai food.

"And my stomach hurts from the flight," Lily added, pushing away eggplant studded with ginger.

They played a halfhearted game of fuck, marry, kill and went to bed on a note of agreement: Beto O'Rourke was marriage material, Andrew Cuomo was obviously a goner, and no one was against one night with AOC.

Ana climbed under the covers next to Margot.

"Do you think we made it fun enough for Lily?" Ana asked.

"Hmm?" Margot was hunched over her phone, lying on her side.

"I just feel like she didn't eat anything, and we didn't really do anything."

"True."

"Margot, why are you being so monosyllabic?"

"Sorry, Ana. I'm trying to finish this fucking work thing, and then I need to see about a new reservation for tomorrow, because the place we had can't do parties bigger than eight. I just put so much work into this, and she could have given us literally, like, three days of notice? Give me ten minutes. So I can be fully present tomorrow."

"I can look into options."

"I love you, but picking restaurants is not your strong suit."

"That's true."

Normally, there was a symbiosis to this dance: When Margot and Ana would share a room on a girls' trip, they'd split off for thirty minutes or so before their pillow talk. Ana would call Silas and say good night, and Margot would review fonts or approve music or tell a client to stop freaking out or whatever it was that she did.

But this didn't feel like that: Margot was holding up her end of the arrangement, but Ana felt ancillary. There wasn't much she could do by way of rejiggering the plan: Margot had all the confirmation emails and phone numbers for the restaurants and the boat.

She didn't want to peel off and call Silas, who hadn't texted her since she'd left. Her wound from their spat was still a little leaky. So she stared at the ceiling, and must have fallen asleep before Margot had the chance to flip over and face her.

When Ana woke up, she had four texts from Bryn, which often happened when Bryn and her husband got high on a Friday night: Bryn would deep dive ugly dogs on Reddit and send Ana a barrage of screenshots. Margot was still asleep, so she rolled to her side, swiped her phone open.

You're not going to believe this!!!

A link to a Facebook post.

Oh sorry I forgot you don't have Facebook.

A stack of screenshots, the first a description of a group: "Pac Heights Mommies and Daddies [No Nannies Please!]."

The second, a post: "Keeping this anonymous because I don't want to stir anything up, but I'm a little concerned about something that's going on at Horizon. Curious if any other mommies in the group have thoughts on this: there's a little girl (fourth grade) who comes from a troubled household (know for a fact parents not in this group) who is cheating off my kiddo. Teachers not doing anything about it, haven't been super happy with kiddo's teacher."

Ana paused, felt her armpits go prickly.

"Anyone else feel Horizon = loose with hiring requirements? Oldest graduated from there a couple years back, not saying my kid needs an Ivy League PhD for a teacher, but I thought we were only hiring teachers with master's degrees at least? Would love any thoughts, curious to hear from parents at SF Country Day and other top schools in area. Also, can we update description of group to include nonbinary parents? Not relevant to husband and me, but want to be inclusive! Thanks!"

"Margot." She elbowed her sleeping friend. "I need to show you this shit."

"Five more minutes," Margot murmured. She must have been up late.

Ana typed back a response: this is obviously about me wtf??? And the virtue signaling NB thing, are you fucking kidding me?

She was sweating through her pajamas. It was still early in San Francisco—she probably wouldn't hear back from Bryn for an hour at least.

She went to the living room, where Lily was already making coffee.

"Lil," she said, "look at this." She shoved her phone in Lily's direction.

"What is it?" Lily asked.

"It's about me. This fucking crazy mom who thinks that me not disciplining her kid who, by the way, is a major problem kid and is not being *cheated* off on a *collaborative* assignment, is somehow a reason to publicly lambaste me for not having a graduate degree? Like, we went to *Hawthorne*, I'm not some delinquent, and also, I am so sick of parents abusing the word *kiddo* to sound cute."

Lily read it. "At least she's being inclusive about nonbinary parents," she said, shrugging, then going to the fridge to retrieve a jug of oat milk.

"No, Lily, that's the worst part. She's just *trying* to sound nice. It's literally not genuine *at all*."

"Hmm," Lily said. "Yeah, I guess that is kind of weird." She seemed bored, distracted.

"Lily!" Ana said. "Do you not see how insane this is?"

Lily shrugged. "It's kind of weird, yeah."

"Oh my god," Ana said.

Silas would understand the specific craziness of the pseudo-woke San Francisco elitism. But she didn't want to give him the satisfaction of texting him about it, reminding him that he helped her get this job even though—it was true—she *didn't* have a graduate degree, and they usually *did* require that.

"Never mind," Ana said, locking her phone. "Let's just have fun." She'd think about this later. She was going to focus on celebrating Lily. Cooper and Hadley and her doubts about the rest of her life would still be there for her to obsess over after the weekend.

After scrambled eggs and sourdough toast—preordering groceries for delivery had been Ana's greatest contribution to the planning of the weekend—they all went to the beach in the bikinis Lily had sent them and shared mushroom tacos and beef tinga empanadas and paper boats of freshly baked tortilla chips dipped in hot sauce. They washed down their tacos with glass bottles of Corona topped with wedges of lime, procured from a cooler Emily had thought to pack. Liza squeezed her lime into her hair instead of her beer. Margot was glued to her phone, half present.

By the afternoon, someone had procured a bottle of champagne and a sleeve of plastic cups from a bag, and they drank it warm, then ran for the waves when the sun got high, played in the surf, warm as a bathtub. A teenager stood at the water's break, twerking for the waves while her friend, lying awkwardly in the sand, recorded her. A group of European tourists threw a ball back and forth.

Everyone except for Ana and Margot wanted to take one last dip in the ocean before it was time to head back.

"Ana," Margot said, pulling her towel closer to Ana's as the other girls ran for the waves, dove in like synchronized swimmers. "I don't mean this in a gossip-y way, obviously. I'm just thinking—I totally might be overreacting. I mean, it's kind of normal, in a sense, before a wedding . . ."

"Oh, good, your phone ran out of battery?" Ana asked. *She* had willingly put her work stress aside to focus on Lily.

Margot rolled her eyes. "Okay, uncalled for. Choosing to ignore. Remember what you said about Lily being skinny in that dress she sent us? I feel like she does look really small." She nodded toward the ocean, where Lily was emerging from the water.

"I don't know," Ana said. "I hadn't really noticed."

It was really bothering her: *loose with hiring requirements. loose with hiring requirements, loose with hiring requirements.* Ana knew she was a good teacher. But it tugged at her—that there was a kernel of truth to it. Horizon *had* bent the rules for her. For Silas.

"She seems thin to me. Maybe?"

"I feel like she's fine," Ana said, snappier than she meant.

"Jeez, okay," Margot said. "I'm probably overreacting. What's wrong with *you*?"

"Nothing," Ana said. "Let's just focus on Lily."

"That's what I'm trying to do, Ana," Margot said.

They stood up, shook out their towels, watched as the wind caught the sand.

Eighteen: Margot

Back at the rental, they were cheers-ing Coronas and peeling off to shower and get ready in shifts.

Margot had locked in a new reservation at a place she thought everyone would like and canceled the boat and talked them out of charging her a fee. She was expecting at least something from Warner: a "We like you guys, this is definitely going to get signed, just awaiting our legal team," or at least a couple of more probing questions, but there was still nothing.

Now, she was sudsing up her hair in the shower.

"I'm coming in," Ana said, pulling back the shower curtain.

"Fine," Margot said, even though the shower wasn't big enough for both of them. "I think I fixed everything for the weekend plans."

"Oh, good." Ana reached over Margot for the body wash.

Margot stepped closer to the wall to make way for Ana. It was an old ritual: Back in college, Margot was so busy that Ana had joked she and Lily were going to start waiting for Margot in the shower.

"How else will we get time with you?" Ana had said.

Margot had shrugged. "It's actually kind of a good idea." She loved efficiency, and socializing during a shower was definitely efficient. "It's not like any of us are weird about nudity."

"I was kidding, but sure," Ana had said, and then it became a thing: Ana would wait to shower until Margot was home—Lily thought it was too weird, and plus, the water pressure was already bad enough—and they'd lather themselves in suds and talk about class and friends and the future. It was often the only time the two of them spent together without Lily.

"What's new with Si? And how are you liking the place?"

"He's—" Ana said. "It's good."

"What?" Margot had her suspicions: Silas, in all his effusiveness and confidence, could suck the air out of a room. Which was fine when you were young and surrounded by mutual friends who could put him in his place, but was tougher when lives started filtering onward and outward. And Ana wasn't exactly the type to confidently shut him down.

Margot had a soft spot for Silas, but it belonged to Silas as Margot's friend, and not Silas as Ana's boyfriend. They'd taken a bunch of the same math classes back at Hawthorne, both of them rising quickly to the top of their classes. Helping everyone else in their study group became a waste of time, so they started studying together on the fifth floor of the library.

"He's just—he's stressed, to be fair. You know, the new role," Ana said, working shampoo into her hair.

"Sure, but people can have new jobs and not be dicks." Silas was impossible when he was stressed.

"He's not being a dick. I just wonder, sometimes, if I should—I don't know. He's not really doing anything specifically. Okay, here's an example. I know I'm not, like, solving world hunger, but Mondays are important at school. It's a big deal to set the tone for the week with the kids, right?"

"Sure," Margot said.

"So a few days ago, he mentioned we should take a long weekend in Napa, play hooky on a Monday. And I told him I can't just skip school, and he looked at me all incredulous, like of *course* I should be able to. And I told him that just because he could take vacation days at work it didn't mean *I* could. It's not like that."

"Right," Margot said. "That sounds reasonable. And he got angry?"

"No, he didn't get angry. I probably sound crazy. He's just so fixed in his world. I mean, money grows on trees for him, and I should be grateful, I guess, that he wants to include me in that, but like, let's say we break up—he's just, he doesn't take anything seriously, and he acts like just because I'm part of his life, I shouldn't, either. I feel like this uptight bitch around him sometimes. I sound crazy. I sound crazy, right?"

Margot wanted to reach out and grab Ana by the shoulders, shake her, tell her she was just as good as any of them. "You're also entitled to personal fulfillment, and you're not his concubine because he's earning more than you." She thwacked her razor against the tile.

"Concubines are for sex. Not cleaning."

"Whatever."

"I do hate cleaning up after him. But maybe that's just what we sign up for. I don't know."

"I don't think that's what we sign up for," Margot said.

"Don't take this the wrong way, Margot—but I don't know if you're the authority on this," Ana said. "No offense."

"None taken," Margot said, even though she was a little wounded: Who was to say that her singlehood precluded her from understanding what was best for Ana—what was best for any of them? "Maybe I can see it more clearly because I'm not in a relationship."

"I don't know," Ana said. "Maybe."

"You deserve someone who can make you feel good all the time." She wondered, for a second, what a life with Alix would be like: if they'd load and unload the dishwasher equally, if they'd stay in bed on weekends for hours, what her parents would think.

"Not *all* the time," Ana said.

"A lot of the time," Margot said. "And Silas—you know I love him—but he can be really—"

"What?" Ana asked.

"Power-trippy," Margot said. "Pass me the conditioner?"

Ana did. "I don't know. I feel like he means well, though. Sorry. I'm being so hormonal right now."

"Don't do that, Ana. Have you talked to him about any of this?"

"I just—love him, obviously. We've grown up together. And you know we're going to Paris this summer? He asked me if I like gold or silver."

"Fuck," Margot said. "Yeah."

"And I feel like—"

"The permanence scares you? All of a sudden, it's like, wait, spending your whole entire life with this guy who once yelled at you because you accidentally put his raw denim in the dryer?" Margot handed the conditioner back to Ana, who worked a blob into her hair.

Ana started to respond, but the bathroom door swung open.

"Finish up, we're leaving soon," Lily said.

They rinsed the conditioner out of their hair, and Ana turned the water off.

Margot knew she wasn't any sort of authority on relationships. But she *was* an authority on Ana. And she knew that Ana wouldn't stand up for herself, and she could see a world in which Ana would continue to cave in seemingly inconsequential moments, until one day Ana had completely forgotten who she was. Margot didn't want Ana's resistance to change to lead her to be a shell of a person living in Silas's shadow.

"Ana, you deserve to be taken seriously," Margot said, wrapping a towel around herself and handing one to Ana.

But maybe that was just a concession of long-term relationships, and maybe Margot's unwillingness to concede to anything at all was exactly the reason she was still single. It was entirely possible that living partially in the shadow of the person you chose to spend your life with was just part of spending a life with anyone at all.

Margot swiped mascara on her lashes and checked her phone. An email from Warner: Just running some things up the chain, looking good, might just need one more quick call to talk through social strategy. W.

Then, a text from Alix, a picture, waiting in line for the concert. You'll have to come to the next one!!

She clutched her phone to her chest like her future was inside it.

Nineteen: Lily

They gathered in the living room for a round of drinking games before heading out. It was almost like the old days, except they had their own rooms and their own clothes and their own tubes of mascara. It was almost a little bit sad, how they could each pack their lives into a neat little private suitcase. It made her miss the days when everyone's stuff was communal. When they shared slinky tops and feelings instead of TikToks.

She wrapped her fingers around her wrist, felt where they overlapped, breathed out a sigh of relief, then breathed in a huff of panic.

It was the way she'd felt during intern season, back when they lived in New York. Summertime, so many girls as young and lithe as baby giraffes, swarming the city, walking purposefully with the knowledge that they had plenty of time to figure it out. She had been like them, too: so sure that everything would unfold as it was supposed to, if she made the right decisions.

It was just too hard, Lily thought. To be getting older and more serious and to have nothing to show for it. She'd evaded the question of career a couple of times already, in the catch-ups of seeing each other: "None of the opportunities have been quite right," she said to Liza.

Emily jumped up and down. "*Ooh-whee,* do we have a night planned for you, Lily!"

She blinked toward a smile.

"We really *do,*" Liza added, wrapping Lily up in a hug.

Lily wondered if the boys were going through the same motions of touching and hugging and screeching. More likely, she thought, they were out polishing off domestic beer after domestic beer and crushing the cans in their hands, waiting for the last guy to toss on shorts and a T-shirt before announcing that it was time to "call it" and head to dinner.

This would be easier without the boys here. This would be easier if she could grasp for the words, let her friends fill in the details—explain that sometimes she felt bored, but not in the way that made her miss work as much as she thought she should. That she was afraid of becoming one of those UPPAbaby moms exactly nine months after the wedding. That she did want to be a mom, but she wanted it to feel like a choice, not a default. That lately, she didn't feel known by anyone, and she felt like a waste of over a million dollars' worth of education.

And it would all be so much easier if she could also just casually mention that it was perhaps possible that there was the faintest trace of that old voice in her head, the one that counted calories. That it wasn't a big deal, and they didn't need to worry because this time she had it under control. But still—she knew, and now they would know, and that would be enough. Nothing to worry about. Just an open dialogue.

They went to a bar, piled onto a white picnic table that faced the ocean, gave their orders to a man in chambray.

There was nothing inherently wrong with a tiny little bit of anxiety, even out here in the cool evening sun, wedged at a table between Margot and Ana, drinking an Aperol spritz and watching the waves crash on the beach. *Acknowledge it. Breathe into it. Accept it.*

Normal, Lily thought as she rapped her knuckles on the table. *Knock on wood,* she thought, five times this time. It was totally, entirely, completely normal to both enjoy yourself and wonder if maybe eating coconut shrimp *before* dinner was just a little bit excessive. Certainly it's what her mom would have been thinking.

They seemed to be enjoying each other, cheers-ing glasses and laughing, sitting intermingled even though no one had prompted them to.

"I want to say one thing," Lily said.

They turned to her expectantly.

"I'm really grateful that you're all here. I know you all came from far away, and it just means a lot to me. And I love all of you a lot."

She watched them beam at her, their faces loose with ease, and she felt a wave of gratitude for these people who'd known her and stuck by her and made her life worth living. Mostly the girls, but even the boys, who bolstered Jack, who in turn bolstered her, and all of it was almost enough to rouse her from the hum of anxiety that was threatening to throw the entire weekend off course.

"We love you so much," Margot said, and they all clinked glasses.

"Try the shrimp," Liza said, handing a plate to Lily. "It's coconut."

"Yum," Lily said, taking one and putting it on her plate. "Jack, shrimp?"

"What are you calling me?" He looked to his friends for approval. He abandoned the joke when they didn't respond. "Yeah, sure," he said, plucking it off her plate, tapping his hand lovingly on her forearm.

She let her shoulders relax. Jack tipped his head back and extended his tongue like a snake, gobbled the entire thing. Lily wrinkled her nose, grateful for her future husband's willingness to divert calories for her benefit. *Knock on wood,* she thought to herself again, five times, ten times, realized the content of her thoughts, tried her hardest to push them away.

Focus, she thought. *I am incredibly grateful. I am having a wonderful time. I am happy to be here and I love my friends and I will not let these thoughts ruin my weekend.*

But then also: *twenty-eight calories.* Although that was regular-size shrimp, and these were jumbo shrimp, so maybe more. And not to mention the coconut. *Two hundred,* she thought. *Two hundred. Two hundred. Two hundred.*

It was almost enough to make her scream.

Everyone was getting along. Margot and Alistair were laughing loudly about something at one end of the table, and Zoe, Ryan, and Eileen were deep in conversation at the other.

"You having fun?" Ana asked, leaning into Lily.

"Yes! Of course!"

"Where's dinner, by the way?" She pictured someplace with cushioned benches, candlelight, and girly cocktails.

"Okay, you're going to love it," Margot said, a hand on Lily's thigh, shocking her from her thoughts. "We actually changed the reservation, because the original place couldn't fit the guys. But this place is, like, way better. It's this Asian fusion place that turns into a club? And it also has a bunch of arcade games—seems kitschy, I know—but this influencer I know from work loves it, and she said it's actually really dope, especially for a big group like this. You know, keep the guys entertained."

"Oh!" Lily said, nodding enthusiastically, lifting her drink to her lips. Of course they wouldn't go somewhere cozy and girly with the guys. It was a silly vision: sitting and chatting, laughing and divulging secrets.

—

The car slowed in front of a restaurant with a flashy neon sign and thick velvet curtains over its door. They got out and filed in, past a bouncer, down a dimly lit staircase.

"Welcome! Congratulations!" said the hostess.

"Thanks so much," Lily said, trying her hardest to seem like she was having the best night of her life.

They followed her to a back corner of the restaurant, past an older guy on a date with two fake-lipped women, then another bachelorette party. The girls slid into the booth, and the guys sat down in chairs across from them, Jack directly across from Lily.

"Hi, baby," he said, grabbing for her hand. "We're getting married."

"We took shots in the car," Keith said. "Sorry, Lil, we got him pretty drunk."

"Shots!" said Ryan, and the rest of them joined in. "Shots, shots!" they all chanted.

"Do Jack's friends have to be so loud?" Margot whispered to Lily.

Lily brushed it off.

A waitress appeared with a tray of shot glasses, one for each of them.

They erupted, laughing and cheering and slapping Jack on the back.

It was loud in here, dark and slightly overwhelming, and Lily felt sober and a little nauseous.

"So the whole menu is a prix fixe thing," Margot said to the group. "Basically I just had them do their most popular items. It wasn't going to be that way, but with all the guys"—she blinked in a way that felt accusatory—"it was the only option. And we'll just share everything."

Lily felt a tightening in her throat, but breathed through it. This was fun. She'd dealt with Margot getting annoyed about less, and everyone *did* seem to be having fun.

"Amazing!" Zoe said.

"Fuck yeah," Keith said. "You're a legend, Margot."

Margot rolled her eyes at Keith, but he didn't seem to notice.

A waitress appeared with plates of food: salmon on rice cakes, wooden trays of dumplings, steaming bowls of something, handrolls stacked like bloated Lincoln Logs.

Everyone dug in. Lily placed a piece of sushi on her plate, grabbed a salmon rice cake, although maybe it wasn't rice but something else. Taro? No. Some kind of edamame cracker?

She looked around at everyone digging in effortlessly, raising dumplings to mouths, chewing, laughing, washing down their food with cocktails.

She looked at her plate and tapped her feet under the table.

She tried to focus on everyone else: They were smiling and laughing and caught up in the magnetism of each other. They were getting along, and they were here for her. And that was what mattered.

But still: She was the only person at this table without a job. What had felt like an advanced step toward adulthood—she was getting married before she turned thirty!—felt, suddenly, like a cop-out: something she'd look back on when she was a bored housewife as a mistake. She should have written a novel or gotten her yoga teacher training certificate or done long distance with Jack for two years so she could stay in New York! She should have looked up the menu ahead of time. She should have planned the whole entire weekend so Margot would have nothing to resent her for. There was a part of her that wanted everyone else to be here, having fun, while she stayed at home, or better yet, while she locked herself in the closet of the pottery studio on Fifth Avenue that used to bring her peace when she felt like the world was going to implode.

"Here, Lil, have some dumplings," Jack said, dropping a few onto her plate with his chopsticks.

"Thanks," she said, but he'd already turned away from her, laughing at some lilted, masculine exclamation from the other end of the table.

—

Everyone was laughing and eating and laughing and eating, and now pressure was building up behind Lily's eyes like she might burst into tears if she didn't get a moment to herself. She grabbed her purse, mumbled apologetically that she really needed to pee, waved off Zoe's offer to accompany her.

"Don't break the seal!" Brent yelled after her.

She pushed open the door to the bathroom. A line of women snaked past a row of sinks.

"Oh, you're a bride, too!" said a woman in a tiara, B-R-I-D-E sticking out at wonky angles, like maybe she'd broken it earlier and one of her friends had attempted to fix it. She looked older. She reached out to Lily, clearly drunk. "Your dress is soooo cute," she said. "I'm Natasha. I saw you walk in. I was like—oh my god, there's another bride here." She cackled. "And she's skinnier than me! Like, go home, baby! This is my day! You want some gum, by the way?" She pulled out a watermelon-flavored stick. Lily took it. "You wanna pee with me?" Natasha said, grabbing Lily's hands. "Brides pee together!" Natasha pulled her into the handicapped stall, wriggled her thong out from underneath her skintight dress.

"What's wrong, boo?" Natasha asked.

"Nothing!" Lily said.

Lily just wanted a single moment alone, to choke back whatever made her feel like crying when she was supposed to be dancing and eating and looking forward to the rest of her life. To sort out the chaos, to make sense of a world in which she was locked in a stall with this stranger; a world in which she cared about everyone around her, but some fluke of her brain made her think about her own body more than the people she loved.

The tequila from earlier must have entered her bloodstream at that exact moment, because suddenly, she had to pee and didn't care if Natasha was there. Suddenly, she wanted to divulge to this thin-lipped stranger that she'd consumed 908 calories so far today and she absolutely hated that she knew that.

She felt emboldened by the alcohol. "Do you ever—I don't know. Doubt, or I mean, worry, not in, like, a big way? But some way?"

Natasha peered at her from under miles of fake eyelashes.

"Oh, honey, I just live," Natasha said. "You should try it!"

Plate after plate. Everyone grabbed at spears of miso-glazed eggplant, bowls of cold noodles, glass plates of cucumber salad, beef medallions resting placidly on plates.

The DJ started playing a mash-up of "My Humps" and something by Calvin Harris.

"What the fuck," Ana said. "This is insane. These are our two best college songs." She was drunk.

"Let's dance!" Lily said, snaking her way around the table, Ana in tow, toward the dance floor. Margot dropped the frown and followed them. Lily felt a jolt of confidence: She still had the power to make everyone else feel important.

Twenty: Ana

Ana was tipsy, and she kept thinking about Cooper's mom and the Facebook post; about her own mom—what would happen if a dizzy spell knocked her over in the shower; what she'd look like on a hospital bed, open-mouthed and unable to escort herself to the bathroom; about Silas getting down on one knee in Paris, sliding a ring onto her finger. She heard Bryn's voice: "You don't have to marry him." She shook the thought away.

They danced, and then they dispersed, siphoning off into exclusive huddles, confident and open thanks to shots of Patrón and sweating cups of vodka soda.

"Not to be a woman hater," Liza said in the general direction of Ana's ear, "but he's hot, right? Even doing that?" She nodded toward Brent, who held a toy rifle at his shoulder, cocked toward the screen. *Bam.* He shot another doe, its guts exploding outward, splattering the ample chest of the game's pixelated heroine, who ran across some cartoonish plane, barefoot and braless.

"Yeah," Ana said to Liza, nodding. "That's fair." Brent's triceps rippled.

"I need more tequila. I'll get you one," said Liza, disappearing.

Ana was glad to have a moment alone. She'd been doing her best to stay positive, to focus on celebrating Lily and smiling for flash after flash of pictures from all her friends' phones. But staying centered on happiness took effort. It was the most random things that pulled her in the direction of everything else: a waiter in Vans like Bryn's reminded her of the Facebook post. An older bartender made Ana squint with fear at the knowledge that her mom would keep getting older and dizzier and older again.

"You okay?" Alistair said, elbowing Ana in the ribs and pointing at Brent. Ana hadn't realized how close he was. "Sorry, does this gross you out?" He gestured at Brent and the screen and the pixelated guts. "Are you a vegetarian or something?"

"Me? No." She paused, caught off guard at his recognition of her daze. She must not have been keeping it in as well as she'd thought.

"Brent gets really into this kind of shit. That's what happens when you marry your high school sweetheart and have two kids by twenty-six." He shrugged. "All that pent-up testosterone has to go somewhere, right?"

"Can't fault him for that, I guess," Ana said, offering a laugh.

Alistair was surprisingly unkempt when you got up close, not at all like his friends, with their poreless faces and oiled leather belts. His pants were slightly too short, exposing sockless ankles. His fingers were long, knuckles knobby, fingernails clean. Ana wondered, for a split second, what Alistair's fingers would feel like inside her.

"Where are you from again?" Alistair asked.

So they were doing this. "San Francisco." Her voice came out sounding more bored than she'd intended. "Oh—or did you mean contextually? College. Hawthorne. But I'm from Wisconsin originally." She tried to add a lilt of enthusiasm.

"Right," Alistair said. "I figured you weren't from New York. Don't take this the wrong way—I mean it as a compliment—you don't really have the same vibe as them. You seem"—he looked up at the wall behind her and puckered his lips—"more normal, I guess."

Normal. Ana knew what this was code for: Her imperfections were human, which is to say actually imperfect, unlike the imperfections of all her friends, which had been ironed out. Not decimated, exactly—no, coaxing one's face into Instagram-filter replicability was for the wannabe rich—but improved, highlighted. It was the way Emily was a bit chunkier than the rest of them, but wore it like a badge of honor, all smoothed out and sexy in the kinds of expensive wrap dresses that made her look feminine and goddess-like instead of thrumming with cellulite. It was the way Liza's nose was a little bit crooked, but because her skin was dermatologist-perfect, one couldn't help but find her nose interesting instead of off. It wasn't that all Ana's friends were preternaturally beautiful, although many of them were. It was, instead, the way physical flaws carried a whiff of superiority when their owner could correct them, easy peasy, but chose not to. It was the way a crooked nose looked like a bummer when it sat atop a pilled viscose dress from Forever 21 but dignified in Alaïa.

"Where in SF, by the way? My parents are in Pac Heights," he said. "You're a teacher, right? Jack was giving me a rundown."

"Don't tell me your parents are in that fucking Facebook group," Ana said.

He laughed, his breath hot on her cheek. "My parents are complete Luddites. So definitely not. But what's this Facebook group? Do people still even use Facebook?"

"Just the mommies and daddies in Pac Heights, I guess," she said, rolling her eyes. "Sorry. I'm just annoyed. A situation at work. Some mom posted about me, we don't have to get into it."

"I would actually love to hear. Do you want a drink, by the way? I'm gonna grab one for myself. Seems like we might need it."

"Actually, Liza was supposed to bring me something, but seems to be lost. Tequila. Please."

Alistair disappeared to the bar and returned to her with two glasses in hand.

"Here," he said. "I got the nice stuff, because we're too old to drink shit." He paused. "So. Teaching. I wish I had the confidence to do something like that. Something real." She'd gotten the speech before, usually from skinny bald guys who turned out to be something equally real, just worse: a garbage collector, maybe, or a bike messenger. She hated the speech, which was usually a thinly veiled brag, a way for boring and cargo-pantsed men to wrap their insecurity about their own careers into a neat little package of condescension poised as praise.

But Alistair seemed sincere.

"Yeah," she said. "I usually love it—" She paused, took a sip of her drink.

"What?"

"Sorry. I'm trying to not focus on this dumb work shit."

"I'm interested," he said, nodding. "Try me."

"Really?"

"Really. Let me guess. The parents suck?"

"Some, yeah," she said, nodding. "It's this mom who posted about me not disciplining this kid who she thinks is cheating off her perfect son. I know I should brush it off, it's just, like—the job is fine, the kids are great, but sometimes the parents look at me in this dismissive way, like they feel bad for me or something? And sometimes even the kids do it. And—I worked at this charter school, and there were so many things that were harder, but the parents respected me, and . . ." She trailed off. "I don't know why I'm telling you this."

"Keep going. Please. So it's important to you to be respected?"

"Not even," she said, thinking it through. "It's just—at Horizon—I guess I feel interchangeable with everyone else? Like, one of the parents asked me if I would ever want to come by and help babysit, which—fine—but it turned out it was practically a housekeeping job, like, she wanted me to do their laundry. And that's fine, I mean, I ended up doing it, actually, and she was really nice, it's just not what I thought would happen when I started working at this kind of school. And it's not like it's a bad thing. I think a lot of teachers appreciate the extra income. Easier than tutoring. I just wanted so badly for so long to get away from being anonymous? I know it's lame to still be affected by high school. Sorry. I don't know why I'm still talking."

"It's not lame," he said. "It's real. And it's actually refreshing to hear someone considering her life so insightfully, like, knowing what's motivating. As much as I'd rather scream around a thirty rack." He stroked his chin. "It's not illegal to want to live authentically, you know. God, I bet my parents sucked when I was in school. Do your parents suck?" He searched for his straw with his tongue, found it.

"Not at all," Ana said, looking up, cocking her head. "Well, my dad's dead. But my mom is fine. Aging, but fine."

"Oh. Sorry."

She shrugged it off. "I was a baby when it happened. Long time ago. It's just—I should be grateful, really. It's a really good job."

"I should be grateful for a lot of things I'm not grateful for. Comes with the territory of being human."

The music throbbed.

"That's—well. Honestly, my mom has been having these dizzy spells and it's kind of freaking me out and I guess it's making me, like, look at my choices and think about them? I don't know. I'm probably overreacting. Dizziness is not that big of a deal. She's probably just dehydrated. What about you?"

He shrugged. His shoulders were bony but broad, made her want to touch them in a way she hadn't felt toward Silas in some time.

"I'm an ecologist. We're gonna run out of drinking water eventually, but I'm trying to push that date out. Sorry to hear about your mom. I'm sure she'll be fine." He paused. "What's the hardest part about teaching? Emotionally?" He shrugged again, the point of a shoulder blade poking out through worn cotton, the tease of his taut, hair-covered lower stomach that he'd unknowingly shown off when his gestures got big.

She looked at the ceiling for a minute, regained her composure. "It's probably the lack of control. No matter what you do, you just—you can't control what they go home to. And it can totally derail—everything, really," she said. "Like, back at Oakbrook—that's the school I was at before, I forget if I told you that already—there was this boy who'd flinch when I got close to him. And obviously—hopefully this is obvious—I'd never laid a hand on him. But you just know with that kind of situation that he's being hit at home. And he falls asleep on his desk. Which, you know—that usually means a kid isn't sleeping at home. Maybe because there aren't enough beds, or maybe because he doesn't feel safe, or maybe because he's hungry. And it's just"—she pushed a strand of hair behind her ear—"really tough. To feel like, no matter whatever I did back then, in some ways it didn't really matter. Ultimately."

"No," Alistair said. "It definitely did!"

"Maybe—" Ana wondered if it meant she was an alcoholic if she only seemed to know herself when she was drunk. "Maybe that's what I'm afraid of? That what I did at Oakbrook mattered? And now I'm just lying to myself. I'm just as bad as all the tech people I make fun of."

Bam. Brent cheered. Liza and Emily high-fived him. A sharp thwack of someone's palm against someone else's ass.

"Why did you leave?"

"What do you mean?" Ana asked.

"That first school. You sound passionate about it."

"Oh," Ana said. "Summer vacation. I had to teach summer school at Oakbrook. And prestige, I guess. It sounds so awful when I say it out loud. Sorry. We're supposed to be having fun, and I'm being professional and lame."

"Would you ever go back?" Alistair asked, ignoring her deflection.

"No," she said. "It wouldn't be a step in the right direction."

He raised his eyebrows as if he could have known these were Silas's words, not hers. "Fuck that," he said.

Ana was in the wrong relationship.

It was abundantly clear to her, all at once, in this restaurant-slash-club that was home to a stripper pole and also a point-and-shoot video game and also a bunch of scantily clad waitresses carrying bottles of Patrón, lit up with sparklers.

She realized it suddenly, then wondered if maybe she'd been realizing it all along, with each self-inflicted blunting of the thin trickles of her rage, which she always stopped before they could become a creek, then a river. Suddenly, now, her rage was a waterfall.

It just felt so good to be taken seriously, for her passion to be understood as not just a conduit to something better, for the fear she'd been holding in about her mom to find its way out of her, all around her, mixing with the thick air from the smoke machines. She wanted her work as a teacher to be seen as a genuine contribution to society instead of what she sometimes worried Silas thought it was: the best she could do. A stopgap measure before she ceded and gave up. She wanted Alistair to keep asking her questions. She wanted to answer them, sidestepping the reality of her relationship with Silas.

Silas didn't understand her, and he didn't understand the world.

It was obvious now, crystal clear as she looked back at their relationship and watched in slow motion as each memory shifted, or perhaps focused, like triangles in a kaleidoscope when they turned into stars.

The writing had been on the wall. They'd met as tutor and tutee, and the rest of their relationship was built from that dynamic. Back then, he'd helped her with econ problems, which had seemed innocuous and sweet, but was suddenly a red flag for everything that was to come: the way he made "lots" of money but Ana actually had no idea how much; the way he said she could quit her job if she wanted to because they'd be "fine," without understanding that a claim like that left her blindfolded and suspended in thin air.

It was the way he guided her toward the options he'd made her believe were best: that she'd tire of the quaint details of the apartment she'd originally wanted them to move into, with its hundred-year-old ironing board that pulled out from the wall. She'd prefer the new high-rise, trust him. She'd be grateful in a year when they didn't have the cat that she wanted, because who knows if they'd want to move abroad or travel for a month? Never mind the fact that Ana didn't like living out of a suitcase or starting over in a place where she knew no one. It wasn't fair, the way he steered her toward what he wanted under the guise of knowing her better than she knew herself. She needed, if not necessarily to be able to control her future, then to play a role in it.

Ana ordered two more drinks from the bartender and paid. She pulled out her phone and texted Silas: When I get home, let's make a chore chart. Then she deleted it, took another sip. I need us to be more transparent about what we each want, she tried, looked at it for a second. Deleted that one, too.

"Do you wanna dance at all?" Alistair asked, a hand on Ana's elbow. "I mean, you're not with anyone, are you?" Had Jack not mentioned Silas?

"Let's dance!" Liza said, grabbing Ana's arm, interjecting before Ana had a chance to admit to herself that she was thinking of answering Alistair's question with a "No."

Twenty-One: Margot

Margot was still looking at the photo from Alix.

"Sorry we derailed your weekend." She felt a hand on her back.

Keith. She nudged him off. "All good," she said.

"I told Jack it was kind of gay to do his bachelor party with his future wife, but he insisted."

Margot prickled. "Oh, do we still say that?"

She'd planned everything for them. On top of all her work. On top of everything.

This was why ex-rowers who worked in private equity were the fucking worst.

"Oh, gay? Sorry. Not, like, derogatory. I have a gay sister. Why, are you gay?"

"Actually, yes," Margot said, and realized before she could stop herself that she had just officially come out for the first time in her life, in a basement in Miami to a man named Keith who rolled up pediatric dental practices for a living and wore a watch that made Margot want to barf.

"Shit, sorry, my bad. Seriously," Keith said.

"Fuck," Margot said, and felt a prickle of tears threatening at her eyes, turned to go to the bathroom.

"For real, I'm not homophobic," he called after Margot.

"This has absolutely nothing to do with you," she yelled back. "That's, like, the whole point."

God, she wished she was home, where she could tell Alix about coming out to fucking Keith, where they could laugh about it together, where Alix could one-up her with some far-cringier coming-out story from one of the lesbians she was at this concert with (there were so many, Margot felt jealous of that, suddenly), which would make Margot feel better. Home, where she could send over a last-minute gift basket to the Infinity guys (pears were in season—they would appreciate that, unless they were imported from far away, in which case maybe they wouldn't). She wanted to be here, enjoying her friends and celebrating Lily, but she wanted even more than that to get home from the weekend and get on with the rest of her life: to tell her friends about Alix, to figure out why it had taken her so long to let herself feel this way about someone, to get a raise and move out of her apartment and live somewhere by herself on a director-level salary, with the knowledge that she'd made it.

She wiped her eyes and emerged from the bathroom.

Margot surveyed the bar. Lily was off somewhere, and Ana was deep in conversation with that Alistair guy again. She checked her phone, grabbed some water. She couldn't risk getting too drunk; she'd probably lash out at Keith, and anyway, she had a big week ahead of her. If all went according to plan, she might even need to be photo-ready for *Ad Age*. She ran her hand through her hair, chugged the whole glass.

Ana was really getting into it with that guy. Margot went over to her, a hand on her shoulder. She kind of wanted to tell Ana first.

"Ana, hey."

"I'll stop hogging her," Alistair said as he disappeared into the throngs of people.

"Why'd you do that?" Ana asked.

"What do you mean?"

"I was having a moment with him," Ana whispered.

"Bro," Margot said. "I'm sorry, first of all, this weekend was supposed to be about friendship and you've been talking to him for hours, and second, I need to tell you something, and third of all, you're in a relationship, and it would be so easy to just leave him and date someone else if you wanted to, but why are you being cagey about it? Like, you're clearly flirting."

Ana's eyes were swimming. She was drunk.

"It's just harmless. Like, it feels good to be actually liked by a guy."

"Do you feel like Silas doesn't like you? Because some of us put a lot of work into figuring out who we are instead of just letting life do its thing to us, and it's kind of lazy to just stay with him because you're afraid of your options." She was being mean. She knew it. She was taking out something bigger on Ana. It wasn't fair.

"What is wrong with *you*?" Ana said.

A server with a sparkler in one hand and a tray of shot glasses and tequila in the other walked past them.

"I need to tell you something."

"No," Ana said. "*I* need to tell you something. You literally have no idea what it feels like to not be good at, like, everything, with absolutely zero effort. And you can be so condescending about it, you know? Like, you really think I couldn't have made a single dinner reservation for this bachelorette party?"

"Excuse me? You think I don't try?"

"No. I know you try. It's just, like, we can't all be independent and just happy all the time and have good things just always, like, happen to us. No offense."

"Some taken, actually," Margot said. "Honestly? You have no idea how hard I work, or how hard things are for me in so many ways, like, living far away from all my friends and figuring out my—" She paused. Didn't want to give Ana the gift of disclosure, not like this. "If you're not happy with Silas, you should do something about it. But you can't just flirt with some friend of Jack's and then get mad at *me* about interrupting. We're not eighteen anymore."

"Just because you put your entire self into some important job selling shit to people who don't need more shit, doesn't mean you're, like, the authority on adulthood, Margot."

Margot shook her head at the ceiling. "Fuck you. Go cheat on Silas. Just don't come crying to me when he finds out."

"Dude," Margot said, her hand on Lily's shoulder, their backs to a high-top in the corner. "Ana is literally being so psycho. She's in that, like, 'poor me, I can't do anything and you don't understand me' mode that she used to get into all the time. She is being such a victim. You good?"

"Yeah," Lily said, raising her glass to her lips. "I'm—"

"What?" Margot asked, looking at Lily, really taking her in now that they were up close. Lily's eyes looked dark and heavy, in a way Margot hadn't noticed when they were outside at the beach. Had Lily been wearing big sunglasses then? She couldn't remember.

"I'm totally good," Lily said, nodding, but she looked like there was something else she needed to say.

Margot's phone buzzed. She fished it out of her purse. She was surprised to see Jenny's name. She let it ring, considered picking up. If it was urgent, Jenny would call back. Margot dropped her phone back into her bag.

"Lil, you sure you're good? Do you want to pee with me?"

Lily shrugged her shoulders, looked like she was about to cry. "Okay," she said, and Margot took her by the wrist and dragged her beyond the thrum of the music and the bodies and the sweat.

Twenty-Two: Lily

It was good to take a hiatus from all the fun, to look privately in the mirror while Margot peed, to confirm with her reflection that she couldn't handle her alcohol anymore. Not at this size. *Not at this size. Knock on wood.* She was drunk enough to feel unembarrassed by her sudden and urgent need to look at her body in the mirror.

Margot called out from the stall. "Lil, can I ask you something?"

Of course Margot had noticed. Margot, who was more observant than Liza and Emily and Ana and Eileen combined. Margot, who would have picked up immediately on the fact that Lily was chock-full of jitters. Margot, who'd pulled Lily aside, who'd take her to the street for a moment of private reconciliation, silencing whatever bouncer dared insist it wasn't an "in and out kind of place." Lily could have burst into tears with relief.

"Yeah, shoot," Lily said, trying her hardest to sound casual.

Margot emerged from the stall, the door clanging behind her. "No offense, but why are the guys here, and why did you not tell us? And two, Ana is pissing me off."

"Oh," said Lily, deflating. "I thought it would be fun?" A half-truth. "And why?"

"Obviously I love her, and know it's your bachelorette party, and it's your fiancé's friends, I just find Keith to be kind of a dick, and I'm not trying to bog you down with this shit, but it seems like things are really weird with Silas, and honestly, I have never liked that guy for her, but she needs to own what she wants, you know? Like, break up with him and tell him to fuck off instead of just flirting with Jack's friend and crawling back home to Silas, which you know she will do."

"I feel like Ana is just being friendly, right?" Lily said. "And what did Keith say?"

Margot rolled her eyes. "He just—never mind. You're right. I'm coming in hot. I just want this weekend to be perfect for you. And the boys threw off our plans. But it's fine! You're getting married! I guess it's time I get used to boys coming first!" She laughed, but she didn't look like she thought it was funny.

"I need to tell you something, Margot," Lily said, leaning in.

"What is it?" Margot asked.

"There's something—I mean, you obviously—" she paused, looked up at the ceiling to stop the tears that were already welling.

Margot's phone buzzed. She grabbed at it, looked at it anxiously, then dropped it back into her bag.

"You know about the whole—I mean, I was so fine in New York, and I guess I didn't realize how hard it would be. I'm happy for Jack, I want this for him, but still—"

Margot's phone buzzed again, and she glanced at it like she was trying to pretend she wasn't.

The alcohol was creeping up on Lily. She didn't mind being tipsy. She liked the way alcohol softened her, made the world appear more gentle, as if it wasn't out to get her. It was what came after that undid her. When she felt her words come out of her mouth before her brain had registered what she was saying. When, suddenly, she lost control, let her face go slack, said things to Margot, in public, at a bar at her bachelorette party, like: "I'm a little bit worried that I'm relapsing. My—you know. Food thing." And then, was met with nothing.

Margot did not rub Lily's shoulders and tell her that everything would be okay, or arm her with a checklist and a plan and a reminder that Lily was completely capable of preventing relapse, that it was normal to need a therapy brushup, that this was fixable.

"Shit, Lil," Margot said, looking at her phone. "I, fuck—I want to talk about this, I—fuck, I don't know why Jenny is calling me four times in a row on a Saturday night, but it's really not like her—give me one second, Lil. Fuck." She swiped at her phone. "Jenny, hi," she said, one pointer finger pressed into her ear. "I'm at a bar, it's—my friend's—hold on, let me get outside."

Margot stuck up a finger as if to say it would be only one single minute, but then she turned into the corner, glanced back at Lily apologetically, and made her way out of the bathroom and off to who knows where, leaving Lily utterly and completely alone.

The bathroom attendant pushed a wad of paper in Lily's direction. "Tissue?" she asked.

Lily looked in the mirror and realized she was crying.

Twenty-Three: Margot

Margot wove through the crowd, shaking her head vigorously at the bouncer to let him know she meant business, and it wasn't a good time to interrupt and tell her she wouldn't be allowed to reenter.

"Say again, Jenny," Margot said into the phone.

"Margot, hi. Sorry to bother you on a Saturday." She paused. Margot didn't jump in to tell her it was fine. "It's Infinity. I just heard. They're moving forward with Ogilvy after all."

Margot switched her phone to the other side, plugged her ear with her finger. "What?"

She saw it all flash before her eyes: the promotion, the one-bedroom apartment without Sabrina, the strutting around the office smiling demurely as everyone called out to her, her parents when they learned the news. "Are you serious?"

"Well, I'm not totally sure. I heard it through a friend. His wife's sister is a CD there and heard it from her account friend. It's kind of inconclusive, but apparently she's dialed in, so . . ."

"So we still have a chance," Margot said.

"I know you're in Miami. But it sounds like they're making a final decision Monday morning. And I think we need to show them how much we want this. Do something big."

"Right," Margot said, holding steady. "Of course. I have more out-of-home concepts. I can finish the deck—it's basically done—send it over, order champagne—"

"Margot, they're in New York right now. I wouldn't ask if the whole agency wasn't basically riding on this. But I think we should go, tomorrow morning, get them to have lunch with us."

"On a Sunday?"

"I totally understand if you want me to handle it. But they love you, Margot. Honestly, I wouldn't ask if I didn't mean it." She paused. Then, more quietly: "I don't think I can land this without you."

Margot held the phone away from her and let herself feel important. "What time?"

"There's a flight out of Miami at nine."

She closed her eyes. "Yup," she said. "Yeah, of course I'll book it. I'll be there. Let's do this."

—

If it hadn't been for the last-minute addition of the boys, or for Ana's refusal to make this weekend about the girls, or for Keith's comment—which wouldn't have bothered her so much if it hadn't caused her to mistakenly come out first to someone as insignificant as him—then maybe she would have pushed back on Jenny.

She watched a group of girls a few years younger than her pile out of a car, all legs and stilettos and giggles.

"Get out, bitch!" one of them yelled into the back seat. The others hooted and hollered, pulling wallets out of designer bags and handing their IDs to the bouncer. He glanced at them, then back at their IDs.

"You sure you're all twenty-one?" he said.

"I'm actually twenty-two," one of the girls barked back.

They'd be dancing, drinking, gyrating, snorting lines of coke in the bathroom, considering threesomes with whoever they met who proved worthy, unconcerned with the rest of their lives. They would be living, while Margot would be missing half a bachelorette party to suck up to middle-aged men.

"Is this, like, a generational thing?" she asked one of the girls in the group, who was wearing tiny sunglasses pulled down to the tip of her nose, even though it was dark out. "Like, this whole not-giving-a-fuck, just-living-free thing?"

"Sorry, what?" the girl asked, running lip gloss over her mouth. She looked at the others, furrowing her brow, and they all giggled. "Lady, you good?"

No one had ever called Margot "lady" before. "Never mind," she said, and pushed her way past them, past the bouncer, back inside.

Twenty-Four: Lily

Lily was getting a little bit dizzy. It was late, it was loud, and she was dabbing at her tears while the paper-towel lady watched. At least the paper-towel lady had a job. The more Lily thought about spending every single day home with a baby, the more it sounded actually really boring. Margot was annoyed and ignoring her. Jack was having more fun than Lily on Lily's trip. And more than anything, Lily just wanted to go home.

She splashed water on her face, tipped the woman, and went back to her friends.

"Jack," she said, going up to him from behind and wrapping her arms around his firm torso.

"Hi, love," he said. "You having fun?"

"Yes," she said. "You guys should stay out as late as you want, but Ana and Zoe said they're getting tired."

"Really?" Jack turned away from the bar. "They look like they're having fun." Ana was deep in conversation with Alistair again, egregiously close. Zoe was getting low, a group of strangers gathered around her and egging her on.

"They're putting on a show for me."

"Well, if you're still having fun, just send them home. They're big girls."

"No way. They came all this way for me. We'll just go home and hang a bit before bed. If that's okay with you guys."

"If that's what you want. You hear that, boys? I'm a free agent!"

Lily rolled her eyes and kissed him on the lips. "I love you."

"I love you more," he said.

She turned away from him and started rounding up the girls.

"Everyone is ready," she said to Emily, nudging her.

"Oh yeah?" Emily said. "I'll call the Uber if you're ready to go. You sure?"

"Yup," Lily said, going to Ana. "You ready, Ana?"

She was laughing at something Alistair was saying. "Wait, seriously?"

"I mean, you can stay here with the guys if you want," Lily said.

"She doesn't," Zoe said, nudging Ana, whispering something in her ear.

Ana rolled her eyes and followed the girls out.

"Sorry," Lily said. "I didn't mean to rush you."

"It's alllll good," Ana said, with some bite. "It's not like I spent a significant portion of my meager salary on this trip."

Lily prickled. "Wait, Ana, I can totally cover more of it if you want."

She'd offered, months ago, and Ana had declined; Lily had assumed Silas had booked Ana's flight with his miles, or just paid for the trip outright. But she'd never asked directly. "Did Silas not—it's none of my business . . ." She trailed off.

"No, Lily," Ana said. "He bought us a couch for twelve grand but thought this kind of thing falls on me, which is true, it does, and it's important to me, so obviously I paid for it. Just—"

"No, of course," Lily said. "If you want to stay later—"

"It's not about that," Ana said. She hiccupped. "It's about—"

Zoe grabbed her. "Alright, Ana. Let's get you home."

"I'm fine," Ana said. "I just think Lily needs to remember that we don't all get to come from money and marry a guy with money and never have to worry—"

"She's drunk," Emily said. "Ignore her."

But she couldn't.

This—not the contracts or the flowers or the caterer or the dress—must be what people were talking about when they said planning a wedding was hard.

Twenty-Five: Margot

They pulled up to the condo and piled inside. Ana beelined it in first, avoiding Margot, clearly.

Margot tried to play it down. "So, I have to leave a tiny bit early, but you guys have brunch and shopping and shit tomorrow, so you won't even notice I'm gone."

"What? Everything okay?" Zoe asked.

"Yeah. It's dumb. I need to go to New York. It's this big account we're trying to land. If we don't get it, I won't get this promotion . . ." She looked around; the girls were sprawled on the couch, short skirts up around their butts.

And I really don't want to be here anyway. Not with Keith and his offhanded homophobia, not with Ana who has never asked herself who she is or what she wants. Not even with Lily, who didn't show an iota of appreciation for all the work I put into planning, then replanning this. Who seems distracted and bored and not really like herself.

"Seriously?" Ana said.

"When did we get so responsible and *old*?" Liza asked.

"Everything is planned, I'll text you all the details. You get it, right?"

"'Course," Ana said. "You're an important businesswoman who's needed elsewhere." She maybe rolled her eyes, but Margot chose to ignore it.

"I'll make it up to you," she said, a hand on Lily's shoulder.

"I get it," Lily shrugged. "Don't worry."

It wasn't long before they all disappeared into their bedrooms, leaving Margot sitting on the couch to book her flight, her face lit by the glow of her phone.

She looked up at the ceiling. She was needed. She was good at this. Lily was maybe a tiny bit annoyed, but she'd feel better after waking up and going to the brunch Margot had planned; she'd preordered champagne for all of them, plus a round of desserts to celebrate Lily—

And then she remembered: At the bar, before the call, before she left, before the girls climbing out of the limo, who were both impossibly young and as young as Margot had been just a moment ago, before she'd had the chance to ask Lily to repeat what she had said, before she could wrap Lily in a hug and tell her it was loud in here and she couldn't quite make out everything but something about food and—

"Fuck," Margot said into the darkness. But she'd fix that, after she fixed the work thing. Land Infinity. Call Lily. Apologize to Ana for coming in hot, but also convince Ana to leave Silas and see that she was right to call her out on her behavior with Alistair. Let her friends know that maybe she was gay after all. That perhaps they shouldn't have brushed her off when Margot mentioned it long ago, that actually, there was so much she'd missed out on, lying to them and to herself. Come out to her parents, get her bridesmaid dress altered, go to the wedding, get on with the rest of her life.

It was all doable. She'd do it, she'd get it done, she always did.

Twenty-Six: Ana

Ana woke up the next morning with a throbbing headache and only some memory of the night before. She'd spent a lot of time talking to that guy, Alistair, but about what, she couldn't entirely remember. She flipped over to see that Margot was already gone. Right: She'd left early this morning.

Bryn had texted back: sorry soooo delayed, was surfing all day, please do not let this woman get to you!!! She is clearly unwell, probably too much Botox! Heard it can go to your brain. You know which parents aren't in this group? OAKBROOK PARENTS!!

Last night flickered back: the way Alistair had hung on her every word, the way Margot had accused her of liking it.

—

At brunch, they sat interspersed with the boys: Keith to her left, Alistair to her right. They bumped knees when he turned to the waiter to order coffee, and she felt a tingle that went up to her belly button.

Lily was across the table, sipping her coffee, next to Zoe.

"You have fun last night?" Ana asked her.

A beat. "Yup," Lily said, then exchanged glances with Zoe.

"What?" Ana asked. Had she done something stupid? Fuck, she hadn't kissed Alistair, had she—

"Where's Margot?" Keith asked, interrupting.

"She had a work thing," Lily said. "Emergency."

Keith and Jack traded glances. "Shit. You sure?"

"She's trying to land this client," Lily said.

"So she's not mad about me saying the gay thing?" Keith asked. "Since she's gay?"

"Wait, what?" Ana laughed. "Margot isn't gay."

Keith narrowed his eyes. "Oh—last night she said—I felt really bad, I said something was gay in a way that was totally uncool, and she called me out, said she was gay and I apologized."

"Um," Ana said, "I think you were drunk." They all laughed, took sips from their flutes of champagne, shared stacks of powder-dusted waffles.

Ana tried to catch Lily's eye, did her best not to focus on how hard Lily was working to avoid the attempt.

Twenty-Seven: Lily

Lily and Jack were home, showered, and in bed by midnight. Lily wanted to feel glad to be back, for Boston to feel familiar after a few days away.

But she couldn't settle. She kept thinking about that time sophomore year when she'd stupidly asked Ana if she could "just ask her parents for money" to cover the Cabo trip they'd all planned.

"First of all," Ana had said, "my dad is dead—*you* of all people should know what it's like to have an absent father—and second of all, money isn't, like, some abstract thing that's doled out according to made-up rules in my family. My mom makes eighteen dollars an hour, remember?"

Lily had felt terrible. Ana had apologized. That was ten years ago now, and since then, money had never come between them.

But Ana had been so biting on Saturday night, so casually cruel, that it had ruined the final twenty-four hours of the weekend. It would have been forgivable if Ana had just said she drank too much and reassured Lily that it hadn't meant anything.

But she hadn't.

And Margot hadn't reached out, either. Not to apologize for ignoring Lily's confession, or for tapping out early, or for bringing semibad energy all weekend long.

Lily shouldn't have opened up about the hardest thing in her world to the only person who could put up walls around herself and her work like the fate of the world depended on it.

She shouldn't have robbed herself of an opportunity to talk it through for real. If Lily hadn't invited the guys, none of this would have happened.

—

They woke up early the next morning. Jack had class, and Lily, who'd slept restlessly, was grateful for the excuse to get out of bed when Jack turned on the shower at six.

Lily had dreamed that Margot apologized over text. It was an uncharacteristically rambling note, praising Lily's vulnerability, thanking her for opening up, promising to come to Boston for a weekend to make up for missing Sunday in Miami. She'd said she was sorry for the bad vibes, she was just feeling territorial, and she felt terrible about it all.

But of course it had just been a dream. When Lily grabbed her phone, there was nothing from Margot. Disappointment settled in her stomach like gravy.

—

"Oat milk?" Jack asked, handing her a mug of coffee.

"Black is good," she said. "Thanks." She scooted herself up onto the counter and accepted the steaming mug from Jack.

"Lil," he said, furrowing his brow, "you *never* drink your coffee black."

"Oh, sometimes I do." She didn't like the way black coffee scorched her stomach like acid, but she couldn't get the image of the stretch marks that slashed the mirror when she looked at herself in the wrong light out of her head. Stretch marks as pale and glossy as oat milk.

Lily finished her coffee and traipsed into the bathroom. Truth be told, she'd ordered a scale two weeks prior. It had been the day after her second-to-last dress fitting, and she'd ordered it in an almost-fugue state. She'd snuck it up to the bathroom, still in its box, and then shame had washed through her and she'd vowed to return it.

But then she'd forgotten to initiate the return, and then she was kind of glad she had it, just in case, and now she was ripping it open with an X-Acto knife and turning it on and placing it on the tiled floor and dropping her robe from her shoulders and stepping onto the scale without bothering to close the bathroom door. She let it beep loudly at the empty apartment, breathed out a heavy sigh because the number was like a failure, and then the blood drained from her face as she heard the sound of Jack's voice at the door.

"Lil?" he said, pushing the door open. She inched her feet over the number, as if Jack would judge her for it, which she knew he wouldn't, but maybe the number was low enough to worry him, which she also knew wasn't rational because men never had any idea how much or how little women weighed. Still, she curled her toes protectively over the number just in case, then fluttered her hands to her face in apology, tried her best to convey with her eyes that she hadn't meant to stand on the scale, it just was sort of there, it got under her, oopsie!

"You weighing yourself?" he asked softly, and it scared her to hear him speak without a modicum of confidence.

"No, I mean, I'm returning it—" She stumbled over her words, tried to come up with something that made sense. But what was there to say? There was no way to extricate herself from the obvious fact that she was standing on a scale, covering the most important number in the world with the fat, puffy permanent pads of her toes. It was a moment before she remembered that she was completely naked, and she moved to cover her body with her hands, as if Jack hadn't seen her stark naked a thousand times before, including just ten minutes prior when she'd forgotten a towel, and run, dripping wet, from the bathroom to the linen closet.

"Lil?" he asked, his face blank and questioning.

She'd never felt so bare. She backed into the counter, just to make contact with its hardness. She craved the contact of fist to hard surface—*knock on wood*—but she couldn't remove her fist from its protective position over her body, so she stood there, hands around her stomach when they wanted to find their way to anywhere else, stranded in her very own bathroom, more naked than she'd ever been in her entire life.

"Lil?" he asked again, going to her, wrapping her in his arms, his shoes and his backpack still on. It felt strange to see him fully dressed like this, walking through their bathroom. His shoes were leaving damp outlines where the dirt mixed with water from her earlier footprints. Her hair was heavy with water—maybe that was why the number was high today?—and it dripped onto the sleeves of his favorite leather jacket.

She was ruining his jacket.

Margot had no idea what was going on.

Ana had no idea what was going on.

And her bachelorette party hadn't even been fun.

"I'm ruining your leather jacket," she managed to say.

He ignored her. "Are you okay?"

It took everything in her not to break down into a waterfall of sobs, and she didn't know why, she was fine, she'd been fine, and then he rubbed her back and dropped his backpack onto the floor, and it looked so stupid and helpless there on the tile, and the tears prickled and then streamed, and she was ruining his jacket, the jacket he loved, the jacket she'd bought him, and she was naked, and the backpack looked so sad—

"Lil," he said. "Lillian."

And then she was off to the races, sobbing harder because he almost never called her Lillian, and suddenly she was convulsing, which she'd never done in front of Jack before.

"I'm just a little worried," he said.

"Why?" she asked, even though it was a stupid question.

"I—Lil, I mean—this isn't—does this have—"

Jack never stumbled over his words. Hearing him talking around something instead of straight through it was so unmooring, it made her want to jump in and rescue him from his meandering, to redirect his conclusion for him: No, this had nothing to do with the obsessive-compulsive disorder she'd been battling for as long as she could remember. Nothing to do with the eating disorder that was entirely behind her. No, she was not a twenty-eight-year-old woman on the verge of marriage who couldn't eat a mini cupcake without spiraling. No, this had nothing to do with their wedding, or the diet she'd halfheartedly started eight months prior, or the fact that she wanted, more than anything, to feel squarely superior to the other girls her age, the girls from high school and Jack's friends' wives and girlfriends and even her best friends from Hawthorne, who posted five-minute wedding-highlight reels with captions like "Best day of my life," and were somehow also attorneys and ob-gyns and VPs at BlackRock. No, this had nothing to do with the grief from her parents' divorce that she'd probably never properly processed, because she'd been pro-divorce—after all, they couldn't stop fighting; it only made sense. It wasn't about them separating. Or the fact that living in Boston was so fucking lonely, about trying to make friends and being met with glazed-over eyes and conversation about things that didn't matter to her at all. It wasn't about quitting her job and thinking she'd get something better, or letting wedding planning become a full-time job and realizing—too late—that she might have been wrong. That it was, in fact, boring and lonely to be bored and alone.

He pulled back from her. "Should we get you some help, Lil? I just—we're starting our lives together. I want you to be happy. Happy and healthy. And safe . . ." He trailed off.

She'd never seen him so concerned, so she composed herself, visualized a zipper that ran from her pelvis to her nose, zipped it up, everything under control. *Knock on wood, knock on wood, don't worry Jack, grateful, perfect, no problem, knock on wood, knock on wood.*

"Okay," she said, nodding, because she sensed that resisting would cause him to worry more. "I mean, some help—maybe you were right that staying home to have kids isn't for me—I mean, yes. Some help can't hurt, right?"

Twenty-Eight: Margot

Warner visibly perked up when Margot caught his eye. The restaurant was bright and modern, all fresh wooden paneling and a skylight that opened up to the bright New York sky. She took a deep breath in, inhaled confidence. She let it out, exhaled worry. Lily would be okay for twenty-four hours. She'd call her tonight.

"Margot," he said, standing. The others stood, too. She went in for a hug, and Warner seemed to relax at her touch.

"Thank you so much for coming," Margot said, flashing them a smile. She'd stopped in the bathroom at LaGuardia to brush her teeth and swipe on some mascara, and even though she was underslept and had spent the last few hours in the stale air of an overcrowded Delta plane, she knew she looked good. She went to Jenny and gave her a half hug.

"Margot, sit, hello!" Jenny said. "So good to see you. We were just chatting about these gorgeous plates." Jenny lifted a ceramic disk and showed it around the table like a picture book. "We were discussing putting a kiln at the hotel, creating dishware on-prem. So much better for the environment—avoiding shipping costs, all that."

"Love that!" Margot said, clapping her hands together. It was so like Jenny to focus on the details before setting the tone. "Sorry I'm late. Traffic was terrible. So glad we're doing this. You guys—Ogilvy?" She nodded in mock disappointment, watched Jenny's face go slack, regretted for a second getting straight to it like that, but before Jenny could backtrack, Warner's face cracked into a smile.

"You are very straightforward with us, Margot," he said. "Are you German?"

Jenny's lips flattened into a forced smile.

"Probably somewhere way back," Margot said, nodding at a waiter as he came by to fill her mug with coffee.

"The Benedict looks great," Jenny said, pointing at the menu.

"We don't want to work with Ogilvy," Warner said, ignoring Jenny. "We like you guys. We think you understand our vision."

"We think so, too," Margot said, nodding vigorously.

Warner took a long sip of his water. "But," he said, placing his glass on the table and looking around the table, "we do have a concern."

"Okay," Margot said, pushing the thoughts aside. "Is it that copywriter who did that really bad proposal for you guys? Because we can have Ellie work on stuff instead. No worries. Or was it Sean? He actually quit anyway."

"No, none of that," said Kevin, or Hans, she couldn't remember which. "It's the optics of signing an agency that works with a gas company and a car company."

"Oh," Margot said, stalling for time. It was true: The car company was a car*sharing* company, and they only used electric cars, but some recent research had surfaced about their battery manufacturing process, and it was pretty terrible. But they were a small account—a quarter million a year, tops. As for the gas company, it wasn't PG&E or anything. It was a Chicago-based natural gas company they'd taken on mostly because the CMO was a friend of one of the creative directors.

"I'm sure we can get to the bottom of this," Jenny said. "It's a dealbreaker? Really?"

"It's critical that we put our mouth where our money is," Warner said.

Margot and Jenny traded glances and let the misuse of the phrase slide.

"Our whole thing is zero waste, you understand?"

"Of course," Margot said.

He continued. "We're dedicated to that. We've divested from oil and gas, even though it's lowering our operating budget. We're printing our business cards on paper filled with seeds. It's the attention to detail, you see? It's critical—"

"For the brand and its perception," Margot cut in. "Of course. We completely understand. The car company is actually a carsharing company, if that helps, and the gas company is natural gas—"

"No," Warner said, cutting her off. "Carsharing—still cars. Gas company, not okay. Zero waste, Margot. I did not start Infinity to make compromises."

"Right," Margot said, nodding. She ran through some quick mental math: She happened to know that the gas company was paying three-quarters of McQueen's typical hourly rate of $300 per person per hour—they'd leveraged the CMO friend to negotiate a discount. As for the carsharing company, RideFlow had demoted McQueen to social media and influencer only, and Margot would have to check, but it was possible they were paying even less than the gas company was.

"What would have to happen for you to be willing to work with McQueen?" Jenny asked. She sounded a little desperate, Margot thought.

They looked around at each other.

"We can't work with you if you keep those clients on."

Promotion. Raise. Living alone.

Having something that none of her friends had: an impressive job and a piece of the world that was entirely hers.

She glanced at Jenny.

Then before she could talk herself out of it, she let the words roll out of her. "Jenny," Margot said, "why don't we get Jason on the phone, ask him if we really need to keep those clients on, right?" She felt a rush of energy snake up the center of her body, explode out into the world like lava. Margot was a volcano. Margot was powerful. She was going to land the client, and she could see the agency-wide email and the highlight reel, after the work had been completed. She could see it all: Her hard work was paying off, and thank god, it was all happening. It was worth it. She felt both weightless and huge, and in an instant, she understood why people gave up their families to spend weekends building something they cared about. She understood why CEOs had their kids raised by sitters. She got it, it was intoxicating.

"I don't think—" Jenny started, but Margot had her phone out, was excusing herself, stepping into the hallway by the bathroom.

Jason picked up on the first ring. "Margot. It's a Sunday."

"Right," Margot said. "Hi, Jason—"

He cut her off. "If this is about those needy German dudes—"

"Let me run something by you. Infinity would work with us instead of Ogilvy if we nixed the gas and car accounts."

"Oh," Jason said. "And how much are we talking?"

"Six million for this year," she said.

"Let's discuss this on Monday, okay? Appreciate you bringing this to me, but I need to talk it over with the rest of the guys."

"No problem," Margot said, but she had already made up her mind.

She hadn't felt this powerful since she'd landed the job with McQueen. "We're going to figure out a way to make this work for you," she said, sliding back into her chair and winking at Warner. "Consider them fired," she mouthed when Jenny looked away.

"We'll chat things over with Jason when we're back in the office," Jenny said, standing and thanking them.

Margot got up, smiled, pumped Warner's hand up and down in hers.

"We've always liked you," Warner said, and Jenny thanked him, but they all knew the compliment belonged to Margot and Margot alone.

PART THREE

Twenty-Nine: Ana

At SFO, Silas was waiting for Ana, engine idling.

"Hi," he said, leaning over the center console to open the door for her.

She shoved her bag into the trunk, then climbed into the passenger seat, leaned across the center console to peck him on the lips, flattened her mouth into a stiff smile that she hoped read as grateful instead of detached. "That was sweet of you to come get me," she said. "Very unexpected."

"I missed you," he said.

She bristled, knew she should have missed him, too. She rubbed the top of his hand where it cradled the steering wheel at two o'clock, felt a pang of guilt that dissipated quickly.

He merged into traffic. "How was it?"

"Really fun. It turned out—so Lily totally didn't warn us—but Jack's friends were there, too. Like a combined thing."

"Really?" Silas said, raising his eyebrows. "That's kind of weird."

"No, it was fun," she said. "They were cool guys. This guy Keith, didn't really talk to him much. Brent, a friend of Jack's from Harvard. This guy named Alistair, pretty cool. An ecologist." She thought back to that night and the parts she was missing. There was no way anything had happened, right? Her friends would have seen her, stopped her.

"An ecologist!" Silas said, eyes focused on the road. "Is he the guy you were talking to?"

"What?" Ana looked out the window so he couldn't see her cheeks go red. She felt guilty for whatever she may or may not have done: a hand too close to his cheek, caught on someone's iPhone camera and posted to Instagram?

Silas was quiet. They raced north.

"Never mind," he said, merging quickly, no blinker.

No, she hadn't done anything wrong. It wasn't a crime to touch an elbow, or speak up close to a stranger in the darkness of a noisy bar.

So why did she wish she was still at the gate in Miami, reading a book and sipping a latte, with thousands of miles between Ana and Silas's indirect accusation?

"Why are you upset about this?"

"Just tell Liza not to post everything on Instagram if she doesn't want me to see your face an inch from some ecologist's. It's not a big deal."

Ana felt the tears, leaned back, willed them away. "I—I mean, we were just—it was *loud*, Silas. It's not—nothing *happened*."

"I never said anything happened," he said.

"We were just talking." Snippets came back to her: Horizon, Oakbrook. "About work, actually."

He shrugged.

They sat in silence all the way home.

Ana's plan was to spend her week off taking leisurely strolls across the length of Crissy Field, packing peanut butter and jelly sandwiches in foil and hauling them up to the top of Mount Tam, where she'd eat them and look at the view. She'd take herself out for kale salads studded with moons of jammy eggs in Presidio Heights or Mill Valley, and she'd wear big sunglasses to hide her face in the event she came across anyone from Horizon. She didn't actually have big sunglasses, and of course she wouldn't run into any of the families, on account of their ski vacations.

She wanted to relax, and if that was too tall an order, then at least she wanted to distract herself from the way Alistair's face opened into a grin like a friendly black hole that wanted to suck up all her knowledge and intellect and personhood. From the way Beth's eyebrows crumpled into unkempt commas when she doubted Ana. From all the WebMD articles she shouldn't have started to read when she'd made the mistake of trying to get a sense of why women in their sixties might be dizzy. Could be nothing. Could be the start of a rapid and dehumanizing decline.

But Ana's spring break was shaping up to be decidedly devoid of kale salads and leisurely lunches and vigorous exercise.

She spent Monday picking up after Silas, plucking T-shirts from the floor and chucking them into the cardboard boxes they were still using as laundry bins, running out to buy a duster, spraying the counter and wiping the counter and then coming back to find a ring of coffee in the exact place she'd just cleaned.

By the time the apartment was back to some semblance of order, save for all the still-unpacked boxes stacked in the living room, which Silas seemed entirely blind to, it was three in the afternoon, and what was the use in going outside when she'd just be back to make dinner in the same amount of time it took to watch half a rom-com?

"Hey," Silas said, emerging from his home office, probably to stain the counter again or splatter the microwave with tomato soup.

"Hey," she said. "Can we tackle the rest of unpacking tonight? Together?"

He turned to the cabinet and retrieved a box of something. "I'm gonna be working late, so probably not. Can you turn that down? One of the partners asked what the background noise was." He let the accusation linger.

"Oh!" she said, jumping up from the couch, even though the remote was right next to her, perched on a cushion like a companion. "Yes, sorry," she said, grabbing it and turning the volume to mute.

"You've got the life, Ana," Silas said, backing away and grabbing a jar of peanut butter on his way back into his office.

"It's my *one* week off," she said to the air around her. *I deserve a break,* she reminded herself. It was one of Bryn's mantras—"You can't let this profession take everything from you, Ana."

Could he really not see that she'd spent the entire day cleaning up after him, getting their place back in order when he hadn't so much as lifted a finger the entire weekend?

He shut the door behind him.

The next morning, Silas asked if she could hang around to sign for a package he was expecting, and she couldn't really say no—he had work to do, and she was free—but by the time the package arrived, it was four in the afternoon, and it was time to make dinner. On Wednesday, she woke up early to surprise Silas with weekday pancakes—it was something he'd done for her when she had a test one time back in college, and she thought maybe a romantic breakfast would remind her how good they were together—but she couldn't find the pancake pan, so she opened a box labeled *kitchen*, then another labeled *kitchen two*, and it wasn't until three boxes later that she finally found the pan, and by then Silas was wolfing down a granola bar and murmuring something about missing his bus to work, and so she was left alone and pancakeless and surrounded by the spilled contents of their lives. She wanted them to unpack together—to prove to herself that they could take this on as a team—but she was getting fed up, and Silas was out of the house, and now was as good a time as any to tackle the rest of these boxes.

She turned on some music and got to work. She finished the bedroom, the rest of both of their clothes, developed an ingenious organization system for the kitchen, broke down twelve boxes and took them downstairs to recycling, then wiped down the counters and admired her handiwork. She'd made great progress: a few more boxes, some art on the walls, maybe a rug for the living room, and they'd be completely moved in.

"Whoa, Nelly," Silas said, surprising her. He dropped his bag on the floor and looked her up and down. "Are you still in your pajamas?"

"What are you doing back?" She glanced at her watch: six in the evening? Had she eaten anything today? Had a single sip of water? "I can't believe how late it is—" She looked down at herself. She'd been so busy, rearranging drawers and hanging up all of Silas's shirts before realizing they were wrinkled, and searching for an iron and ironing his shirts and hanging them back up before even getting to her boxes of clothes, which she also finished unpacking. "I guess I was just so busy, I didn't even have lunch, but look at the kitchen, I found the good pancake pan, finally—"

"I'm gonna run to the gym," he said, disappearing into the bedroom.

She followed him. "Si, I unpacked all your stuff. Your workout shorts are in the dresser—"

"Ana, fuck, did you wash my blazer?"

"No, of course not—" She'd run a few loads of laundry—was it possible it had fallen in with the T-shirts and underwear? She knew not to wash his blazer, obviously, and she was pretty careful with that kind of thing, but maybe she'd been so in the zone—

"It looks like shit," he said, a shrunken wisp of a jacket dangling from his outstretched wrist. "This thing was two grand."

Two grand? Her face was hot.

She bent down to pick it up.

He pushed his way past her.

She was six hundred feet up Mount Tam and already out of breath.

It was kind of fucked up. Silas was clearly going through something—work stress? Transition panic? Anxiety? Depression? They'd been together for ten entire years, and he'd only been a dick for the past few weeks, and anyway, it wasn't like he'd *asked* her to clean up after him because he was disproportionately funding their shared lives. He'd never even suggested it.

But on the other hand, wasn't it possible that this was not an isolated incident at all? That it was the same shit he'd pulled a million times before, except magnified because they lived together?

She waved at a fellow hiker, breathed in the gentle shade of the redwoods, breathed out the stress of everything else.

"On your left," said a gravelly voice.

I get it, you're fitter than I am, she thought to herself. All these stupid Mill Valley moms and dads, wealthy and idle and skinny. All that kale.

"Ana?"

She swiveled. Okay, now she was officially going batshit crazy. She needed to get back to her routine, to eat regular meals and get outside and—or maybe she wasn't crazy—"Wait, Alistair?"

Thirty: Lily

It had been Jack's idea: "Why don't you go back to New York for a few days, see your mom, check in with Barri in person?" He was going away for the weekend anyway—a friend from law school had invited Jack and a few other guys to his parents' place in Lake Winnipesaukee to start studying for the bar.

Part of Lily wanted to stay home, have the relaxing weekend she'd been trying to have for ages: This time, hopefully, Annette and Gina wouldn't pop in unannounced. She had enough of the details figured out that she could absolutely take a weekend off from wedding planning, finally get that massage she'd been meaning to get, take herself out to dinner at one of the restaurants Jack didn't like, page through a book or get a head start on writing heartfelt notes to each of her bridesmaids. That was another thing she was falling short at: showing the people in her life how much they meant to her. Being effusive with thanks.

Margot called and she let it go to voicemail.

She'd been screening Margot's calls—she'd only called twice, but still—the prospect of returning her call and answering the inevitable "Did you have a fun weekend in Miami?" seemed cataclysmically difficult. What was she going to say? *I melted into a puddle of my own tears just moments after you ignored what I was trying to admit to you, and I spent most of my bachelorette party stressed that you weren't having fun, and I'm actually not nearly as busy as I thought I would be in this stretch between bachelorette party and wedding, and Jack thinks I need to go back to treatment, and logically I agree. But there's a familiar part of me that wants to ignore Jack. And the voice in my head that tells me to avoid treatment is at odds with my need to not disappoint anyone in my life. And also, I'm kind of hurt that you were more focused on your annoyance at the guys being there than what's clearly going down with me.*

What would Margot say to that?

And anyway, those weren't the kinds of things you said to a bridesmaid between the bachelorette party and the wedding.

So she hadn't called Margot back. And she hadn't booked a massage at the place she liked in Back Bay, either, because if she booked a massage, she wouldn't leave Boston for the weekend, and if she didn't leave Boston for the weekend, then she'd slip into eating, or not eating, all her meals by herself, because alone was the only reasonable company in which to pick at spinach leaves and cut grapes in half.

No, she couldn't do that to Jack. Not this close to the rest of their lives.

—

The train to Manhattan was crowded. Lily walked to the final car and found a seat in an unoccupied row, shoved her overnight bag into the rack above, and made herself comfortable by the window. She texted her mom: arriving around 4, see you soon, xx

Her mom texted back immediately: Great Lil!! Come right home, I have a surprise for you. Love you. Mom

Lily smiled at her mom's refusal to send a text without signing it. She tucked herself into a pair of noise-canceling headphones, hit play on jazz that felt like a hot bath, and woke up to the conductor announcing they'd arrived.

—

The dog was so excited to see Lily that she peed on the carpet, but her mom might as well have, too.

"Genevieve, down," Gina scolded, going to Lily, wrapping her up, taking her bag, shoving a coconut water in Lily's hand. "We're going to have an amazing weekend. I got you the coconut water you like, and your favorite black-and-white cookies, and I was thinking we could either go out tonight, or do bagels and lox, like you love."

It had been an old tradition: Back when Lily's parents were first divorced, and her mom was finally freed from the burden of cooking the hearty dinners Lily's dad insisted upon after a long day at work, Lily, her brother, Jacob, and their mom had worked their way through every type of breakfast for dinner, eaten mostly in front of the TV, which could have been sad, but it wasn't. They watched in familial contentment, laughing at the same parts, finishing their dinners at exactly the same time, playing Uno even though they were too old for it, cleaning the dishes together, which they'd never done before.

They were doing this without him. Or at least that was how it had felt to Lily.

"That sounds good!" Lily said. She couldn't remember the last time she'd allowed herself a cookie or a bagel.

"Do you need to change or anything? Drop off your stuff in your room. We're going to be picked up in—" She glanced at her watch. "Oh! Ten minutes! Go, Lil! What underwear are you wearing?" She reached for Lily's shirt, pulled it up to examine her bra. "Nude. Good."

Lily hugged her sweater back around her abdomen. "Okay," she said, suddenly wary. "What are we doing?"

"A surprise!" She clapped her hands together.

"Mom, you know I hate surprises," Lily said, but it came out sounding less like she was slightly annoyed and more like she was scared. "I mean, it's fine, sounds fun," she revised, then went to the room that used to be hers.

"You really didn't need to get a limo," Lily said.

"It's only once that your daughter gets married!" Gina said, giddy as they slid into the smooth leather seats. "Well, maybe twice. Who's to say. Do you think I need more Botox before the big day?" She furrowed her brows and pointed at her forehead.

"I'm not getting married for a few more weeks," Lily said as they merged into traffic. "And no, I don't. Where are we going?"

"Okay, I'll tell you." Gina bared her teeth in excitement, let out a little squeal. "Do you remember that dress you loved when we first went shopping?"

Lily had chosen her dress a year prior, after trying on so many that had all blended together. Mermaid, ball gown, sweetheart, sheath. Three cities, six stores, and ultimately, Lily had settled on the first dress she'd tried. Silk, strapless, slinky, cream. In it, she'd felt like someone who'd never struggled with anything at all. "I think it's the one," she said, and she and her mom had gone back to the Garment District to order it.

"Oh, not the Clara," the woman at the store had said.

The designer, apparently, was "taking a sabbatical" and wouldn't be taking on anything new. "We can totally find you something similar, we're really truly very sorry." The woman looked like she was about to cry, and Lily had waved it off—there really were plenty of other dresses she liked almost as much.

"Seriously, don't worry," Lily had said, placing a hand on the woman's arm. She looked thin and tired, her nerves frayed, maybe from all the brides whose perfect days were contingent on so many details that Lily knew weren't actually relevant to happiness at all.

She'd opted for something that was imperceptibly different: still sleek and beautiful and expensive. Plus, it had fit perfectly, which meant they didn't have to build in extra visits for fittings. They sold her a brand-new one they had in the back, and said they'd get her in once or twice to take up the hem a half inch if she wanted, but even that wasn't really necessary. Lily and her mom took the dress home that day, and it had been hanging in paper and plastic in Gina's closet ever since.

Lily tried to recall that first dress—the Clara—and how it differed from the dress that was hanging at her mom's now, but couldn't. "I vaguely remember," Lily said, looking out the window as they sped past a Jack's Wife Freda that had long ago been a shoe store where Lily had gone for a pair of patent Mary Janes with a slight heel that she'd worn for her bat mitzvah.

"Well, Lillian," Gina said, hands on Lily's knees, "don't even ask me how I did this. Okay, I'll tell you. You remember Rachel, right? Samantha's mom? I think she was two years behind you at Dalton. Maybe she's Jacob's age. Anyway, Rachel went to Yale with Clara—you remember, the dress was by a Clara? That's the woman who makes those dresses—I, of course, had no idea. But I ran into Rachel at Pilates a few months ago, she looks like hell, by the way, and we were chatting after class, the quality at that place has nosedived. Anyway, she was telling me all about Samantha, who you should absolutely reconnect with, she's in Providence studying medicine and married some guy Rachel hates. And so of course I mentioned your wedding, and she happened to tell me that she was going to Greece for a weekend with a friend who is a wedding dress designer, and it just all came together: Her friend was Clara, and I said, 'Not *that* Clara,' and it *was* that Clara! It turns out she was just taking some time off because it got to be too much and she hardly needed the money, but was happy to take on a one-off request, so Rachel hooked it up, Lillian, is what I'm saying, and the dress is waiting for you, and we're going to see it, I'm just so excited!"

"Oh!" Lily said, stiffening. It was too much, sort of a waste of money to buy a second dress when she was already so happy with the first, but her mom looked so thrilled with herself for tracking it down, and there was only so much to be happy about in this world, Lily thought, then realized that maybe she was starting to get a little bit depressed.

"So we're going to see it!" Gina said, as if maybe Lily hadn't heard.

"Wow!" Lily said. "That's great, Mom. Thank you. I can't believe you found it."

"I thought you'd be so excited, Lily! And I know this is overkill"—she gestured at the limo—"but I thought: Why not, right? And if we buy the dress, I don't want us to have to wrestle it into a cab. It's just not worth the risk. And we have it for the night, so we can go out to dinner, or go home and do bagels. I thought you might be tired after your travel day. Whatever you want, Lily!"

But it wasn't whatever she wanted, not really, because if she chose going home for bagels or leaving the dress for the next person, Gina would be disappointed enough that Lily would regret stating what she wanted. It would be easier to play into her mom's fantasy for the evening. "This is great, Mom, thank you."

The shop was small and white, carpets as plush as clouds.

"We have the Clara right here for you. I'm Lydia, by the way. The dressing room is over there. There's a chair in the dressing room, if Lily doesn't mind."

"Oh, she doesn't," Gina said. "I gave birth to her!"

Lily forced a smile, went to the room, shimmied out of her jeans and sweater while her mom settled in.

"Lily," Gina said, fumbling with her purse, "I don't want you to feel like you have to get this just because I roused Clara from the dead for you."

"Right," Lily said.

"It's an option, but if you prefer what you already have, then wonderful! You can keep that, or get this as a backup, or even get it and we'll have it shortened for the reception. It's totally up to you." She tucked her purse under the chair, got her coat off.

Lily watched as Gina took in her body, and she moved instinctively to cover herself.

"Here it is," Lydia said, letting herself into the dressing room and shaking the dress on its hanger. "I'll help you in, okay? Turn around, here you go, that's it, are you wearing any makeup? We have face shields for that, don't want to get it on the dress."

Lily shook her head. Lydia eased the dress over Lily's head, and Lily sucked in, a little worried it wouldn't zip, and she'd have to face the reality of her body in this mirror with her mom and this stranger behind the curtain with her, and she was afraid it would be a Herculean task to manage herself and not fall apart.

"Oh, it's a little big. Is this not the size we meant to order?" Lydia asked.

"It's not zipped," Lily said.

"No, it is," Lydia said. "Here, look, can you see your back in the mirror? Come out, we have doubles in the main area."

Lily followed her out, twirled in the mirror, and Lydia was right: It was zipped, and it was gaping.

"We wanted a four," Gina said. "You were a four when we went shopping back in February, weren't you? What size is this?"

Lydia fished the tag out of the dress. "A four," she said, furrowing her brows. "Lily, were you planning to lose weight for the wedding? We can alter it, of course, plenty of our brides go down a size or two for the big day, it's just cutting it a little close with timing, you're getting married, when is it—six weeks? We can make it happen, I think."

"Lily," Gina said, tilting her head at her daughter, "you didn't tell me you were losing weight for your wedding. I did notice that—"

"I wasn't," Lily said, reddening, wanting to avoid falling into that old pattern of convincing her mom that everything was fine. "Or, I mean, I didn't," she added, which was clearly untrue. "I'm just—I didn't realize, or mean to, or, I mean, I've been walking a lot—" She pulled herself together, pictured the zipper inside her, zipped it up and took a deep gulp of air, and said that maybe they should just stick with the dress she already had after all.

"Well, that one's not going to fit," Gina said, a thread of alarm working its way into her voice. "Lydia, can I call you tomorrow to figure out alterations?"

"Sure, of course," Lydia said. "We'll hold on to this here."

"Thanks," Gina said. "I'll help Lily out of it."

Lily smiled apologetically, followed her mom into the dressing room and let her zip Lily out of the dress that was supposed to be her dream.

—

Neither Lily nor Gina revisited the prospect of going out to dinner. They got back in the limo, Gina told the driver to take them home, and they sat silently, no shopping bags at their feet or wedding dress laid in plastic across the unoccupied seats.

"Lily," Gina said after ten minutes that felt like forever.

Lily grunted noncommittally, suddenly tingly at the prospect of discussing what was happening in her mind and her body with her mom. She wanted to be different from her mom: less vain, more serious. But here they were: two women who ordered Cobb salads without dressing and didn't have jobs.

There was a silence, and Lily wondered if her mom was working up the same confidence Lily was trying for: a willingness to bridge what was unsaid between them. But all Gina said was, "Let's do bagels, okay?" Then she looked up at the ceiling. Lily watched her mom watch the lights change color, red to blue to green and back to red, and she pictured the zipper again.

Zip.

Knock on wood.

"Lily," her mom said, "we're going to have to talk about this."

Zipper zip zip.

"About what?" she asked.

Her mom sighed, and Lily wondered when Gina had started to look so old.

"I'm worried," Gina said, her back to Lily, as she cut the centers out of their bagels and tossed them in the trash. The kitchen was neat, the whir of the fridge dull and familiar.

"Okay," Lily tried, slow and even.

"Lily," she said, turning toward her, grabbing a butter knife from a drawer and plunging it into a tub of cream cheese. "I'm—I don't know how to say this. I'm worried about—I tried to bring it up, there have been times—" She blinked, looked up at the ceiling. "I should have mentioned it. I just didn't want to make you self-conscious, and they told us, back at Hope House, they said to not comment on your weight, right?"

Lily nodded, surprised that her mom remembered the lessons she thought were indelible only to her.

"The last thing I want is to make things harder for you."

"I know, Mom," Lily said.

"I want this wedding to be everything for you," Gina said.

"I want that, too," Lily said. She took in her surroundings: the stainless-steel fridge, no magnets; the stack of cookbooks Gina had owned as long as Lily had been alive; the painting of a nude by her great-grandmother in the corner of the dining room, just off the kitchen. She felt like a doll in a dollhouse, like she'd been manufactured to fit in her surroundings, which had been manufactured to fit around her, but still, something felt just out of reach: She was supposed to be gearing up for the best weekend of her life, and she felt far away from her friends; no closer to a job; concerned that "wife" was the only thing she was about to have going for her.

"I'm going to see Barri while I'm here," Lily said. An offering.

"Good," Gina said. "Maybe you tell her about this, the dress, or—well, it's your therapy appointment. You talk about what you want to talk about. Have you told your friends?"

"I will," Lily said.

Gina pushed Lily's plate in front of her, and didn't say anything while Lily pushed its contents around.

Thirty-One: Ana

The sun was high overhead, and the trees laughed in the wind.

"What are you doing here?" Ana asked, suddenly self-conscious: She knew there was an underwear line showing through her shorts, she knew her hair looked insane, she wasn't wearing a stitch of makeup.

Alistair placed his hands on his hips. "I'm just visiting my parents. I figured why not see them right after Miami, and they're the best, but I needed a little bit of time alone, you know how it is. What about you?" He tapped his thighs with his hands. "Oh, duh, you live here, you told me that."

His arms were so taut, his skin shockingly smooth in the light of day, his chest trim and fit and somehow also as broad as the sky. She let her eyes drift down the plane of his stomach, the waistband of his shorts.

"I've been meaning to get out here all week," she said. "But I haven't made it out, and—" She stopped herself before she told him that she'd been cleaning and cooking and unpacking.

"No pressure," he cut in. "I love a solo hike, so I totally get it if not, but I have another sandwich if you want to walk together."

"Oh!" Ana said. "Yes, definitely, that sounds great!"

If Silas found out, he'd flip: accuse her of DM'ing him, of inviting him here, no matter what she said.

But she wasn't doing anything wrong by walking with a friend. It wasn't a sin to hike with an acquaintance. And plus, he was here, and it felt like a minor miracle, and if Silas was mad, then fuck him.

"Seriously, I can totally leave you alone," Alistair repeated.

"No, sorry—I'm spacey, not enough coffee yet—" She mustered a laugh. "I'd love to have a hiking buddy." She flinched at her use of the word. Buddy? Really?

Alistair seemed nonplussed. "Great," he said, grinning his wide grin and gesturing for her to lead the way.

They sat at the summit and chewed sandwiches.

"That guy's on my team," he said, pointing toward a man in neon shorts.

"At work?" Ana asked.

"No," Alistair laughed. "It's a game my sister and I used to play when we were young. When you see a person whose vibe you like, you select them. It's kind of an ongoing accumulation thing. Parachute shorts are always an automatic for me."

Ana nodded, pictured Alistair, tiny and towheaded, giggling with his little kid feet in a pool somewhere, sitting next to his sister on a summer vacation fighting over passersby.

She panned the surroundings. "Can that dog be on my team?" A boxy-shaped thing with an overbite.

"I was planning to call him next," Alistair said, elbowing Ana in the ribs. "But fair's fair. Yes. Boxer McChewy over there is yours. I get that guy." He nodded toward a totem pole made of the stacked heads of various woodland creatures.

"*All* of them?" Ana laughed. "That's not fair."

"Loophole." He shrugged, laughed. "You can have the ranger over there. Hey, how's your mom, by the way?"

A drop in her stomach. "God," Ana said. "Honestly, I've been so busy, I need to call her."

He chewed thoughtfully. "I've been thinking about the thing you said about Horizon."

"You have?" She feigned interest in the fog, thick in the trees around them, so that he wouldn't notice her cheeks had gone red. "Did I go on too much? I thought, in Miami, that maybe I had—"

He put a hand up. "No, not at all. I've been thinking about it because it's a metaphor, right? Oakbrook is you. Horizon is who you think you should be."

"What do you mean?"

"I'm not trying to mansplain your priorities to you," he said. "It just sounds like you know yourself, and I wonder if you're giving yourself enough credit."

"Hmm," Ana said, because of all the things she'd considered, underestimating her own sense of self had not, she realized, been one of them.

Later that afternoon, she was back at home, making a posthike smoothie and putzing around. Maybe Ana was being weird, traipsing around the house, still in her hiking shorts, feeling uncharacteristically fond of herself, underwear line and sweaty hair and all, but she was going with it. The fresh air and the hike had invigorated her. Maybe all these overexercised moms were onto something. Or maybe she just had a crush on Alistair that was propelling her into motion, waking her up from the rest of her life.

She showered and took herself out to dinner, almost called Margot, then remembered they hadn't really spoken since the Miami spat. She tried Lily, but got her voicemail. Oh well. She was eating a kale salad on Union Street, twenty thousand steps into a Thursday, and felt refreshed enough to brave the rest of the semester.

Silas was already in bed when she got home.

"You're being weird," he said.

"What do you mean?"

"You're, like, weirdly happy," he said, rolling toward her. He was unshaven, his face closed off and unreadable.

"Isn't that a good thing?"

"Were you with anyone today?" he asked.

How could he possibly have known? "What do you mean?"

"I don't know. You were gone all day. Were you alone the whole day?"

"I mean, there were people around me. This is a densely populated city."

"But you weren't with anyone specifically? It's fine if you were. I'm just wondering."

She thought for a second. What was the use in telling him, in making the Alistair thing out to be something that would worry him, when it was totally innocent?

"Right," she said.

"Okay," he said, rolling over and shutting off the light.

Was there any way he could have known about Alistair? "Silas? Are you, like, mad at me?"

"I'm just not sure what's up with you, Ana. You just seem off lately, to be honest. Like, I know it's your spring break, but if I had a whole entire week off, I would be grocery shopping and figuring out about that overhead light thing we talked about, not just bopping the fuck around, hiking with some guy and lying to me about it."

It felt like a slap. "How did—"

"Rodge saw you on Mount Tam. It doesn't matter. Who is this dude, Ana? Were you seriously not going to tell me?"

Her breath caught in her throat. "I just—he was just there, and I didn't want to make a thing out of it—"

"*Who* was there?"

She didn't have time to lie, to consider all the threads of a story she'd have to keep straight if she said it was a stranger, or an old friend from high school, or a friend of Margot's, and anyway, her mind was racing too fast to pin down a relationship that Silas would both believe and be okay with. "He's visiting his parents, Jack's friend—"

"This is fucking rich," Silas said, standing from the bed and going to the closet. "It's the dude from the Instagram story, isn't it?"

"Alistair," Ana said as her chest filled with pins.

Silas pulled a T-shirt down from its hanger and pulled it on over his bare chest, like armor.

"It wouldn't have been so weird if you weren't hiding it," he said.

"I wasn't hiding it, I just don't think I need permission, and it wasn't even planned," she said.

"I'm going for a walk," he said, and slipped his feet into shoes, trotted out of the apartment like one of Ana's students at recess.

Ana wrinkled her nose with indignation, wished she'd had the ability to twist this into his fault, but she knew that he wasn't really being as controlling as she wanted to make him out to be. That he had a point.

She grabbed a broom and swept the whole apartment, vowed to apologize to him as soon as he was back.

But then he'd been gone for two hours. That was a lot of walking, and it was making her really nervous. She'd done all the dishes, unpacked the last of three boxes, and still, Silas wasn't home.

She was starting to feel desperate. She wanted to call him, tell him to come home, apologize for hiking with Alistair, for not telling Silas how much she appreciated the coffee ice cream back when he'd bought it for her, so many years ago. She wanted to tell him that she'd continue to choose him. That they could get through whatever this rough patch was. That she'd thought about it, and she was a gold girl, and she wanted a round diamond, and she couldn't wait for Paris. But if he thought she'd look better in silver, or platinum, then maybe he was right. Either way, it wasn't about the ring. It was about their shared lives.

The front door opened.

"Silas," she said, going to him, reaching for his shoulders, taking in the kismet of it: Just as she'd decided to apologize, to fully welcome him back, as much as she could, he'd come home. If this wasn't a sign.

"Look, Silas, I've been thinking—" She followed him to the fridge. "I'm really sorry. About all of this. I don't even know what exactly devolved—"

He grabbed a coconut water. "Devolved?" he asked.

She took a deep breath. She was trusting herself—speaking without second-guessing, letting the words land uncensored, exactly as she meant them.

"I should have told you about Alistair," she tried again. "I don't know why I didn't. It's really not a big deal, though. I really—I won't talk to him again, or I mean, I will at Lily's wedding, but not in any kind of intentional way, okay? I shouldn't have made you uncomfortable. It's the last thing I wanted." She heard the desperation in her voice. "I'm just really sorry. I know things have been hard since we moved in, and I know I've played a part in that—"

"Ana," he said, swiveling to face her.

There. He was going to forgive her, tell her they'd figure it out together, that he was sorry, too. It would be like the time they came back from a trip with his family to Turks: He'd apologized to her before she'd even realized how badly she'd needed for him to tell her that he hadn't meant what he said when he told his mom, in front of her, that Ana's job was "mostly fun and games." He'd been drunk, he didn't mean it, he didn't think it at all, he had just been feeling insecure.

She'd been shortsighted, thinking that tepid interest from a stranger during an alcohol-infused weekend meant anything compared to what Silas had given her over the last ten years. All the times they'd eaten fried eggs in the dining hall and taken thermoses of spiked hot chocolate to see Margot's lacrosse games and gone camping in Acadia, sharing one sleeping bag because they couldn't bear two layers of baffled nylon between them. All the times they'd walked the hills of Pacific Heights, holding hands and making up stories about the people inside the pretty houses, then returning to his place to fuck or play Monopoly even though he didn't like Monopoly. That day in Napa, both of them wine drunk and twenty-six. An older couple had given them some canned advice: "The most important thing is that you get along" or something, and Ana and Silas had looked at each other and tried not to laugh, because they'd been together for eight years and still missed each other on the nights they spent apart.

"Hey, Si?" Ana said, suddenly emboldened. If they were going to build a life together, he was right—she needed to be honest about everything. "I—you know Horizon is an amazing school, I mean, obviously—you went there. So of course you know. I, just—I'm wondering if I'm more—" She searched for the words. "Impactful, I guess. At Oakbrook. Or somewhere like Oakbrook."

"What?" he said, eyes wide.

"I know," she said. "It's not like I don't *like* Horizon. I obviously love the kids, and I've learned so much—"

"Seriously?" he said, his eyebrows thick across his forehead. "Are you serious?"

She blinked.

"Ana, our entire relationship is at risk. I just walked the city talking myself through breaking up with you—"

She stiffened.

"And this is what you're thinking about? Leaving Horizon—the job I helped you get—to go back to Oakbrook? If you want to quit your job, fine. Quit your job. But don't go back to the place that made you miserable. You were crying, like, every single day, and I was the one taking care of you. But honestly, forget all that. Go back if you want." He looked like he was on the verge of tears. "But that's what you're thinking about? Not us? Not the misery of the entire time we've lived together, or the fact that I invited you to Paris and we've hardly even talked about it, like you're not excited about what's obviously a proposal trip? Or how *weird* you've been ever since we moved in together?"

"Silas," Ana started, waited for the tears to prickle at her eyes, but was met instead with hot fire in her chest. "I don't—that's not fair."

"No," Silas said, "it's not. It's not fair to ask me to pull rank for you at Horizon, then to give it all up, then to go back to a job that made you miserable as if I won't be the one picking up the pieces when you get depressed about shit that's not even your responsibility, just like it's not fair that you're hanging out with some random guy while I'm at work making money to subsidize *your* life."

"I didn't *know* you were planning a proposal, not that—I mean, Alistair is just a friend, Silas. He—you don't know what it's like to feel dispensable, Si. You've never been interchangeable."

He waved her away. "You always do this, Ana," he said, and she realized he still hadn't taken off his jacket. "That's really great for you that Alistair thinks you're special." He was spitting. "You just—you look at everything through rose-colored glasses. You romanticize the past. You never take anything seriously. Life isn't all optimism and sunshine and stickers on math quizzes, you know? You just think you're so special."

"I don't think I'm special," she said, her breath catching in her throat. Fuck the fried eggs and the thermoses of spiked hot chocolate and the day in Napa and the advice from the older couple they'd thought they were above. "You're the one who's gone your whole entire life as this golden boy who everyone—and most people—" She took a deep breath. It was so unfair: the way her ability with words rose to every single occasion but this one. "It's just exhausting, sometimes, to be this background character. At work. With my friends." She paused. "With you."

"I've worked for everything that I have, and you know it."

"That's not even relevant," she said.

"I get it, Ana, you're like, this tortured, misunderstood soul." He rolled his eyes. "Honestly, sometimes you could suck it up a little, you know?"

Something sharp and hot rose in her solar plexus. She wanted to slap him. "As if you've ever sucked it up in your life."

"Please tell me how my promotion to VP is a result of anything besides sucking it up every day and working my ass off. Please, Ana, tell me how *you're* sucking it up by grading math tests and marking the girls' answers correct even when they're not."

It hurt, to have him hurl this private secret that she'd shared with him once, a guilty admission, back in her face. It sounded so stupid now that he voiced it out loud: What would happen to these girls once they were met with the world, which was run by people like Silas who believed everything was a meritocracy and had no idea how untrue that really was?

"I thought you wanted to be moving forward," Silas said. "This just—it's objectively backward."

"Not everything is linear."

"Actually, yes," he said. "Stuff like this—leaving a job at Horizon that I helped you get to go backward to the place where you were so unhappy before—not to mention, this makes me and my family look really stupid, and good luck if we ever want *our* kids to go to Horizon—is linear in the wrong way. It's pretty fucking black and white."

"Do you even—you used to, like, care about my fulfillment, Si. Remember?"

"I care about our future, Ana, and you're being a baby about this. It's in direct opposition to the life we want."

"The life *you* want, maybe," she whispered.

"Maybe you need to think about whether or not you actually want to be in this relationship." His gaze was paralyzing.

"I do," she said, but as soon as it was out, she wondered if it was entirely true.

He'd taught her Econ 100, and then he'd taught her how to be a person in the world. Now, they had an extra bedroom and she was just starting to feel like maybe she belonged, or if not belonged, then at least could speak the language of belonging with proficiency if not fluency. She was doing it. She was living this life with him. Alistair was totally irrelevant, and Jesus god fuck she did not want to start over, to make a profile on a dating app and tolerate boring dinners with guys who wanted to talk about their IPOs. She was almost thirty and she wanted to have kids and if he broke up with her she might miss her window! Maybe this was a panic attack, her breath was quickening and she wanted to melt into the floor because she disappointed everyone and all she did was try, and try and try and try and fuck up and she was such a failure, and her boyfriend hated her, and there were all these wildfires.

She tried her hardest to slow her breath, but let a few hiccups out, because maybe Silas would take pity on her if he heard how much she was suffering.

His silence felt like tectonic plates were shifting beneath her to expose a gaping hole, straight into the center of the earth.

"I think you should stay somewhere else tonight," he said.

She almost laughed at the absurdity of it.

"I'm serious, Ana," he said. "I need some space from you."

"It's my home, too," she said.

The apartment was sharp and cold around them. He blinked rapidly.

In a quieter voice: "Where?"

"You're an adult. You can figure it out."

She wanted to slap him, or hit him, or fuck and make up, or jump out the window, or curl into herself and turn into a rock and stay a rock for all of eternity. She wanted to be anything but sentient.

She threw a change of clothes in her backpack, grabbed her laptop and a phone charger and her wallet, slipped her feet into shoes, squinted at the elevator keypad through eyes blurred by tears, poked at the L button. Once outside, she let the tears seep out of her like blood.

She tried Lily. Voicemail. She called Margot. Fuck the Miami fight. But voicemail.

Deep breaths. In and out. She could try her mom, but she'd tell her to come home to Wisconsin, as if that would help at all. Or worse, she'd tell Ana that the dizzy spells had been getting worse. That things were bad. Ana couldn't bear hearing that right now. She could try one of her other friends: Zoe or Liza or Emily, but she didn't have the energy to explain herself, to fill them in on the background information about the minutiae of her relationship with Silas that they'd need to fully understand in order to be appropriately mad on her behalf. She needed Lily or Margot. She needed Lily to tell her what to do, to walk her through the next night or year or decade of her life, to hand her the reins to her own life the way she used to hand Ana a statement necklace to borrow for the night. She needed her friends to wrap Ana up in confidence, show her who to be.

But they were elsewhere, moving on with their lives the way she'd been trying to move on with hers.

Thirty-Two: Lily

Lily had both divulged almost nothing to her mom and wished she'd divulged less. So she spent the rest of her weekend in New York avoiding her. On Saturday, she went for a run—"I'm going to stop for a smoothie bowl after," she lied. That night: "I have dinner plans with Liza," she said, then went to see a movie alone.

Her mom was gone most of the day Sunday for her monthly lunch and shopping with a couple of fellow divorcées, so Lily stayed in—picking through a bag of dried mangoes and watching stupid TV with Genevieve curled in her lap.

—

On Monday, Lily walked the twelve blocks to Barri's office.

It smelled like incense and patchouli. There was a new framed poster in the waiting room, and it felt like a betrayal: Barri had gone on updating her space for clients who weren't Lily, while Lily wasted away in Boston. It was childish to feel so attached to Barri, she knew.

"Lily!" Barri said, emerging from her office with arms outstretched. It had freaked Lily out, the first time Barri had gone in for a hug, but now it was comforting, and for the first time since she'd left Boston, Lily felt herself relax.

"You crying already?" Barri asked, and Lily realized that she was.

"Come inside, come," Barri said, ushering Lily toward the familiar sofa littered with mismatched pillows made from Barri's kids' old sports jerseys. She took a deep breath, looked up at Barri, and let her tears fall.

"When you're ready, Lily."

Lily told Barri about the therapy appointment with Jack, the frosting tasting with Gina, the coconut shrimp at the bachelorette party with the guys, the rival bride in the bathroom in Miami, Jack and the backpack and the leather jacket and the scale. Once she started talking, she couldn't stop.

"What I'm interested in, Lily," Barri said, interrupting her once Lily had started to go breathless, "is why you haven't, at any point in all of this, shared with anyone what you're going through—"

"I have," Lily interrupted. "Jack and the backpack, I told you."

"When I say 'what you're going through,' I'm actually not talking about the eating-disorder thoughts or the need to weigh yourself, although I certainly would like to revisit that. I'm talking about everything else." She paused, and Lily watched her flutter her eyelashes in a way that Lily used to find obnoxious.

"When was the last time you said no?" Barri continued.

"I said no to lunch," Lily tried.

Barri didn't laugh.

"A joke."

"It seems like leaving your routine has resurfaced your need to please everyone, Lily, and I'm wondering why. I'm wondering why you haven't told your mom that you need her to butt out, that you actually don't care about the peonies as much as she does, and if she cares so much then she can take that on. I'm wondering why you never let yourself get angry at your mom for blindsiding you with that therapy appointment, which, by the way, is kind of a conflict of interest. Your mom paid for it? We'll come back to that, that's not really ethical. I'm wondering why you didn't tell Jack that you'd prefer the guys didn't join you in Miami, or if you were okay with it, why you didn't tell Margot to stop complaining about it."

"That would have been rude," Lily said. "They'd bought their tickets—"

Barri tapped her foot impatiently. Lily loved this about her: She didn't beat around the bush or feel all sorry for Lily the way some of her previous therapists had. "Lily, who are you angry at?"

"No one!" Lily said, a little offended, actually: No one had wronged her, and she wasn't about to start blaming other people for problems that were hers. Yes, it was her wedding, but it was also her *family's* wedding, and she *wanted* her mom to be involved.

She enjoyed spending time with her mom, trying on dresses and eating—or not eating—bagels together. She liked the shopping part, even if her mom could be a bit critical. It was even a good thing she'd gone back to try on the dress: At least now she knew she'd made the right choice in not getting the way-too-big Clara.

"Pretend I'm your mom," Barri said, and Lily almost laughed.

"Can we not?" Lily said. "Maybe next time. I just can't."

"Lily, just try."

Lily rolled her eyes. Hated Barri. Loved that she didn't treat her like an eggshell. "Why are you so obsessed with never aging?"

"Good, Lily," Barri said "How do you feel about my eating habits?"

"Barri, this is too much. Can we talk about something else?"

"We cannot. How does it make you feel, Lily, when we have lunch together and I scoop out my bagel?"

"I mean, I get that you had your own stuff, and I know you don't mean to hurt me." She looked at her hands. "Can we be done?"

"No hedging, Lily. You don't have to worry about hurting anyone's feelings. Focus on the anger. What else, specifically, do you notice?"

"Don't buy me cookies then refuse to eat one yourself then get mad when I don't want one," Lily said, heat rising in her chest. "Sorry. I know your dad said shitty stuff to you when you were a kid."

"Lily."

She took a deep breath. "You act like I should be better than you and not care about the stuff you care about, but you should have thought of that when you told me I looked pudgy after a summer at camp, or when you told me my hair was a color that would look mousy when I got older, or when you said that Ana wasn't as pretty as my high school friends, or when you said that Dad was going to upgrade to a younger model back when he still loved you for being you, and then you made it happen, and he wouldn't have done that if you could have just believed that you were as good as you obviously are. It's so fucking exhausting, Mom, and I have no idea why you made such a big deal out of me spending money on Wi-Fi on the plane when we went to Chile last year, as if I'm this irresponsible spender, but I'm not, I'm really responsible and you never trust me and you always need to be in control and I don't even care about peonies and if it was up to me I would probably just not even have this stupid wedding," Lily said, then sucked in a surprised breath of air, because she hadn't known any of what she'd said.

"There it is, Lil," Barri said. "Good." Barri nodded, as if listening to a rhythm that only she could hear. "Good, Lily."

She was exhausted.

"Your homework, tonight, is to share a part of this with your mom. Are we back on Zoom next week?"

"Yup," Lily managed, nodding, picking up her stuff. She checked to make sure her phone had been off: What if it had somehow recorded what she said and sent it to her mom and made her mom feel terrible?

"You are not responsible for her feelings," Barri said, reading Lily's mind.

"I know," Lily said.

"Look, I think you're experiencing a significant relapse with regards to your anorexia, and I need you to consider more intensive treatment. I'm going to set up an intake at a place I like in Boston." Her face was solemn. "I just need you to be open to it."

Lily wanted to protest, but instead she just nodded. It felt good to be directed. To not have to think.

Thirty-Three: Ana

Ana was walking down Chestnut Street, watching the couples go in and out of restaurants, her overnight bag on her shoulder.

She could technically go home and curl up on the couch, but that felt like letting him win. A prickle of pride down her back made her want him to suffer. She'd stay out and he'd worry. She could book a hotel, stand crying in the shower for as long as she needed, tuck herself naked into starched sheets and order room service she couldn't afford in the morning. That was an idea.

But the hotels were so expensive. What was she doing here, living in this stupid city, inching toward destitution, reliant on a man who didn't even like her, walking at night with her clothes packed up on her back, practically homeless, maybe soon-to-be single? Forget the Paris trip, forget bringing a date to Lily's wedding? She tried to hear Bryn's voice: "You deserve to rest."

She could talk to Bryn on Monday. They were back at school on Monday.

No, she couldn't wait. She needed to hear Bryn's voice now. She took out her phone.

"Hi," Bryn said, picking up on the first ring. "Why are you calling me at nine thirty at night? Are you finally ready to go out? On a Thursday? Damn, girl. But fine, let's do it."

Ana choked out a laugh-sob.

"Oh, Ana," Bryn said, her voice softening, which made Ana cry harder. "What happened? Where are you? Do you want to come over? Max made curry."

"Okay," Ana managed. "That sounds good," she sniffled.

An hour later, Ana was wrapped in a blanket, eating her second bowl of chicken coconut curry, sitting on the couch, Bryn stroking her leg, Max pitched forward in a chair, hands together, eyebrows raised in disbelief.

"So he kicked you out of your own house?" he asked.

"I mean, he's entitled to some alone time if he wants it," Ana said, shrugging.

"Oh, Ana please," Bryn said, extending her leg to kick at her playfully. "He's a fucking dick. Sorry. I know this is, like, your person or whatever. I just don't like him at all."

Ana laughed, even though it wasn't really funny. The apartment felt good: warm and bright, all soft and mismatched, worn furniture and healthy plants, nothing like the monochromatic and stainless-steel sharp angles of the home that Ana wasn't allowed to be in right now.

"Permission to speak freely?" Bryn asked.

Ana and Max both looked at her, like, were you not going to already?

"Look, Ana, don't take this the wrong way, but I don't get why you're with him."

"I know he can be a little intense . . ." Ana thought for a second. Silas could be cruel, but when he employed his cruelty against their common enemies—the broker who'd tried to get a fee from them that Silas wasn't willing to pay, the Wi-Fi company—Ana felt close to him. His cruelty was like a shelter: one he invited Ana into, willingly, exclusively, because she was special and he wanted to protect her. "But he's actually a really good boyfriend most of the time."

"You lack confidence, and I'm sharing this not as a criticism but as an observation of a fact, but you're beautiful and intelligent and very much a grown-ass woman, and if you want to be with Alistair, all you have to do is do that, and if you want to tell Beth to fuck off, tell her to fuck off, and if you want to go back to Oakbrook, just tell them, and they'll either take you back, or they won't. You're smart and capable, but you're also not that special, Ana, and I know you hate change, but you are capable of weathering it, and you need to look in the mirror and realize your self-worth and that your life can be what you want it to be if you just admit to yourself what it is that you want, okay?"

"Damn straight," Max said.

"The thing Cooper's mom said, it just stuck with me."

"Oh, please. She's just projecting."

"I know."

"It's just not that easy to know what I want," Ana said. "I mean, you're so good at it . . ." She trailed off. *But I'm not,* she wanted to say. *I'm still just a girl, I feel exactly like I did at seventeen, I don't know what I want, it's not easy to have needs, I don't know if I'll ever find someone who can give me what Silas can give me, who can get me a job I'm not even qualified for, who can help me fit in in a place like this, when I'm really just the daughter of a vet tech from suburban Wisconsin.*

"You'll stay tonight," Bryn said. A statement, not a question. "We'll set you up in the office."

Thirty-Four: Margot

On the plane back to Chicago, Margot got upgraded to first class for the first time in her life. Jenny had booked another flight; for some godforsaken reason, she preferred flying into Midway. *Good thing,* Margot thought, *because how awkward would it be if Jenny had to walk past me back to coach?*

After takeoff, she sat back with a glass of white wine and opened her laptop to send a quick email to Claire: Hi! Wanted to send you a quick update on the status of Infinity. They're basically in (yay!), but still a little conflicted about our relationships with RideFlow and People's Gas, which I want to chat with Jason about asap. You and I both know the value of Infinity is way WAY higher (as we know, People's Gas is more of a favor-type account anyway; you and I both know they're very lo prio for the agency). Can you book something for me, Jason, and Jenny first thing tomorrow? Would be great if you could pull stats on profit for those clients to help me make my case. We gotta get rid of em!! Thanks Claire. Sorry for the Sunday email. M

Back in Chicago the next morning, Margot walked into the office with her head held high. "I heard things are looking good with Infinity," Amelia said, rolling her chair to Margot's desk. "Claire told me the news. I literally want to be you when I grow up."

Margot blushed and flipped her hair. "It was a team effort," she said. "And it's not totally final yet. And maybe I was still a little drunk from the bachelorette party?"

"That's my girl."

"Margot." Jenny's hand was on her shoulder. "Can we talk?"

"Of course," Margot said, turning to wink at Amelia. "I think Claire has a room booked for us in ten, but you want to debrief first?"

This must be it: conversation. Jenny would tell Margot how critical she'd been to getting this deal signed. They were so close. Jenny was going to offer Margot $120,000, and Margot would think it over before asking for $140,000. It was a lot of money, but she'd practically single-handedly landed the firm an additional six mil a year, and more than that, she'd shown what she was made of, and they'd want to keep her around. She was still young and capable, and there was so much more where this came from. They'd be stupid not to give her exactly what she wanted.

Jenny led the way into a conference room, and Margot sat down and placed her elbows on the table. "What can I do you for?" she asked, then shook her head. "Sorry. That was weird. I've never said that in my life."

"Margot," Jenny said, sitting across from her, "there's no way to sugarcoat this. I'm afraid I have some bad news."

PART FOUR

Thirty-Five: Ana

The next day Ana woke up in a tangle of sheets, and for a split second, she felt blissfully well rested. And then she remembered with a shock that everything was wrong and nothing was hopeful. That she had slept in Bryn and Max's office; that on Monday she'd have to face the body odor of fourth graders who were one week riper than they had been before spring break; that she and Margot still hadn't made up after their fight in Miami; that her ten-year relationship was on the brink of being over; that she hadn't called her mom that Sunday or the Sunday prior.

She threw the borrowed pillow across the room, then placed her feet onto a vintage rug. She picked up the pillow. Put it back where it belonged. Fluffed it, folded her sheets and deflated the air mattress, dressed slowly in the change of clothes she'd packed hastily last night.

—

"Coffee?" Max asked, handing her a mug. "I already made you a latte."

"I should get back home," Ana said, accepting it and thumbing at her phone, hoping for something: an apology text, an *I miss you, please come back* from Silas. But there was nothing.

"You can stay the weekend, you know," Bryn said, popping up from a lounge chair, letting a stack of newspapers fall to the floor.

"I wouldn't do that to you," Ana said. "It's the last weekend before you're back to work. You don't want me around."

"Ana, please. We spend every second with each other. Stay. If you want."

She checked her phone again, knew there would be nothing. Thought about Max's curry and pushing the inevitable conversation—what would that conversation be?—with Silas to next week.

"Maybe it's not the worst idea in the world," she said.

—

On Friday, Ana, Bryn, and Max went for a walk, then to a movie at Balboa Theater. On Saturday, they had brunch at House of Pancakes on Taraval, then walked the hour to Ocean Beach. On Sunday, Ana checked Silas's location: He was in Marin, probably biking, so she skedaddled home and picked up a few essentials, including a new change of clothes for her first day back to work tomorrow.

The place was a mess: an empty wax bag from Arsicault lay prone on the counter, surrounded by flakes of some previous day's pastry. A greasy pizza box sat drenched in the sink. Ana sighed, felt in her stomach that this home didn't feel like hers at all. She rode the bus back to Bryn's house, and apparently looked sad enough for a kind old lady to tap her on the shoulder and ask if she was okay.

"No," Ana said. "But thanks for asking."

—

On Monday, her students were antsy and raucous, emboldened with the confidence of being home with their parents for the week, staying up late or going out for ice cream or bossing around their ski instructors, and it showed. It was like the whole class had collectively gone through the emotional part of puberty in the week they'd been gone, and now they were back and all they wanted to do was break rules and not listen to Ana at all.

Ana straightened up the room, checked the time, and walked the hallway to Beth's office.

"Ana, Ana," Beth said. "Come sit."

Ana sat, trying her hardest to smile at Beth in a way that conveyed that she and her boyfriend of ten years were not on the verge of a breakup, that she loved her job, that she hadn't spent her break sneaking around with a guy who wasn't Silas and wondering if Cooper's mom was right about her and whether she'd be anything without Silas—and it was seeming more and more likely she was about to find out.

"So," Beth said.

"How was your break?" Ana asked.

"Oh, Mike and I stayed around. Nothing special. How was Hadley today?"

"Great, as usual," Ana said. In a sea of hormones and callouts and children who disappeared for ten minutes during class—Ana had had to revoke their privilege of leaving the classroom to use the bathroom whenever they wanted—Hadley had been the only one, throughout the entire day, who'd done her work diligently, who'd broken Ana's heart when she drew a tiny smiley face after her name at the top of her worksheet, and below that: "You're my favorite teacher."

"Well, that's good," Beth said. "But I do want to talk to you a little more about what's going on with her."

"Okay," Ana said, taking a deep breath in, letting it out slowly.

Beth thwacked a stack of papers onto her desk to line them up, turned away to file them in a cabinet.

"Look, Ana, I'll cut to the chase. Hadley is, as you know, unfortunately going through some tough things at home. Her parents are going through a divorce, and it looks like Mom is taking custody and will be moving with Hadley soon."

"Where? Marin?" Ana was used to the exodus that happened once parents made enough money to secure a place in Mill Valley or Larkspur. Then she reddened: Of course that wasn't the situation here. "I mean, probably not Marin," she said, correcting herself.

"Ohio, actually," Beth said, rubbing her face. "Cleveland. Apparently Hadley's mom got a job there, and Dad has been dealing with some health issues—" It made Ana even more impressed with Hadley: She was going through this, and she was still writing notes to Ana and paying attention and remembering to bring back the books from the school library she'd borrowed over break.

"We'll miss her, of course. And, Ana, I did speak with Cooper's mom again. She called me this morning, and she'd love for us to have a retribution circle and give Hadley the chance to apologize to Cooper in front of the class."

Ana waved Beth away. "But we have no reason to believe she actually cheated. And we need to be supporting Hadley right now—*especially* right now. I mean, that sounds like a lot, right? I'm worried about her. It doesn't seem fair to put her on the spot like that, especially when we have no idea what happened."

Beth paused. "Ana, I see your point. But it's just a community-building activity. It's not punitive. And we want Cooper to feel comfortable, just as much as we care about Hadley. I know you don't see it this way—I don't either—but Cooper's mom feels like Horizon has abandoned its responsibility, hasn't lived up to its moral standards. She feels like the standards—well, she thinks the teachers need to be held to the standards they were held to back when her older son was here, five years ago, right? Before your time, of course. But Julien—you remember, at Amherst?—he had such a good experience here, and of course Cooper's mom is a little—well, the reality is, Ana, her opinion does matter."

Ana stared at Beth blankly.

"Ana, are you with me? Cooper's mom? Who is on the board?"

Ana held Beth's gaze. Maybe her blood pressure had lowered after a week away from this place, or maybe she was stepping into her own maturity, or maybe, more likely, her life was already unraveling so quickly that this was practically irrelevant compared to everything else that wasn't working out: Her relationship was effectively over, and she wasn't nearly as hung up about it as she should be. She'd be going to her best friend's wedding solo. She'd have to find an apartment.

"I understand that Cooper's parents are big-time donors—"

"Oh, Ana, it's not that," Beth cut in, waving her hand over her face, pulling a KitKat bar out from her purse and taking a bite. "We take all parents' concerns seriously at Horizon. You know that. It's just that Hadley is departing our community momentarily, and Cooper will be here a lot longer. Just host a circle time and discuss it all, have Hadley and Cooper, I don't know"—she waved a hand in the air—"talk about honesty or put on a skit together about it. It's important that Cooper's family knows we're hearing their concerns."

Ana nodded slowly. "I guess I could do that," she said, but inside, something had shifted: She wasn't going to plan a skit for her kids so that Hadley could apologize to Cooper.

She wasn't going to let Silas off the hook, either.

Ana walked the two miles back home—*her* home, she reminded herself, that she had every right to be in—the wind heavy in her hair and on her face, the bougainvillea that climbed up the sides of the mansions taunting her with its permanence. *We were here before you,* they seemed to say, *and we'll be here after you, on the top of the hill overlooking the bay.* She bit back tears, but the wind off the bay stung her eyes, and they watered anyway. She wiped them.

Her phone buzzed in her pocket, but she ignored it. She was one with her indignance, her frustration, the unfairness of it all: that the Coopers and Scotts of the world would always win. She wanted to be alone with her rage, she wanted to bottle it up so it was fresh when she saw Alistair at the wedding, so she could share with him the extent of her, so he could witness it and look at her with that intensity that made her feel like what she was doing mattered.

She rode the elevator up to her apartment, went toward the door, was relieved to see that Silas's shoes weren't there. She checked his location: SFO. Of course! He was in London this week! It felt weird for him to be crossing an ocean without so much as having reminded her.

But it would give her a week at home in her own apartment, gathering up the courage to be real with him later.

Thirty-Six: Margot

"It's not your fault, Margot," Jenny said, sitting across from her in the Big Room. "You did everything you could."

"What are you talking about?"

"It came down to the relationship they have with that VP at Ogilvy. I mean, that's not what they said. They said Ogilvy was way cheaper, had a client list more in line with their values, but that's obviously not true. You know as well as I do that Ogilvy works with whoever pays them. They work with fucking Chevron. But anyway. Not the point."

"Maybe we can still convince them," Margot said. "What if we go to them, or throw in a free influencer campaign, or tell them we'll work pro bono for a month, or—"

"Stop," Jenny said, putting her hand up, inches from Margot's face. "It's done, Margot. It's not your fault. It's okay, though. Thank god we didn't fire those two clients, right? Jason was telling me earlier this morning that the natural gas people might actually have a new campaign they want to work on with us. Which is good, because to be honest, the agency is going through—don't repeat this—a bit of a tough time. Seems we were a little behind on some tax things, and our cash flow has seen better days . . ." She trailed off.

Jason pushed open the door. "Uh, Margot, can you tell me why the *fuck* Lori Fucking Stafford from People's Gas just called to say it's a shame we've 'fired' them—her words—because Con Ed just bought them and their marketing budget has tripled, but not a problem, because Con Ed works with Ogilvy anyway and Lori's always been 'curious about the hype'? I'm sorry, am I missing something? Because last I checked, we have an in-progress Out of Home Campaign for them, and it's paying for my kid's fucking preschool."

"What are you talking about?" Margot said, heat rising from her chest to her cheeks.

"Does 'we gotta get rid of 'em' ring any bells, Margot?"

"Wait—" She opened her laptop, went to the email. "That was to Claire—she didn't forward it to them, did she?" She typed in Claire's name, found the email, opened it. "There must be a mistake."

A response from Claire: Just a heads up, Margot, I think you accidentally cc'd Lori and Brian?

Fuck fuck fuck fuck fuck fuck fuck.

"I'm sorry, I can explain—or, I got ahead of myself—it must have auto-filled, I guess because I had emailed them both recently—I mean, it doesn't matter—"

"Margot, how would you feel if the agency you were paying admitted to your face that you were a low-priority account? Do you realize how unprofessional that is, even to say to Claire?" His lip was quivering.

"Fuck," she said. "I've never done anything like this. I—" She felt her breath quicken. "But we can get them back! I have a good relationship with Brian. Maybe he hasn't seen the email yet? I can just let him know it was a mistake. And Lori went to Hawthorne, so I can pull that lever—" She felt like she was going to fall through the floor. "I'll do anything. I'll ask them to lunch, I'll say I had a psychotic break."

"You don't have some kind of authority to just fire clients, Margot," Jason said, taking off his glasses and rubbing his eyes. "Are you kidding me? Do you understand the kind of precedent this sets?" He replaced his glasses. "Do you have any idea how hard I've worked to build this agency from nothing?"

"Of course. Let me fix it. You know I can."

"Margot, stop." He put a hand out, rose to stand. "You're taking a month out. I don't know what else to do." He stormed out the door.

"He can't just—"

"Margot, of course he can," Jenny said. "It's his agency. He can do whatever he wants."

"But it was a mistake!" Margot said. "You always say that it's important to make mistakes, that that's how we learn—" She sounded whiney, even to herself.

"Yeah, I'm talking about showing up five minutes late to a meeting or sending last week's version of a brand template. Not firing a significant portion of our recurring revenue when we're already struggling." She stood. "Do you realize how bad that looks for me?" She let out a huff. "Margot, I adore you. You're brilliant. But I have two children who depend on me. This isn't, like, some game to see what I can get away with. Do you realize—" She rubbed her eyes. "This is really, really bad."

Margot's voice came out quiet. "I know. But a whole month?" The expanse of her unplanned days unraveled in front of her. "What will I do with myself?" She shook her head. "Can't I at least try to fix it?"

"A month without pay isn't that long, in the scheme of things," Jenny said.

"Without pay?"

"Margot, Jason's right. This sets a really bad precedent. Consider yourself lucky you're not getting fired. And take the opportunity to slow down and reflect."

That night, she shared the news with her parents over the phone.

"Have you ever thought about law school?" her dad suggested. "Maybe this is the perfect opportunity to reassess. And you've always been such a logician." It wasn't exactly true, but her mom chimed in anyway: "You have been, sweetie!"

"You think?" Margot asked from her bed, her eyes red and puffy. She wasn't interested in the idea at all, but she was anxious to be busy again. She wanted to believe that energy wasn't finite, or if it was, that she hadn't used up her entire allotment. That she hadn't lost her judgment permanently. That she could still beat out everyone else at something that required raw intelligence and preparation, both of which right now felt entirely out of reach. She wanted to do things, not just sit around and think about herself.

"Of course, Moo! I think that maybe you'd like being your own boss."

"Why not, Moo-y?" her mom said, closer to the receiver. "You're way too good for that place anyway."

She wanted to tell her mom that she was wrong, that in fact, Margot wasn't good enough for it at all, that she wasn't good enough for McQueen O'Doul, that she wouldn't land director by thirty or live alone anytime soon, that she'd tried so hard to be brave, and now she was jobless and in the closet to everyone except some rando named Keith.

"That place is a riot anyway," her dad said. Margot had brought her parents in once, early on, back when she was still enthusiastic and optimistic, because showing parents around was something that one of the creative directors had recently made cool. That was before she'd lost the firm two clients. Before she'd become the laughingstock of the entire agency.

Margot's parents had been entirely too enthusiastic, just like Margot, really—touching the golden awards and swiping their hands across all the textured surfaces: marble, knotted maple, leather. "This place is a *dance* hall!" her mother had exclaimed, and one of the pierced and tattooed skinny guys who was either a copywriter or a senior copywriter had raised his eyebrows at Margot, as if to say, "Who are *you* to bring these people *here*?"

Nothing about working there was meaningful in the grand scheme of things, but still. Margot was at the helm of a million tiny emergencies: the restructuring of briefs when high-maintenance influencers decided they weren't willing to adhere to the vision McQueen had aligned on; using Google Translate to verify the required disclaimers in Chinese-language versions of an ad they made for Intel; getting a persnickety creative director to revisit a concept when the client still didn't like his fourth go of it. She was all of twelve hours into her "sabbatical," and already, she deeply missed her job: the invigoration of barking at men who were older than she was and getting them to accomplish things; seeing an ad on TV while she was out at a bar and knowing she'd been part of making it; supervising celebrities whose names she'd toss around casually as if they weren't supervised by all kinds of Margot-equivalents who worked for all kinds of McQueen-adjacent agencies.

"I don't know, you guys. I'll think about it. I'm exhausted," Margot lied. "I'm gonna go to bed."

"Love you, Moo," they said in unison.

Margot woke at seven the next morning, like usual. She jumped out of bed and was halfway into her favorite knee-high power boots when she realized, actually, she didn't have anywhere to be.

"Fuck," she said out loud.

She had to run it off. She kicked off her jeans and pulled on a pair of shorts, laced up her sneakers, went to the lake.

Thirty-Seven: Lily

After four nights of sleeping in her childhood bed, Lily was ready to go home. On Tuesday, she took a train home to Boston and told Jack that her time in New York had been "fine." On Wednesday, Lily made a Pinterest board of all her bridesmaids' dresses and shoes, and asked Zoe if she could please pick something a little subtler. On Thursday, she chatted with the florist and her planner.

And on Friday, she walked the six blocks to the outpatient treatment center Barri had picked for her.

"You sure you don't want me to come with you? Even just sit outside and wait?" Jack had asked.

"No, I'll be fine," she'd said, but now she regretted it, wished he was there.

—

She just didn't expect it to be so much worse than the last time she'd stood at the window of an eating-disorder clinic. At least last time, she'd had her whole life ahead of her. She'd been fourteen years old, and the greatest challenge of her life had been memorizing her Torah portion and convincing her mom to let her wear heels. Yes, she'd had to miss a month of school, but Dalton had hardly cared: She was a model student, and her parents were happy to hire a tutor, and they set aside the work she was missing, and she finished it during the one hour reserved in the day's schedule for academic catch-up.

But now, there were no tutors or teachers checking in. No friends whose parents prompted them to send teddy bears, delivered straight to her bedroom.

And maybe that was her fault, for being secretive. Or maybe it was her circumstances, or her self-consciousness, or her friends' fault, whom she hadn't shared anything with, but they also hadn't asked.

She felt lonely and pathetic. For a moment, she wished she had a boss she was close with: a woman like Mariana, her first boss at twenty-two, whom she could have told everything to. Mariana would have responded with a no-nonsense text: Lily, take all the time you need, get better, and seriously, don't worry about that project, I'll cover for you, we're not saving lives here.

"Name and age?" asked the woman at the front. She was graying and gentle-looking, her chin like a knob on the bottom of her face.

"Lillian Rosen, twenty-eight," Lily said. Half her life ago, she'd put this behind her for good, and vowed to never let negative thoughts about herself express themselves as fear toward carbohydrates. She'd taken copious notes in three marbled notebooks, learned to mix Odwalla juices into her meal routine while she was still putting on weight, discovered relative freedom from everything that had plagued her for as long as she remembered, talked herself into feeling excited about graduating from the children's department and into the women's, which inexplicably started at age fifteen.

Fourteen years since and she was right back where she started. It was dizzying. She felt like she was floating. She had felt that way, maybe, for months now.

"Right this way," the woman said, handing Lily a clipboard and motioning to a chair.

It was just a day program. That was something. And she had agency this time, could sign herself out at any point. If she decided to do the program, that is. Which she still hadn't. Deep breath in, deep breath out, tap her feet on the floor, toe heel toe heel, knock on the grainy texture of the walls, not wood but there was probably wood inside them somewhere. The world was soupy around her.

"If you'll just follow me," said a woman in a striped sweater, her hair pulled up in a claw clip shaped like a dachshund. "I'll show you where lunch is. You'll be a little late, but that's on us. We like to show our prospectives what they're getting into before they commit. It's a little atypical, I know. But we do focus on choice here, within reason. Will you join us for lunch? If you do join us, you'll have to abide by our dining room rules, of course."

"Um, okay," Lily said, offered a smile.

The woman pushed the door open and ushered Lily through. "Everyone, this is Lily."

They looked up at her: a woman in pearl earrings, her hair slicked back. A twentysomething with brown hair who was almost pretty, except her nose was too big for her face. A man with sad sunken eyes and a girl who didn't look old enough to be here, clad in a T-shirt with a cartoon cat on it where her boobs should have been. Below it, in bubble letters: ONE COOL CAT.

"Hey," Lily managed, hands finding their way to her stomach, covering the expanse of her width before they could judge her. She shook her head. She didn't need to do that. She was here on purpose, she reminded herself.

She pulled out a chair next to the COOL CAT girl and sat. It wasn't her first rodeo. If she wanted to leave, she could.

"Hey," said the woman in pearl earrings, "welcome." She rolled her eyes, but in a way that wasn't unfriendly.

"Thanks," Lily said, blinking and wishing she'd put on makeup, like a shield. "So, does the food come to me, or?" She looked around.

"Oh!" said the woman in the striped sweater. "Sorry, I thought Caroline in intake would have explained that to you! We encourage clients to serve themselves from a buffet. For your first meal, you'll take one thing from each tray. If you decide to move forward, a dietitian will customize a plan for you, of course."

Lily stiffened, swallowed something back. "Sure," she said. She was a good sport. She was here to heal. And more control over her choices was a good thing.

She followed the woman into an alcove with plates of premade salads.

"So, you'll take one item from this section," she said, gesturing to a row of plates, "and one from here."

At least the food looked better than the sticky pink yogurts they served on the adolescent unit at Hope, or the soggy buns she'd been forced to dunk into the remnants of her spaghetti, or the reheated bowls of formerly frozen raspberries that counted as an "extra" but still somehow didn't fulfill any of the actual food group requirements.

"Then you'll pick a caloric beverage and a dessert from here."

"Oh, I don't do dessert," Lily started, then remembered where she was. "Sorry. Habit."

The woman smiled at her. "Good catch."

"Well, okay. Thanks." She waited for the woman to disappear, but instead she felt a hand on her shoulder.

"I'll just be in here to help—to make sure—it's just a policy. Not that we don't trust you."

Lily nodded. "Right," she said. "Got it." She reached for a set of tongs, piled a turkey pinwheel and two clementines and a square of chocolate onto her plate, thought about all those calories, and stood there watching the drink machine and mustering up the courage to fill a whole glass with juice.

"Well?" Jack asked, an arm on her leg, a blanket stretched over both of them on the couch. "How was it?"

"It was okay," Lily said, suddenly exhausted. "All things considered."

"Tell me about it?"

"Maybe tomorrow. I just need to sleep."

He nodded, and she wondered if she seemed like a ticking time bomb, the kind of woman a man with everything going for him might not want to marry in five weeks' time.

She kissed him on the cheek, traipsed into the bedroom, fell asleep without brushing her teeth. She woke briefly to Jack climbing in beside her, but maybe she was just dreaming. Maybe it was all just a dream.

Obviously, it wasn't. She was genuinely anorexic, and she was absolutely back for her first official day of outpatient treatment, and she was very much choking down spoonfuls of oatmeal topped with cherries, banana, and almond butter, and she had three missed calls from her mom, whom she was avoiding, because she had no interest in coughing up the details of all this, and being forced to calm her mom down about it—"No, don't worry Mom, I'll be okay!" "But your wedding, Lily! Is this my fault? Is this because I said the comment about weight gain that time? Is this because I took you out of treatment too soon last time? Tell me what I did!"

Her wedding was five weeks away, and at this rate, she'd be twice the size of both the dress she'd been planning to wear for an entire year and the dress her mom had tracked down last week. She hadn't spoken to Margot or Ana directly about any of this, and now she was bubbling with resentment: because they hadn't asked, and because it seemed like ever since she stopped working, they stopped taking her seriously. Was that in her head? Why hadn't anyone asked her what it felt like to be jobless in Boston? Were they worried they'd set her off? Didn't know how to talk about it? Secretly thought she was a failure, a waste of a liberal arts degree and a tradwife sellout?

She and Jack were basically in a snow globe together, and thank god he was there, but it felt like every time she could see him clearly, close enough to touch, someone lifted them up and shook them and snow fell all around them, enough to get in her eyelashes and obscure her vision, and here she was, one life behind her and one life ahead of her and a full serving of carbs in her belly.

She stirred oats in her bowl, looked up at a supposedly inspirational poster featuring a girl climbing a rock face: IF I CAN DO IT, YOU CAN! it read, which made no sense. Who was this poster to assume that Lily was more capable than this cankled, rock-climbing stranger?

"Lily?" asked Caroline from intake, who was supervising breakfast this morning. She had finished her own oatmeal and was on to peeling a clementine—the staff ate with the clients (they didn't call them patients here, Caroline had explained), which was supposed to make the whole thing feel more natural and less like Caroline was a prison guard, silently judging everyone from her vantage point at the head of the table. "I'm going to ask you to share with Ashley here what you're feeling." Lily turned to Ashley, who was clinking her spoon against the bottom of her bowl. "Ashley is—what, Ashley, six weeks in?"

"Right," Ashley said. "Lily, I know it's super cringe, but it gets more normal. Anyway. Don't worry if you cry or anything."

"I didn't—I mean, I've been in treatment. It was harder then. This isn't supposed to be, like, a whole thing—"

"Lily, it's fine," Ashley said. "On my second day, I literally ran away. It's normal to cry over oatmeal."

She searched Ashley's eyes to make sure she wasn't poking fun, but all there was in her face was sincerity, and it would be funny if it wasn't so absurd.

She tried to choke back the tears. But Ashley's eyes kept getting kinder, and everything, in that moment—not just the dried cherries or the oatmeal or the sliced banana or the heap of almond butter or the lack of coffee or the lack of water or the toast *on the side* as in *in addition* to the oatmeal, but also the wedding and the joblessness and the way her mom had surprised them with a couple's therapy appointment instead of just saying, "Hey, Lily, are you okay?" which is probably in retrospect what she should have done—it all felt like way too much. She felt that panicky feeling that she hadn't felt since middle school: She was out of control, the world was expanding, and she couldn't think of everything she'd ever known, and all she wanted was paper and pens to map it all out so she could take stock of every fact in the world. How could her brain be the size of a human head when the world was infinite? And how, in all the vastness of infinity, could she be here at a holistic outpatient treatment center for eating disorders, in the city of Boston, crying in front of a stranger over a bowl of oatmeal?

"Seriously, Lily," Ashley said. "Just try to let it happen."

She nodded. She tried.

On the third day, Lily made it through her bowl of oatmeal without crying, then cried in a group therapy session led by a potbellied man named Bruce who posited that maybe Lily had been working too hard for too long to make everyone else happy. It was embarrassing—not necessarily to cry in front of others, but to cry over something so obvious. On the fourth day, she conquered a turkey sandwich with mayonnaise and then almost puked, and by the fifth day, Caroline mentioned that maybe it was time to schedule a family session with "anyone who is an important part of your support system."

Jack wasn't judgmental about any of it. He was a perfect gentlemen, bringing her flowers after her first week of treatment, leaving a card on her pillow that professed how proud he was, that elucidated all the myriad reasons he was over the moon about marrying her, that eloquently stated all the ways in which this "rough patch" would pitter out into irrelevance in the grand scope of their lives together, and he was just so happy she was addressing this now, before the rest of their lives took off.

She was absolutely grateful for all of this, and she was not even nervous to have him in for their first family appointment, even though she wondered if maybe she should have been.

"It sounds like he's a really wonderful support system for you," Caroline said.

"He is," Lily said, nodding gratefully.

"And who else might you want to have in?"

"Oh, Jack is plenty," Lily said, resolutely. Caroline wrote something down.

Lily would consider involving more people, too. Her mom, eventually. Probably not her dad, to be honest; she hadn't mentioned any of this to him, and she didn't have the energy to do so now, especially since they only spoke on the phone quarterly or so anyway.

She knew she could involve Ana and Margot in a session, if she wanted, and they'd show up and forget about the weirdness in Miami and apologize for making her bachelorette about them. They'd check in with her, just like they'd done back at Hawthorne, when she'd told them about her eating disorder and they'd promised to help her never relapse again.

But that was then: before she was old enough to have fine lines on her forehead. Before she was in a relationship with Jack, the kind that left little need for outside scaffolding. And besides, her friends hadn't exactly proven themselves as worthy of holding Lily's secrets during the bachelorette party. Certainly Margot at least had had the chance.

Anyway, Lily didn't want to burden them.

This was just what happened as you got older: People drifted, ever so slightly. They relied on their primary partners for their primary needs. It was a little sad to think that she'd be standing at the altar surrounded by these women, feeling like maybe none of them knew each other as well now as they did back then. But that was life.

She'd tell them about her spiral, but she'd package it neatly. She'd tell them, but she'd let them know once she had everything back under control.

Thirty-Eight: Ana

Ana spent an uneventful week working and not communicating with Silas except to answer a text that asked if he'd forgotten his adapter, could she check if it was plugged in by his desk? It was not, she'd written back, and he'd thumbs-upped the text, then sent her an emoji of an octopus, which was a shorthand they used to use for *I miss you.*

Ana let herself believe that maybe they'd work it out.

He had to stay the weekend—"Client entertainment," he'd forewarned.

The following Monday, Ana stirred in bed at the sound of Silas's footsteps and the wheels of his suitcase on the floor. She reached for her phone: It was nearly two in the morning.

"Ana," he called out, "I have such a great idea." He came barreling into the bedroom, sat down at the foot of the bed, dropped his backpack. His eyes were glassy but bright. "I mean, everything that's been—" He was slurring. "Like, fuck that Alistair guy or whatever, and fuck this city, you know? We should just move to London! Why not?" He leaned over her, grabbed at her hand, planted it on his cock; it hardened under her loose grip. "San Francisco is beat. Maybe we just need something new."

She retracted her hand. "Si, first of all, welcome home, it's good to see you. Second of all, we *just* moved in. Actually, we still haven't *even* moved in. I spent an entire weekend at Bryn's house, and we haven't even really talked since you were away for a whole entire week. We haven't talked about anything. Are you drunk?"

He grabbed at her hand, placed it back on his crotch, and she withdrew it again. "I may have enjoyed some whiskey in first class."

"I think we should move to London," he said.

She propped herself up on her elbows, pulled the covers up around her like a shield. "Si, stop. We—I mean, this is serious. Do you actually want to move to London?"

"You don't even have to teach in London, Ana"—he hiccupped—"or quit your job! Just hang out for a bit." He smiled as if it was funny.

"I have a job. A life here. I don't *want* to just relocate. That would be a big deal. Is this actually what you want?"

"Ana, baby," he said, falling back onto the bed, "I'm so horny."

"Si," she said, "seriously. Do you actually want a future with me? Like, sometimes I feel like the Paris trip"—she looked around at the blank walls that were sharpening into more blankness as her eyes adjusted to the dark—"and we're—is marriage even what you want? With me? Or is it, like, your friends start to get married and you spend one week in London for work, and you just—"

"Ana, can you chill?"

"You're drunk," she said.

"I'm Silas," he said, laughing.

"What am I even doing?" she said to the room, looked at him, waited for the weight of her realization to rouse him from his alcohol-induced idiocy, or maybe it was bigger than the alcohol, but he was already face down on the bed, snoring, purring contentedly like someone who'd never not gotten what he wanted. Like someone who, if Ana left, would hardly even need to lift a finger to reinvent himself. He'd have a nicer apartment in London and a hotter girlfriend with better tits and a better job by Christmas.

Hot tears soaked into her pillow. No one had told her love would become this disappointing.

—

She couldn't sleep. And Silas was breathing along, as comfortable as he ever was.

She tried breathing in and breathing out. She tried breathing out more forcefully, to see if she could wake Silas then claim it had been by accident. She tried listening to an audiobook, first in her AirPods and then out loud. Eventually she gave up and went to the living room, laptop in tow, browsed shows, finally settled on something terrible.

She half hoped that Silas would come in and tell her to turn it down, that he wasn't drunk anymore, that he was sorry. He did want to go to Paris. He'd picked out a ring, that's why he was being weird. Ana wasn't out of her mind to think she didn't belong in this world. She belonged, she absolutely belonged. He loved her, and he'd never let her sleep at Bryn's house again.

She woke to the ring of her phone. She looked around, felt like death. Was it already daytime? How long had she slept? She grabbed it.

"Mom?"

"Ana," she said, "I had a bit of an accident."

"Mom, what happened?" She was sitting up now, alert and awake, the whole city of San Francisco melting around her.

"I didn't want to worry you. I'm at the hospital, on the East Side. They're taking good care of me. They don't know yet what happened, but I fell at work, and they're running some tests. I had another dizzy spell. Ana, the doctor is coming in, I have to talk to him—"

"I'll book a flight now," Ana said. "I'll be there as soon as I can."

"You don't have to," she said. "I'm okay, really. You have school."

"Of course I'm coming," she said, her voice cracking.

Ana started throwing underwear and socks and jeans and shirts that maybe didn't make sense for the weather into a bag. She couldn't remember what month it was, or what the temperature was like in Wisconsin at this time of the year. It was April, right? Was that spring?

"Ana, what are you doing?" Silas asked groggily from the bed.

"I'm going to Wisconsin," she said, throwing a swimsuit into her suitcase just in case. Why? What would she need a swimsuit for? Her mom was either dying immediately or in thirty years, and she was thinking about swimming?

"Is this because of last night?" he asked, still prone atop the comforter, his voice muffled by the pillow. "I was drunk, I know. It's—foggy."

"No, Silas, my mom is in the hospital," she said. Last night she'd been making waffles for dinner, writing in her Notes app the points she'd make so that Silas would understand her, and her mom had slipped in her scrubs at the animal hospital where she worked. She'd been watching a TV show on the couch and her mom had been loaded onto a stretcher, bumping down the road in the back of an ambulance. She'd been drifting off to sleep, and a nurse who was Ana's age had been taking care of her mom, and Ana had been here, covered in a cashmere blanket that had been a move-in present from Silas's mom.

"What do you mean?" Silas asked, still face down.

"My mom is in the hospital, Silas," she said. "I don't know what I mean. I'm going to Wisconsin."

He rolled over, pushed himself to sitting. "You want me to come?"

"No, just go back to sleep," she said, zipping her bag, slinging it over her shoulder, going down to her waiting ride, secretly hoping he'd follow her but deeply aware that he wouldn't.

Her mom looked more saggy than Ana remembered, her hair fanned out across the pillow, her chest rising and falling in rhythm with the beeps of the machines. Her eyelids fluttered, and Ana leaned in, breathing in the chamomile scent of her mom mixed with the overwhelming antiseptic of the hospital room.

"Mom," she said, "I'm here."

"Ana, hi," she said slowly. "If I knew it would bring you home, I would have knocked my head on tile years before."

"Oh, Mom," Ana said.

But her mom was smiling.

It was maybe a stroke, but they had yet to confirm it. Or if it wasn't a stroke, then it could be a tumor. Or it could also just be a random fluke thing, or an issue with her nervous system, or nothing at all.

"So you have no idea?" Ana asked. "Sorry. I didn't mean to say it that way."

"That's okay," said the doctor, who looked too young to know what was going on. "We have an idea of a few possibilities, but we're still ruling some things out, to be safe. We'll take good care of your mom, okay? I've ordered an MRI, and once we review the results, we'll have a better idea of what's going on."

"Okay. Thank you." She sat, watched her mom breathe, listened to the sound of the air that whistled out of her partially closed mouth, a tired kazoo. She thumbed at the place her third eye was, pretended she believed in anything at all.

Her mom had been angry. It had been one thing to help Ana pack, to kiss her on the cheek and send her off to Hawthorne, to pay her biannual tuition bills, or at least the amount of them that hadn't been covered by the school. It had been one thing to visit Ana on parents' weekend, to make conversation with Lily's parents and Margot's parents and explain that there wasn't a dad, that he had died long ago.

But it had been another thing entirely to send Ana off to Hawthorne and expect that it wouldn't change her. To send her there with a public school education and zero knowledge of the Hamptons or Nantucket or any of the places everyone was always going and expect that she'd stay the same.

At first, Ana had flown home over breaks: Thanksgiving with her mom and her aunts and uncles and cousins; Christmas in Sun Prairie with Aunt Kate; the weeks of January before school started in her childhood bedroom, tearing through novels and containers of Chinese takeout.

Ana had lobbed a few low blows: She'd said something bratty when her mom bought her knockoff leggings from Target instead of the Lululemon Aligns she'd asked for; she'd asked her mom if she'd ever been to Europe, even though she knew the answer was no. She threw her friends' holiday plans in her mom's face: Lily was skiing in Aspen, and Margot was in Santa Barbara with her family. Ana's mom had sighed and looked at the ceiling, told Ana that she was doing the best she could. And for the life of Ana, she hadn't been willing to believe it.

She'd pulled away, and she'd told herself that it was just the way things were: Lily's family invited Ana and Margot to Aspen for spring break, and they'd both gone; Ana's mom had put up a bit of a fight about it, but ultimately she'd coughed up the money for the plane ticket and told Ana to have fun. All three of them landed internships in Boston that first summer, and they'd shared a single room in a two-bedroom apartment; the other occupant was a recent grad whose roommate was away for the summer, and they'd thought she was impossibly sophisticated and mature with her PR job and her leather tote. Of course Ana knew that both Margot and Lily—especially Lily—could have afforded not to share, but back then, it hadn't been about that. It had been about maximizing their time together, about piling into one bed to stroke each other's hair at night. It had been about staying out late and giving each other a nod when a guy approached them, or a quick headshake, because none of them had developed their own opinions about who they were or what they liked. Not yet.

It had been a good summer, and Ana remembered the sense of relief at the end of it, because they'd had fun and they didn't have to say goodbye. They would board the bus to Hawthorne and move into their sophomore apartment, and they'd start another year together, the three of them, best friends forever.

It was that summer when Ana got out of the habit of returning her mom's calls. She was always busy, and she was never alone. It was a once-in-a-lifetime summer, and she wanted to maximize it. She wasn't like Margot and Lily, who'd have more experiences like this for the rest of their lives. Who had the time to call their moms on their walks back from work, who didn't have to spend every single second soaking in all they could, just in case it was all taken away in an instant. Because for them, it wouldn't be.

It was the one thing in which Ana was completely alone.

By junior year, Ana and her mom had come to an understanding, or at least that's what Ana told herself. She had learned to move and speak with the hurried confidence of people raised on the coasts, people who had chosen to spend sixty grand a year to live on an isolated college campus they rarely left. They had so many unspoken patterns that were completely novel to Ana: None of them wore foundation, because their skin was already perfect. They all owned the same types of fur-hooded parkas and spoke to their professors like equals. They were always lining up at the package room picking up things they'd charged to their parents' credit cards, then abandoning those same things at the end of the semester and casually replacing them in the fall.

Ana hadn't grown up poor. She'd grown up solidly middle class—it was a good thing her dad had thought to take out a life-insurance policy and she received a hunk of money from Hawthorne that changed her life permanently. Her mom could afford to send Ana money for books and snacks and a new winter coat. There were kids who had it so much worse.

But she'd been eighteen, and nineteen and twenty and twenty-one, and she'd been focused on everything she lacked. It hadn't been enough to have landed a scholarship and two best friends and Silas. She wanted to have landed Silas and also have attended boarding school with one of the guys Silas knew from lacrosse camp. She wanted to have shown up on day one of Hawthorne with a Barbour jacket and an awareness of the concept of a semester school.

It had felt like the greatest injustice in the world, back then: to have been at Hawthorne but to not have been prepared for Hawthorne. To try to find the words for that, only for her mom to tell her that she'd changed, that she missed the sweet girl Ana was before, as if Ana could have held on to the kind of naivete that even Lily had thought, for a second, was some kind of self-aware bit. As if she could have told her new friends about cheese curds, and stayed soft and wide open and still survived.

It had felt so unfair: the way her mom praised Ana in public for getting into Hawthorne ("Did you know they accept only nine percent of applicants?"), for getting A's at Hawthorne ("Grade inflation isn't even a thing there!"), and then turned around in private and chided Ana for being a Hawthorne girl. "You're not better than home because you go to this school, Ana," her mom said once. "Don't forget where you came from." Ana had shaken her head, told her friends about how her mom just didn't get it, had chalked it up to jealousy, and then when Silas's family invited her to spend Christmas with them winter of junior year, she accepted.

Ana hadn't known at the time that it would become some permanent sort of fissure: trading her mom for Silas. Or that now, in this hospital in Madison, ten years after setting foot on the Hawthorne quad for the first time, she'd want to reverse the trade.

A nurse brought in a cot, and Ana curled up on it, waking every hour or so when someone came in to check on her mom.

The MRI was pushed, and then it was pushed again. Her mom slept, and a nurse helped her to the bathroom, and Ana listened sadly to the trickle of pee on the other side of the bathroom door.

Thirty-Nine: Margot

Margot completely understood the use case for alcoholism. It was unbearable being here with herself, walking up and down Mag Mile as if she had somewhere to be, pacing past Zara and her former office. There were so many things she could be doing with her Tuesday afternoon that were not anxious laps on arguably the worst street in Chicago, but she couldn't think of any of them. It was like the evaporation of her job had melted her brain into a puddle.

She ducked into a bar she used to love, ordered a dirty martini, waited for the alcohol to deliver her to the solitude of wisdom that came to her when she was tipsy.

"Can I buy you another drink?" said a guy, sliding in next to her.

"Sure," she said, "but don't expect anything."

He raised his eyebrows at her. "I would never. Hawthorne?" He gestured at her key chain, face up on the bar. "Me, too," he said. "Not a lot of us out here. In Chicago, I mean." He nodded at the bartender, gestured toward Margot's drink. "And a Miller for me." He looked her up and down. "Why are you alone?"

The last thing Margot wanted was to get into it with a stranger. What was she going to say? "I took a risk at work, and it was almost the career move of a lifetime, but then it totally backfired, oh, and by the way, it cost me an important conversation with my friend who is probably anorexic, and I know I should call her to talk about the fact that I abandoned her when she needed me at that club-slash-arcade in Miami—I know it sounds kitschy, but it was actually a really good vibe—but for some reason I can't bring myself to call her, and it's not for lack of time, because actually I'm on a bit of an unpaid sabbatical, and no, it's not like being fired at all, why do you ask?"

The bartender set a martini in front of her.

"I like to go to bars alone," Margot said. "I like to sit and write about my week. Reflect on my accomplishments." She pulled a dog-eared journal out of her bag.

"You really have your shit together, huh? I'm Noah, by the way."

"Margot. And yes. Well, no. I don't know. In some ways."

He chuckled. "But what are you, twenty-four?"

She raised her eyebrows. "I'm twenty-eight."

"Oh," he said, "you look good for twenty-eight."

"Do you think that's a compliment?"

"Sorry—I—fuck. Let's start over. Hi, I'm Noah."

"Honestly, Noah, I'm single and I like being single and I appreciate the martini." *And the next person I date is going to be a girl.* She raised her glass and tipped it toward him.

He extended both palms toward her. "Fair enough," he said. "Well, enjoy the martini, Margot."

He grabbed his beer and moved to a table alone, left Margot there at the bar at four in the afternoon on a Tuesday to try to write down something she'd accomplished that week. But she couldn't think of a single thing.

—

She called Lily to check in, but voicemail. Then Ana to apologize: also voicemail.

It wasn't like she'd been doing nothing: She'd gone to a spin class and she'd had lunch with Amelia ("Seriously, I'm so jealous you get to take time off," Amelia had said as if Margot was on vacation), and she'd half watched three seasons of *Love Is Blind*, bought and returned three pairs of jeans, a skirt, and four bras, all of which looked great in the store but then not as great when she tried them on again back home. She felt like that about everything, actually: Her entire life was like a new outfit, uncomfortable and unflattering and a little bit itchy.

By Saturday evening, she was going crazy. She'd subsisted on popcorn and sadness for an entire week, and she still had three weeks to kill before going back to work. Her body felt bloated with salt, her skin dehydrated. She felt more tired than she'd ever felt before. It was a sinking, heavy, all-encompassing exhaustion, one she'd never felt before but knew instinctively wouldn't be resolved by sleep. All the sleep in the world wasn't enough to unshroud Margot from this cloak of doom, or regret, or reality, or whatever the feeling caused by fluorescent lights in your eyes was called. It felt like something was searing into her while also crushing her while also anchoring her to the bed and holding her there, and she wanted to open her eyes to check in on whatever was bothering her so much, but she didn't have the energy. She couldn't do it. She'd never felt so incapable in her life.

How could a person go from top of her elementary school reading group to most popular girl in middle school to top of her class in high school to Hawthorne student body president to Magic Margot at work to a blob on a full-size bed? How had she not realized how tired she was? Surely this weight had been knocking around in the cavity of her chest for some time, trying to alert her to its presence, ricocheting across the inside of her ribs.

She was exhausted, but her feet were restless, kicking sheets up around themselves like squirrelly children on a playground. It was unfair: that her own feet could betray her like this, staying awake when she was finally ready to sleep. She wanted to scream or pound a pillow, but she couldn't. She couldn't move. She was like a squashed bug or a discarded orange peel or a woman who'd sacrificed everything for a goal and failed marvelously at that goal and was now faced, alone and in the great state of Illinois, with picking the pieces back up.

—

Margot let herself wallow until she fell asleep with the heft of her stupidity thick on her chest like a weighted blanket. She woke up around four in the morning, wearing jeans and a bra, her breath stale against her pillowcase. She wriggled out of her jeans, unclipped her bra and tossed it across the room, and willed herself back into a state of unconsciousness.

—

The thing was, Margot had always been like this: revved up in the direction of her goals. Her friends knew this about her, knew to grab her by the arm when something was serious, to redirect her toward them when she swayed like a sapling. They knew her well enough—Lily knew her well enough—that if Margot didn't give them what they needed the first time, then they needed to ask her again. On some level, Margot thought as she yawned, a sudden jolt of energy propelling her toward the bathroom, Lily was at least a tiny bit responsible for not trying harder to talk to Margot earlier about what she'd done. On some level, so was Jenny: She could have yanked Margot's arm during brunch that day in New York, told her to slow down a minute, bucko, let's think about this before you put the idea of firing two of our clients into the world—our lowest-paying clients, but still paying clients—and we'll reassess, come to a decision privately. What was the point of surrounding yourself with people who knew you if they didn't hold you to standards better than the ones to which you could hold yourself?

Forty: Lily

Lily was almost two weeks in, sitting on the yellow couch in the group therapy room. She was picking at her cuticles when Bruce called on her. She'd gotten used to the routine: starting the morning with a regroup, eating breakfast together, splitting off for Relationship Management Group or Life Skills or Facts About Nutrition.

"I wanted to circle back to what you said about your friends."

"What did I say about my friends?"

"You said that you didn't need to share any of this with them," he said, his eyebrows bouncing on his forehead. "If I may, I'd like to share a hypothesis." He went on before she could answer. "It seems like maybe you're avoiding talking about all this with your friends—the two girls you mentioned, right? Because they're the closest people to you, in a lot of ways, outside of Jack."

"That would probably be my mom," Lily said, even though she still hadn't told her mom that she was in treatment. "Anyway, I feel like this is just what happens. We're getting older. I don't know. We're not roommates anymore."

"Lily," said Bruce, "I appreciate that you're close with your mom, and I have a number of thoughts on that, which I'll save for tomorrow, but do you remember telling us last week about Margot not noticing in Miami that you were struggling, when you expected her to see that something was wrong? Or about Ana's rant on privilege, and how much guilt it brought up for you? I'm wondering if perhaps you haven't wanted to be totally up front with either of these friends, because on some level, you don't want them to know they're capable of hurting you."

"That's ridiculous," Lily said, even though it wasn't.

"Do you think that maybe it's a defense mechanism? You're used to having all the power in these relationships. You've always had answers. Maybe it's tough for you to fully relinquish that."

Lily blinked, wanted to protest, but she felt light and fluttery inside, knew that he was onto something, knew that calling her friends out on how they'd hurt her was kind of like avoiding carbohydrates: a means to an end, but one that would ultimately backfire.

—

Ana picked up right away.

"Do you remember when Margot would always be gone?" Lily asked. It was the next day, and she was sitting across from Bruce, who agreed that he'd give her privacy if and when Ana picked up.

"Of course," Ana said. "It was just us."

Bruce nodded, stood, shut the door behind him.

"Right," Lily said. "Sorry. I'm just gonna get into this before I can't. I don't know if I ever told you this outright, but at that point in time, I had just been used to competition with everything. Every girl at school. It was just the New York way—I know that sounds kind of cringey. But it was true."

"Right," Ana said. "That makes sense."

"I guess, you were just—you brought this openness. You were so—you just sort of taught me how to be vulnerable. Do you remember when we went swimming? That time—"

Ana cut her off. "Of course. At night, the last week of classes? You had that final—"

"And I was freaking out, and you dragged me to that rocky beach?"

Ana laughed. "You didn't want to go in naked because you were afraid of the cops."

"Right," Lily said, breathing in what it felt like to be remembered. "But that wasn't—I knew that cops didn't give a fuck about that, right? I just was scared of my own body? I was just so uncomfortable in my skin. And I remember you stripping on the rocks, and I remember how you just had this freedom—" *Feel the floor, Lily.* "That just changed everything for me. The way you could slow down, be so earnest, I guess. You taught me how to see people in a different light. You taught me that it doesn't always have to be a competition. You were my first true ally."

"Oh, Lily," Ana said.

"And I loved—love—you for that. And I was so—" She hated saying that she was hurt. It sounded so desperate. "I have to tell you something. I'm back in treatment, and it's honestly not a big deal, and, like, I'm gonna be fine, and it's not as bad as last time, honestly, but I guess I was—sorry, my therapist is making me do this, it's really fine—but I guess I was hurt when you didn't notice that I was struggling, like, hardly eating in Miami and being weird, and you kept talking to Alistair, and you said some fucked-up drunk shit, and it felt like you cared about him more—"

"Oh, Lily, I'm so sorry," Ana said. "It wasn't—I'm so, so, so sorry. I was just so in my own head, and I thought maybe you looked like you'd lost weight, but honestly, I thought—I didn't want to make it worse by bringing it up, and shit has been so weird with Silas, and that's not an excuse. What did I say?"

"It doesn't matter. It's okay," Lily said.

"I'm really so sorry," Ana said. "You were my first true ally, too."

She could hear beeping on the other side of the line. "Where are you?"

"Oh," Ana said, "I'm in Madison."

"Oh! Seeing your mom?"

"Yeah, well, this conversation is about you. But yeah. She's kind of in the hospital."

Forty-One: Ana

She finished apologizing to Lily, drank a glass of wine from the hospital cafeteria to accompany her tears, and waited.

So she'd been wrong not to say something. She'd been wrong to get drunk, to not apologize for whatever she had said when the vibes seemed obviously off the next morning. She hadn't worried enough, about the way the sun had bounced off Lily's rib cage, at the hollows in Lily's clavicles that had glistened behind swaths of white linen, about the darkness under Lily's eyes that Ana had assumed was a symptom of jet lag, but Miami and Boston were both on Eastern time, and that was only one of a million things that Ana had completely failed to realize.

Her breath was shallow in her chest as she sat, feet curled underneath her. She hadn't eaten in hours, but she didn't feel hungry. She didn't know if it was afternoon or night, and she resisted checking the time in the corner of her phone. Better not to know. Better to stay suspended. Very soon, her life could split into a before and an after.

She wondered what it would feel like to have a sibling—an older brother who'd been to medical school, or who was married to a woman who knew more than Ana knew about anything. Who'd be here any minute now, walking through the doors and wrapping Ana in a hug and telling her that it was perfectly natural to have pulled away from her mom during the time that she did, that it hadn't been selfish—or maybe it had, but no matter: She'd been young, and it was young people's right to think only of themselves.

If Ana's mom died, Ana would be completely alone. Good thing she'd made up with Lily, she thought, then pinched herself for even thinking about her mom being dead.

"Ana?"

She must have fallen asleep. Her neck was stiff, and her left leg was asleep. "Sorry," she said.

"We're not quite sure what's going on with your mother—your mother, right?" He didn't stop to wait for an answer. "Her MRI came back negative, so the good news is we've been able to rule out a stroke. We're running through a few more tests, just awaiting her blood panel."

"Right. Thank you." She had a million questions, but she didn't know how to ask any of them. Before she could shape her lips around the words that would at least be better than silence, he'd already left.

There was no reason to hold her here, they said after a few more hours. Go home, keep an eye on her, don't worry too much. Sometimes these things happen. It could be anything: a pinched nerve, maybe. Not a big deal. Or just a part of aging. We'll wait for the tests and we'll let you know what we find.

"Are you sure?" Was this what it felt like to be a new mom, suddenly in charge of someone helpless? Shouldn't they check her qualifications before releasing her mom into her care? Ana wasn't ready for this.

"I'll send someone in with the discharge papers," he said.

Ana's mom looked frail on the bed, but a bit of color had returned to her cheeks.

"Ana, you didn't have to come," she said. "And what is going on with Lily?"

"You were awake for that?" She'd taken the call from the hallway, figured her mom was still out cold from whatever they'd pumped into her veins. "Are you sure you're okay to leave? Do you want to stay?"

She pushed herself to sitting. "I think I'll be okay, Iguana," she said.

It had been a long time since anyone had called her that.

It had been at least eight years since Ana had stayed overnight in the house she'd grown up in. Eight years of grasping for reasons to not come home, which usually presented themselves without too much effort: It was impossible or too expensive to get all the way back to Madison. Lily's family badly wanted a friend of their daughter's to join them in Aspen. There was a storm over Wisconsin or Ana had a great opportunity on campus or why would she go all the way home when Silas's family wanted her with them at their Providence house for Christmas anyway?

The house was smaller and older and crumblier than she remembered. She'd forgotten about the glass balls in the front yard, suspended on metal baskets. The sincerity of it all: a welcome mat that really meant welcome; decorative plaques all around with family values that had been lifted from the pages of a catalog, indistinguishable from the family values of the house next door. It had driven Ana crazy for years, although she'd lacked the words to describe it back then: It was the predictability, the repetition. It had made her feel bored and restless. It had made her thirsty for the kinds of lives that Lily and Silas led: intentional and curated and full of irony. But now, as Ana's mom took her coat and put on the kettle, Ana wondered if maybe she'd been wrong. Maybe there was something real about the plaques on the wall: In this house, we hug tightly. It was true, at least: Ana's mom did hug her tightly, even after Ana had refused to visit for eight whole years. She thought of Silas's mom, who never hugged Silas with both arms, who still hadn't told Ana she loved her.

"It's been a while since you were here," said her mom.

A thread of guilt stirred in her chest. "I know," she said.

The teakettle whistled and Ana looked around. The place was mostly unchanged, from where she stood: photos of Ana, push-pinned to a bulletin board in the shape of a cross; the carpet, thick and beige and shaggy.

She wheeled her suitcase into the room that used to be hers.

—

The next morning, she called Beth.

"Ana, hi, how is everything?" Beth asked. "Bryn told me what happened. Take all the time you need, of course. But do keep me posted on the status of things. Bryn can handle the next few days, and that sub Rachel—do you know her? I don't remember—she can stay on as long as we need, she said."

"Thanks," Ana said. "I just don't know yet, is the thing. We're awaiting results . . ." She let her voice trail off, clutched an Uglydoll that had been sitting, waiting for her, perched against the pillow of her childhood twin bed, for a decade now. It made her feel too sad to function.

"I'm keeping you and your mom in my thoughts. You take care, okay?"

—

They spent the morning waiting at a café, new since Ana had last been home.

"You're sure you're feeling okay?"

"A little tired, but that's it."

Ana nodded. They hadn't yet negotiated these new terms of their togetherness: Ana checking in on her mom, and her mom letting her. She kept picking up her phone and scrolling Instagram and putting her phone down and smiling apologetically.

"How's Silas?"

"Oh," Ana said. She licked her teeth, considered explaining that Silas had called her three times since she'd left, but Ana hadn't picked up or returned any of his calls, because she didn't want to pretend like everything was normal, and she didn't want to wait for an apology that probably wouldn't come, and she definitely didn't want to apologize to him when she really hadn't done anything wrong. It was easier to just ignore him.

Around them, people buzzed, a group of women sat and chatted, matching novels on their laps.

"No one has a laptop," Ana said.

"What?"

"I mean, everyone is just talking." She hadn't meant to say it out loud, but there was just so little to talk about. It was crazy: that you could come out of a person's body and still, sitting across from it, have nothing to say except a bland observation about your shared surroundings.

"Why would they have a laptop at breakfast?"

"Fair question." It was just something she'd come to accept: all the work, all the multitasking, all the obsession with money and progress and disruption. It was sort of a relief, in a way, to be sitting here in this café with her mom, not feeling like the only person in the world who wasn't trying to IPO.

After breakfast, they went to a movie, Ana driving her mom's Toyota Corolla—the same one Ana had borrowed and kissed boys in a decade prior—her mom in the passenger seat, watching the trees outside the window.

"Ana," she said.

"Yup?" She merged out of the city, let muscle memory guide her toward the theater. She hadn't seen a movie in ages.

"What's it like for you? Being back here?"

"Mm? Fine," Ana said, stealing a glance in her mom's direction. "Look, Mom—"

Silence, except for the sound of the air-conditioning and the whir of the tires. Ana didn't know what to say: how to explain to her mom that leaving this world had felt as critical as breathing. That she had needed to invent herself, to start over in a world where glass balls in yards were a joke, something to point to while driving up to someone's cabin in Maine or Vermont. She had needed to become who she was outside the confines of the limits that had been imposed on her, to learn what she was capable of when the options weren't held up in front of her like a magician's hand of cards: vet tech like your mom, or nurse like Aunt Ruth, or teacher like Aunt Kate, or anything else you want to be, but we don't really know that much about it.

And yet, she had become a teacher. The irony had never occurred to her. She'd tried so hard to leave, and she hadn't gone far at all.

"You're here now," her mom said.

"I guess so," Ana said. They drove the rest of the way in silence.

Ana's mom was definitely going to die. But not yet.

"We need your mom to better monitor her blood pressure. We're starting her on thinners, and we do need her to come back in for a follow-up in two weeks. But her prognosis is good. She'll need to take a week off work, but she'll be fine."

"Oh, thank god," Ana said into the phone, taking her turn with the doctor after her mom had finished. "Yeah, that should be fine. Her clinic said they can be flexible. Thank you so much." She felt the weight of all of it fall off her: She could go back home. She could get back to her world.

They celebrated over hot dogs and cheese curds, then walked down the street for paper dishes of ice cream. It was still chilly out, but the snow had melted, and Ana realized that at some point in all of this, the world had rotated into spring.

"You know," Ana said, sitting next to her mom on a bench, drunk with relief and sugar, "in San Francisco, all the ice cream flavors are like Arbequina Olive Oil or Roasted Pineapple Coconut."

Her mom chuckled, then licked a spoonful of mint chip. "I've never heard any of those words in my life," she said.

"I'm serious," Ana said. "Dairy-free lingonberry is a legitimate flavor option at the place Silas likes."

"Ana, be serious," her mom said, her brow furrowing.

"We have a flavor in our freezer called Matcha Indignation Chip," Ana said.

"You're teasing me." Another spoonful to her lips.

"Mom, I'm deadass. Silas likes to eat his Matcha Indignation Chip with dairy-free whipped cream."

Her mom's eyes crinkled into something both new and familiar. "Don't tell me you eat that, too."

"No," Ana said. "I mean, I do, but I don't like it."

She cocked her head. "Why don't you just get coffee?"

"I—" She didn't know how to explain that Silas used to buy her coffee ice cream all the time, and then he stopped, and now they lived together, and even though they shared a freezer and Ana could buy her own coffee ice cream whenever she wanted, she didn't. It wasn't really about the coffee, it was about reminding Silas that she deserved to be taken care of—not just $12,000-couch taken care of, which wasn't even something that interested her, but remember-my-favorite-flavor taken care of. Why hadn't she told him that? Why had she tried to make herself feel like an expensive couch that she didn't even want was enough?

"Does he actually like that flavor?"

"I think so," Ana said, her voice cracking.

"Ana, what's wrong? I'm okay, everything is fine. You don't have to stay here, if you don't want to. Do you miss Silas? I'm sorry for putting you through all this—"

"No, no," Ana said. "Sorry. I'm just tired." She looked at her mom apologetically, watched her eyebrows raise in familiar disbelief.

"I know my own daughter, Ana. But you just talk to me when you're ready."

Forty-Two: Margot

Margot started the second week of her forced sabbatical scrolling social media and sleeping. By three, she'd been out of bed four times to pee. At five, she grabbed a half-empty bottle of wine from the fridge and a travel mug from the cabinet. She filled the mug to the top, then wished she'd left the wine in the bottle so she wouldn't have to clean another dish. She abandoned the bottle on the counter, took the mug back to bed, and drank it thirstily while something she'd chosen earlier streamed from her laptop in the background. It was a documentary, or it was about friendship, or it was a reality show. It was background noise, the rise and fall of voices of people who didn't know that one week prior, Margot had been effortlessly crushing everything. And now she was a mashed potato of a person. A wine-drenched mashed potato who'd failed everyone who was important.

Margot was good at everything. Except this: grieving the life she'd built for herself, lying around aimlessly and trying to avoid thoughts like, *What if I just took a lorazepam and jumped into the lake?* and lounging around at home all day in yesterday's underwear—these were things she was not good at at all.

The next day was the same: popcorn and wine and watching something terrible and scrolling and scrolling and trying to avoid sitting with it: the failure, the anxiety that prickled through her, the fact that she was still thinking about Alix and no one except for Keith even knew.

The following day, she decided to force herself out of the house. She dressed, brushed her teeth for the first time in too long, slipped on a pair of sneakers, and grabbed her keys. Walked down Clybourn, past a clothing shop where she'd bought the shirt she'd worn to present that first idea to Infinity, past a restaurant where she and Jenny used to take clients. She was aimless and bored, and she missed everything. A farmers' market across the street sharpened into view. She'd buy some lettuce, make a salad. Not let her aimlessness kill her.

—

She picked up a head of cabbage, tossed it in the air.

"Are you gonna buy that?"

"Oh, yes, sorry," Margot said, digging around in her bag for a wallet, handing a crumpled five to the woman, her age, maybe, in a linen shirt and a denim apron, its pockets edged in leather.

"You need a bag?"

Margot shook her head, tucked the cabbage under her arm, meandered over to an empanada truck to buy herself a snack.

She sat down on a bench with two meat-stuffed empanadas the size of her fist.

"Hey."

Margot looked up. The girl with the leather-edged apron held her cabbage in front of her.

"Your cabbage. It was rolling away. You can't just put a cabbage on the ground when you're at the top of an incline like this. Cabbages are round, you know? It's just basic physics."

"Oh, thanks," Margot said, taking the cabbage, realizing that she didn't even know if she liked cabbage. Why had she bought it? Besides coleslaw, which wasn't seasonal at all, she couldn't think of a single reason to use it.

"Are you okay?" asked the stranger, lingering.

"What?" She was pretty. The woman. Freckles bloomed across her cheeks, her blond eyelashes refracted the sun. "Yes, sorry. I—"

The girl raised her eyebrows. "Didn't we—Margot, yeah?"

"Alix?" She felt the blood rush to her cheeks. "What are you doing here?" *Why did you never text me back?*

"I quit my job," Alix said, shrugging, gesturing to the cabbages. "It was just way too much, you know? I was stressed out of my mind, like, constantly. A friend asked if I wanted to help out with her farm stand. That's her." Alix gestured to another girl in an apron. "And I was like, you know what? I would absolutely love to manhandle vegetables instead of wireframes. Blast! I never texted you back! I was just thinking about you last night, actually—not like that!—and I was like, I wonder what that pretty straight girl with the intense job from that bar is up to."

Margot snorted, in spite of herself, and felt the urge to tell her everything: about McQueen and Infinity, about the way she'd built her whole life around success, about the fact that she'd thought she was getting closer to *something* as she approached thirty, but it turned out she wasn't getting anywhere at all. About the way that Alix, this stranger she'd spoken with one singular time, had lit up something in Margot that she'd spent twenty-eight years only vaguely aware of. That she was alone on a park bench on a weekday with a cabbage in her lap, and she didn't even like cabbage. She was a shitty friend and a shitty employee and she didn't even know herself at all.

"Oh my god. I'm sorry. I'm such a mess. I just—do you ever wish someone would come collect you off the pavement?" She shook her head. "I didn't mean to say that out loud. I'm jealous of a cabbage. Fuck me. Sorry. Thanks for—" She gestured at the cabbage.

"Why do you think I quit my job?"

"Ha," Margot said, and she watched Alix make her way back toward her booth. "Alix?" she called after her. "When are you done with work?"

Forty-Three: Ana

Aunt Kate came over to her mom's house, bottle of wine in hand. The three of them were cooking lasagna together, and they were buzzed by the time the oven dinged.

It had been only a few days in Wisconsin, but it was starting to wear on her: the monotony of the days, making coffee for her mom and walking the aisles of Target.

Kate filled Ana's glass again. "So you're telling me, Ana, that you work your ass off, you make less money than you used to, and you actually miss making a difference in the lives of the kids at Oakbrook?"

"It's not exactly that," Ana said, wanting, suddenly, to defend Horizon and Beth and even Silas from her mom and aunt's perception of them, but she didn't sound convincing, even to herself.

"Well, it sounds exactly like that," said her mom. "Katie, you've probably seen teacher friends of yours go through this kind of predicament, right?"

Katie snickered. "Right. Yes. Of course. Because there are so many high-end private schools here in rural Wisconsin." She rolled her eyes. "No, honestly Ana, this sounds like bullshit. I mean, I deal with bullshit every day, don't get me wrong. I have twenty-six kids in my class, and most of them have undiagnosed ADHD. But that's just seventh grade for you, no matter what. But teaching is hard enough as it is. You really have to find a job that feels right for you."

"They're great kids," Ana said. "I love them."

"All kids are great," said her mom. "Of course. But you left a job you liked even more, for less money and worse parents? Because Silas went there?"

"I don't work there because Silas went there. I work there because I care about teaching, and I love the kids, and it's a good school—"

"I just don't get it, Ana," Kate said. "You made more of a difference at Oakbrook. Those kids needed you. You deal with political bullshit at Horizon. They don't really seem to trust you, no offense. They pay you less. I don't know. What's your long game?"

Ana refilled her wineglass, wondered if maybe she had a point.

A few days later, Ana promised her mom she'd come back at some time in the summer, but it really didn't seem like there was any reason for her to stay any longer on account of her mom's health. She was fine, at least for now, and if anything changed, Aunt Kate was only fifteen minutes away. Ana had a job to get back to and a relationship to salvage and a bridesmaid's dress to get tailored. It would have to be a rush job.

She landed at SFO at 7:35 in the morning, which meant she could make it to Horizon before school started, as long as she didn't stop home. She felt a renewed sense of confidence. Yes, there was bullshit, but she was dealing with it in the name of her future. She was at a top-ten private school, and that was a national ranking, not just California.

"Ana, hi!" Bryn said. She was erasing the whiteboard from yesterday's lesson. The kids would be here any minute.

"Thanks for holding it down," Ana said. "How were they?"

"Good, fine. We wrapped up the geography of Australia lesson and—oh—the fish hatched! Go look! Rachel has her master's in marine biology, so she built out this whole lesson around the life cycle of the fish, and then they hatched the next day! It was insane. Oh, Rachel, hey, you know Ana, right?"

Ana swiveled to see a statuesque brunette in dark-wash denim and a cashmere sweater. Her skin was glowy, and a shiny ring announced itself from her left hand.

"Ana! It's so good to meet you," said Rachel. Then, in a low whisper: "I'm so sorry to hear about what happened with your mother."

"Oh, thanks," Ana said, and wondered about the circumstances of so many diamonds on the wrists and neck and hand of a marine-biologist-slash-substitute-teacher.

"My dad's a cardiologist, actually, so if you need anything, please let me know. And you're Silas's girlfriend, right? He was so cute back at Horizon! I graduated two years before him. Tell him hi, I know he's up to so many big things!"

"Oh, you went to Horizon," Ana said.

"Yup! I'm just back in SF for the year, finishing my dissertation. Beth told me all about everything, so I agreed to just come in for a bit. Needed a break from all the dissertating anyway, you know?"

"Of course," Ana said, nodding.

"And I owe it all to Horizon, really."

"Rachel wanted to be a marine biologist ever since she went here," Bryn said, widening her eyes.

"Great!" Ana said. "Well, thank you so much for filling in while I was gone. Seriously, really huge. Are you, I mean, are you filling in for another classroom this week?"

Rachel looked at Bryn. "Oh! Bryn didn't tell you? Beth has me staying for the rest of the year! She wasn't sure if you'd need to leave again, and anyway, the kids are loving this marine biology unit, so I figured, why not! Seriously, you'd be doing me a favor." She reached for Ana's forearm, touched it lightly. A plume of something expensive-smelling. "I *cannot* work on this paper for another second. It's fun for me, and will maybe take a little bit of a load off you?"

"Oh, great," Ana said, but she couldn't help feeling like she'd been displaced.

That afternoon, Rachel led a lesson on orcas that had the kids more engaged than Ana had seen all year. Then she took them out to the playground to outline the shapes of different sea creatures to scale, from goldfish to blue whale. Bryn helped them measure, and Ana served as a floater, ostensibly answering any questions as they came up, but in reality standing idly as the kids lobbed their questions at Rachel. They seemed to gravitate toward her, and Ana knew this was probably in large part because she was new and exciting. But still, it stung. At closing circle, Rachel paired the kids up to share their rose, bud, and thorn from the day, and Ana tried to intervene—Hadley and Cooper weren't a good match, she whispered to Rachel—but Rachel furrowed her brow, shrugged her shoulders, and said that they seemed like they were doing fine, Beth had helped supervise a little "classroom exercise" between them while Ana was gone, and it had gone well. And to Ana's very selfish dismay, Rachel seemed to be right. They were talking quietly and diligently, cooperating on the prompt, trading off serving as scribe. Ana wanted Hadley to be included. She wanted Hadley and Cooper to get along. So why did it feel like heartbreak?

Ana hadn't been home in days. And things had been weird and distant between her and Silas the whole time she was gone, but she could sense from their texts the night prior that he was willing to give her some grace, all things considered: her mom, the red-eye last night. And she knew he wasn't holding anything against her, because he'd sent a bouquet to her mom, then one to her for good measure.

Silas was home, sitting on the couch, waiting for her.

"Hi!" she said, leaving her suitcase by the front door and going to him. "It's so good to see you." And it was: She was relieved to realize that he did indeed feel like home, that he smelled like the world they'd spent ten years building, that he was wearing the shirt she'd bought him for their five-year anniversary, which they'd spent in Sausalito, holding hands and feeling the California breeze and feeling like no one had ever once been this lucky.

"Ana, baby, it's been days. Come here."

She let herself fall into his chest. There was a battlefield of discarded boxes and ice cream cartons across the island. She ignored them. "Si, I've been thinking."

"Me, too," he said.

"I know I didn't want to, but if you really—I mean, it wouldn't be bad for me to be within direct flight access of my mom, and a change isn't a horrible thing, I guess. I just feel like we got off on the wrong foot here, for some reason. I don't know." Maybe a smaller apartment would actually help them corral their mess. Perhaps it would mean Si would spend more time outside it, creating messes at coffee shops and coworking spaces and anywhere that wasn't theirs.

She wanted a reset. She wanted Ana and Silas to be back to Ana and Silas.

"Ana, what? That wasn't a real idea," Silas said, pulling back from her, grinning. "I was drunk." He rolled his eyes and smiled like it was a joke they were both in on.

"Oh," she said, shrinking.

Suddenly, the decorative plaques with their simple platitudes seemed smart. Genius, even. She and Silas had never in all these years defined anything—not expectations, not boundaries, not what either of them actually wanted. His life had structure, and hers bent to accommodate it: planning a move that was just an idea, as if relocating across the fucking ocean wasn't a huge fucking deal. Her wants were incidental. Her contributions invisible. And for the first time, she saw how lopsided it all was: how little space there had ever been for her within the life they'd supposedly built together.

Maybe Aunt Kate had been right: Ana wasn't making a difference here. And that would be okay if at least she felt seen. If at least she could come home after a week from hell and a workday from hell and Silas could wrap her up and understand her, tell her that he knew how hard she worked at everything, that he loved her for it, that he respected her for it, that he appreciated that she'd considered London, that she could get any kind of job she wanted there, that he was proud of her, that he loved her, that to him, she belonged.

Silas stood up, went to the freezer, and grabbed a pint of ice cream.

Tears prickled at the corners of her eyes.

She wanted to tell him what she now realized they both already knew. That the relationship was on its last legs. That the writing had been on the wall for a while now, hadn't he seen it, too? That they'd been struggling ever since they moved in together, maybe even before that, it was just that Ana hadn't had the courage to admit it. She wanted to say she deserved space and respect, even if she would never earn as much. That he should go date someone from his own tax bracket, and let her do the same. That his family would never accept her, that she was sick of feeling guilty because he subsidized her rent when he was the one who wanted to live the way they lived in the first place.

"Remember when you used to get me coffee ice cream?"

"What?" He turned.

"Why did you stop?"

He searched the floor for a second, looked almost boyish. "Wait, what? You never went to the store and got *me* ice cream," he said.

"It was *your* thing," she said.

"I never asked for it to be," he said. "Why are you making a big deal out of this?"

"Because it's important to me," she said.

"*This* is what you're focused on? Right now? How's your mom?"

"She's fine. But I'm trying to talk to you about caring." She paused. "You're always trying to argue your way out of things. Like, Silas, I'm not trying to win an argument here. I'm just trying to tell you that you used to make a bigger deal out of showing me you care. And you don't anymore. Do you realize that?"

"I pay your rent, Ana," he said. "Isn't that a *bigger deal*?"

She stiffened. "You think you have the upper hand. All the time," she said, "and you're right. That's the thing."

"What do you mean, *upper hand*? We're not colleagues."

"You know what I mean. Don't be ungracious with me."

"Congrats on the vocab word."

"*Ungracious* is, like, a fifth-grade word."

"I get it. You're a teacher."

"Honestly, Silas, do you even love me?" She paused for a second, surprised that the question had made its way out of her, but what did she have to lose at this point? She gave him a second. She waited for him to crumple, to look up at her with realization: He hadn't meant for this fight to turn into anything that would bring her to doubt his undying love! He hadn't meant for her to feel confused, worried, sullen, scared! He loved her, endlessly, and actually, he was planning on proposing this weekend, secretly at the beach, and he was nervous, and that was why he was being terrible!

"That's a stupid question," he said instead.

"That's not an answer." She bit down on her lip. "Jesus. You know, Silas, you're like—" Oh no. It was coming. "You're *still* a Horizon kid. Honestly, you're worse than the Horizon kids. You expect the red carpet to be rolled out for you at all times. You see everyone as support staff, even me, just there to enhance your curated experience of the world. It's immature, and honestly—I don't know, I should have realized—I just, I thought it wouldn't matter. I thought I'd come home from my mom almost dying and you'd give me some slack. That we're two mature adults who don't have to make a whole thing of our different circumstances.

"But it's not even—the money is like, so secondary to that. You are so entitled, and you don't understand that some of us have to take life seriously. I just—all this time, I've been worried about not being good enough for you, and I just should have realized that maybe you think you're too good for me. That that's the thing that's wrong."

It was the indignity of having nowhere to disappear to after making a good point in a fight that undid her.

She paced.

"You're not better than me, Ana. You act like you've struggled, but you really haven't. But work at Oakbrook if you want. I don't care. Contrary to popular opinion, I do want you to be happy. It's not like I don't love you."

"Silas," Ana said, "I don't think I want to do this anymore."

Suitcase. Bryn's house. Max shaking up a cocktail, ferns everywhere, cat on her lap.

"Is it permanent?" Bryn asked.

Ana was in shock, still suspended in the moment that came before the real pain. It was like when she got her bikini line waxed—she was still the only person she knew who didn't go for the Brazilian—in the split second after the sound of ripped-out hair and before the sting that came after.

"I don't know," Ana said. "Two years ago, I saved all this money for a single cashmere sweater, and then I put it on and it was so itchy, because I guess I have weirdly sensitive skin, and instead of returning it, I kept it in my closet and never wore it, even though I needed that three hundred dollars. And I just, like—I don't know what kind of sweater I like the best, but it's not cashmere."

"Girl, what?" Bryn exchanged glances with Max.

"I think I thought I wanted a certain type of life, and now that I have it, I guess I realized I was wrong," Ana said. "But I'm afraid to give it up completely."

"Is there such thing as postbreakup clarity?" Max asked. "Like, postnut clarity but for girls?"

Bryn smacked him. "Can you not?" she said.

"Ana, I'm kidding," Max said. "Lightening the mood. And you can stay here as long as you want." He winked.

"I really appreciate that," Ana said,

Max placed a glass in her hand. "This is bay leaf–infused gin with a bubblegum reduction. You might hate it. But I think it's my best work yet."

Ana took a sip, screwed up her nose. "This is disgusting," she said, and started laughing, and then she was crying, her whole life in front of her like an unwound spool of thread.

—

Bryn and Max were going to bed.

"The office is all set for you. But watch TV, do whatever," Max said. "Mi casa es su casa. Mi liquor cabinet—"

Bryn cut him off, pushed him playfully. "She gets it."

"You guys, seriously, thank you."

"Don't mention it," Bryn said, then turned, leaving Ana alone with her thoughts.

—

She couldn't sleep. It was painfully late. She really needed to talk to her mom.

"Ana. Are you okay?"

"I'm surprised you picked up," Ana said.

"I always keep my phone on. Just in case you need something at night."

It almost broke her: the hundreds of nights that her mom had been available for her. The hundreds of nights Ana hadn't needed her. She let out a breath, gained her composure.

"Look," she said, "I know this might be hard to hear, and it's maybe not permanent, I don't know. It's so new. Silas and I kind of broke up."

"Oh, fucking finally."

"Mom, what?"

"That guy was never right for you, Ana. He was such a prick. Do you remember at graduation when he kept thanking me for coming, as if it was his party and his ceremony and I was there for him?"

Ana coughed out a laugh. "No," she said, "I don't, but honestly—I mean, Mom, you hated him all this time? And you never told me?"

"Ana, baby, it's your life. It's not my place."

"Mom," she said, wondering if perhaps she'd worked so hard to stay away from exactly the place she needed to be right now, "maybe I'll come back to Madison for the summer. Stay with you and figure out what's next."

"Oh, goody, Ana," she said. "I'll stock the freezer with coffee ice cream."

For the rest of the week, Bryn and Ana ate oatmeal together at the kitchen table, then took the bus to work. Ana knew she was starting to overstay her welcome, and she knew she should tell Lily about the breakup—was it a breakup?—so she could redo the seating arrangements, and she knew she should tell Margot about it because that's what friends do, but she didn't yet have the wherewithal to make it real, let alone to go back and start packing up her things. Facing him and their apartment would really put the nail in the coffin: It was over. She'd have to start over. Did she want it to be over? Ten years, and then back to first dates? Did she even want to stay in San Francisco?

"I have such good news," Rachel said to Ana, a hand on her shoulder as they watched the kids on the playground. "I just chatted with Beth, and it looks like Horizon is going to keep me on for a few hours next year to teach science!"

"What?" Ana asked, a little offended. Had she not been teaching science correctly? Had she been stupid to think that not having a PhD in marine biology would be a relevant factor to her employment as an elementary school teacher? Was this tweak in staffing at Cooper's mom's request?

"It's actually perfect," Rachel said. "You'll get to have a little more downtime in the day, which I'm sure would be welcome—I mean, you do so much as it is—and I only have class three days a week next year, so it works out perfectly. My dissertation adviser is actually tight with Beth—they did their PhDs together at Cal—did you know that Beth has a PhD in biology? And anyway, he and Beth agreed that it's kind of the perfect situation. I'll get to help out in the classroom, which is great for Horizon's emphasis on STEM, and plus, it will actually count for my mandatory classroom hours, even though technically those are supposed to be spent with undergrads."

Concentric circles. Always the concentric circles.

"And I said to Ant, 'Let me do this, because I'll be honest, women are pushed out of STEM long before they get to college, and the younger I can get to them, the better.'"

"Oh," Ana said, because what was she supposed to say? "Actually, Rachel, I don't want you in my classroom, because I don't support girls learning science?" Or "Actually, Rachel, it's not that I think you're wrong about women getting pushed out of STEM, and it's not even that I don't like you, it's just that this is my classroom and I want ownership of it, and I suddenly feel like a failure?"

"So it's a done deal," Rachel said. "I mean, as long as you're good with it, of course."

"Of course," Ana said, straining through a smile. "Why wouldn't I be?"

But she wasn't good with it. She wasn't good with the way exceptions were made for everyone who knew everyone. It made her miss her mom and Aunt Kate and the declarative wall plaques. She wanted to add another one: In this house, not everything is about concentric circles.

Forty-Four: Margot

The market was alive around them: kids crying for ice cream, vendors offering samples of peaches to passersby, women smelling the bottoms of melons and packing them into straw bags.

"Girl, this is not a real job. I can leave whenever. But I should tell you: I don't get into it with straight girls. I end up falling in love, they get weirded out—it's a thing."

"Yeah," Margot said. "About that. I'm, like, not?"

"Oh," Alix said. "In that case." She turned toward the booth. "Sadie? I'm out for the day. See you later."

—

"So you took a risk and it didn't pan out," Alix said. "Big whoop." Margot had wanted to head home and change, meet up with Alix after she'd had a chance to wash her face like she meant it and put on something at least vaguely less atrocious than what she was wearing, but Alix had shaken her head like Margot was crazy, told her she had a plan.

"You ever done the architecture tour?" Alix had asked. "I've lived here for five whole years and I've never done it."

Neither had Margot.

So here they were, two near-strangers, except they didn't feel like strangers at all, on the roof deck of a boat, ostensibly learning about the architectural gems of the Windy City, but really ignoring the guy with a microphone and leaning into each other a little bit too close.

"Yes," Margot said, "but the thing about me is that my risks always pan out." It wasn't the kind of thing she would say out loud to most people. Not even to Ana or Lily. It was part of her shtick: to be humble and put on like everything came easy. It surprised her: how willing she was to be honest in Alix's presence.

"Girl, you know that just means you're not taking big enough risks, yes?"

But that was the thing: Everyone was always praising Margot for the limbs she went out on, how she got more done in a day than most people got done in a week.

"I just didn't expect that a cabbage farmer would be the one to push me harder than most people in my life," Margot said. "No offense."

"Ha," Alix said.

"I'm only saying that because you're more than *just* a cabbage farmer."

"And what if I wasn't?" Alix asked. "It's kind of a thing I've been toying with. Like, I grew up in Boston, right? Went to one of those private schools that's supposed to get you into Harvard, or Wesleyan at the very least. And I've had my identity so tied to that. And it's weird, because you hear gay people talking about how much work they put into discovering themselves, you know? My friends who are late-in-life bisexuals are always talking about that. But it wasn't like that for me. I knew I was gay from, like, kindergarten, and it was never a thing in my household—I mean, my dad is a gender studies professor at MIT, if you can believe that."

"That's cool," Margot said. "My parents are academics, too."

Alix kept going. "So they always accepted me, it was never a question. I never even came out officially, right? It was kind of always known. So you would think as this gay woman in a straight world, I would be comfortable with questioning, but actually, I never was." She knocked her ankle against Margot's. "I'm not blaming my parents or progressive education for embracing me. I'm just saying: leaving Google for cabbage was my true questioning and coming-out, if that makes any sense at all." She laughed.

"Huh," Margot said. "Actually, it really does."

—

Six hours later. Hot dogs, mustard, a diner, one milkshake, two straws.

"So tell me about your exes," Alix said.

"So we're getting into it," Margot said.

"We're in it already," Alix said, waving a fry in the direction of their shared shake.

"Honestly, I don't have any."

"Is there something crazy wrong with you?"

"Kind of," Margot said, because it seemed like a crime that for so long she'd focused so wholly and entirely on work.

—

Neither of them said it, but Margot was pretty sure Alix didn't want the night to end, either.

"Beer, maybe?" Alix asked.

"Beer."

They went to a nearby bar, ordered something on draft.

Margot gestured to Alix to wipe a spot of foam off her nose. "So tell me more about quitting your job."

Alix swallowed, thought for a second, fidgeted in her barstool. "When I was a kid, I used to have these themes of things I would think about. I called them Thinking Themes. I never told anyone about them, they were just for me. Usually they lasted a couple of weeks."

"Like, interests? Hobbies?" She was a little tipsy. "Girls?"

"No. I've never really—I guess, when I was young, like, tween young, I had this clarity of thought, by which I mean I used to think thoughts. Does that sound dumb?"

"Kind of," Margot admitted.

Alix continued, "I had this moment. I was in the bathroom at Google, peeing, right? And I was thinking about the ways in which the tile in the bathroom matched the layout of this new product I was working on. Like, the number of tiles—the proportions were the same. Whatever. Not the point. The point is, I realized my current Thinking Theme was visual proportions for the design of an internal tool for a multibillion-dollar company. And my Thinking Themes used to be, like: how people manage conflict. Forgiveness. How we could incentivize people to install solar panels. Why my mom can say sorry and my dad can't. Simple shit, you know? I was a kid. But the point is, I used to have Thinking Themes that at least kind of mattered.

"My brain was half developed, and I was thinking about stuff that matters twice as much as the stuff I'm using my fully formed, highly educated brain to think about now. I'm thirty-two years old, and I don't own my own brain. I'm just a repository of Figma files.

"And I just—one day I was flexing when I was out with friends. You know, that thing when someone says they worked seventy hours last week, and then someone else one-ups them? I was bragging about having worked eighty-five hours, and I realized that that had become something I was proud of. And I, like, wouldn't say I've ever dealt with serious depression, but for a couple days after that, I started to wonder what it would feel like to just go to sleep forever. I wasn't going to actually do anything. But it scared me. That I was wondering."

"So you chose cabbages."

"It was kind of, like, cabbages or death."

"Can I kiss you?" Margot asked.

"Girlypop," Alix said, "I said one kind-of-deep thing, and we're drunk, and you've never even been with a woman before. Sleep on it, and if you still want to in a week, we can discuss."

That night, Margot dreamed that she brought Alix to Lily's wedding, and that Lily and Ana kept referring to Alix as Margot's "bestie." Margot kept trying to tell them that she *wasn't* a bestie, but every time she piped up, her friends rolled their eyes and pushed her away. "Margot, please," dream-Lily said. "This is clearly just a phase. You're sexually attracted to your job, remember?"

The following two weeks before Margot took off for Maine passed with a little less pain than the previous one. Partially, Margot was getting used to the routine of not having a routine, and while she was still miserable enough to avoid shaving any of her body hair or eating anything that wasn't takeout, she was at least showering and eating *something*.

Can you guys FT to talk through some day of logistics?? she texted Ana and Lily.

Just voice memo me? Lily said. Sorry soooo busy with planning stuff. Lily hated voice memos, so that was kind of weird. And Ana didn't respond at all.

Strange, but it was the final few days before the wedding, so surely Lily was pulled in a million directions, and knowing her, there wouldn't be a single detail she'd let slide. And Ana was known to be a not-so-great texter. It wasn't like she could have her phone out during her workday.

Or maybe they were just both still mad at her for leaving early.

Well, she deserved that, maybe.

They'd deal with it in Maine. Certainly, they'd dealt with worse things before.

Forty-Five: Lily

Lily was two weeks into treatment and had graduated to tier three of four, which, as far as she could tell, had absolutely zero tangible repercussions, but felt kind of good anyway.

—

She was locked in a therapy room, doing what she'd promised her therapist she'd do. Something that had been gathering momentum since Ana had mentioned that her own mom was having health issues. It made Lily want to hug Gina and shake Gina and smack Gina all at the same time.

"Lily!" Gina said after the first ring. "How are you? I had a thought, and you can tell me I'm crazy, but what if we put Carol at the same table as Ari? I just think they'd get a kick out of each other, you know? Is that weird? You're not saying anything. Never mind. It's a stupid idea."

"Look, Mom," Lily said, "I need to talk to you about something."

"Is it the peonies? I told you we should have splurged on them. Are you having doubts about the ranunculus? It's not too late." She sounded a little breathless.

"This is really hard for me," Lily said. It was something Bruce had been pushing her to try: "You can always just be honest," he said. "Name the feeling. Even in conversation." It was actually less awkward than it seemed.

"Okay," Gina said.

Lily took a deep breath. "I think you're a really great mom." She paused. "I am so appreciative of everything you've done for me. I love you so much, and sometimes I think about you alone at home with Genevieve and I feel so guilty and I think I should move back home with you to take care of you."

"Oh, Lily," Gina said, "that's ridiculous. And you know I'm so busy, with the girls, SoulCycle, book club, walking."

"I know," Lily said. "And I love you so much, and I also need to tell you a few things."

"What? You're pregnant? Don't worry, we'll get alcohol-free champagne. Although, truthfully, I had champagne before I knew I was pregnant with you, and you turned out fine."

"Mom, no," Lily said.

"Okay, because if you were pregnant, I wouldn't be upset. I'm not getting any younger over here."

She could do this. "Do you remember when I was young and you told me I was gaining weight—it was fourth grade, maybe—and you had me stop eating dessert for a week?"

"No, Lily, I wouldn't do that—"

"Mom, you did, and it's okay. But every time you get a Cobb salad with no bacon and no blue cheese and no dressing, or ask me if I've been working out, or tell me someone looks fat, it just wears on me, okay? And you think I'm so perfect, and you think I'm so caring and diplomatic, and sometimes I just feel so much pressure to be caring and diplomatic and perfect and be for you who Dad never could be."

"Oh, Lily," Gina said.

"I love you," Lily said. "But sometimes you need to let me be disappointed. And deal with it. And be uncomfortable."

"Okay," Gina said. "I can hear that."

"Fuck, I'm sorry," Lily said. "Was that too mean?"

"Oh, Lily," Gina said, her voice cracking, "no, never. You've never been too mean. Is that all?"

"One more thing: I'm back in treatment."

Gina could cancel the wedding. She could eat the cost, no problem, and let Lily focus. Gina could come to Boston right now, or give Lily some space. Gina had a million ideas and a trillion and one solutions.

"Jack and I want to go on with it. I can take the weekend off, and I'll go back to treatment after," Lily said, and she was relieved to find that it felt true.

She'd talked it over with her treatment team, and they were all in agreement: She could handle the wedding, if she wanted to. She was going through the motions of therapy with compliance and willingness, and it wasn't like they could force her to stay, even if they'd wanted to. So it was settled: The show would go on.

Forty-Six: Ana

The wedding was two days away, and presumably, Silas still had a seat at a table next to Ana. And also presumably, Margot would be seated on Ana's other side, and they still hadn't spoken since the bachelorette weekend, except for one perfunctory logistics call.

She dashed off a quick text: L, i'm so so so so excited for your big day. so, terrible timing, but Silas has like a really contagious cold and i just don't think he's gonna make it. so pull him off seating chart. I'm so sorry!! he feels really bad.

There. No need to bog Lily down with the details now.

Technically, Silas hadn't been uninvited to the wedding, Ana thought as she shoved her suitcase through the X-ray machine at SFO. *But showing up would be psycho on his part.* She wanted to confirm that with someone who'd agree, but stopped herself just before giving Margot a call. Too much to wade through before they could get back to trading reassurances.

> omg i hope he's ok!!! do you want to just stay with margot then at my mom's? cancel your hotel room?

That would actually be huge. She couldn't really afford the $400-a-night hotel on her own. Sharing with Margot might be a little awkward—they still hadn't really spoken since Miami—but they'd fought and made up plenty of times before. Why would this time be any different?

actually yeah! Perf!!

Ana and Margot both arrived at the house in Kennebunkport that evening. They were staying in the room they'd always stayed in when Gina had let them use the house for weekends or birthday celebrations during college.

"You girls need anything?" asked Gina, ducking in. "You know where the drink fridge is. And the hot tub is open."

"Thanks, Gina," they called out in unison.

The windows were open, and the breeze through the windows smelled like getting tipsy off White Claws and eating hot dogs at the beach. The house was simple. Big but cozy. There was a tiny powder room off the kitchen. Above the sink, copper pots hung from the ceiling like stars.

The three of them had stayed here plenty of times over the course of their youths. It was only an hour's drive from Hawthorne, and a ten-step walk from the beach. They'd always spent their first night in the hot tub, listening to the trees and playing Confessions, a game they'd made up freshman year when they were still just learning how to be vulnerable with people they hadn't always known. Its rules were simple: You shared something about yourself or your dreams or your fears. It couldn't be about boys.

But tonight, it was just the two of them, and they were both tired from travel, and it seemed sacrilege to play Confessions in the hot tub without Lily, and anyway, it seemed like Margot felt exactly like Ana did: We'll get to the bottom of everything between us, but let's not jump into it. Not yet.

"I'm gonna go for a walk on the beach," Margot said. Then, as an afterthought: "You could come if you want."

"I'm gonna read in bed," Ana said.

Margot nodded, slid her feet into Birkenstocks.

—

Everyone else who was invited to the rehearsal dinner trickled in the next day. Ana went into town with Liza, who also wanted a doughnut and an iced coffee from the place they used to love, and Margot went for a jog with Lily's cousin Arabella. They'd see Lily later, at the rehearsal.

Ana sipped iced coffee and smiled and laughed and tried her hardest to seem like someone who wasn't maybe newly single and in a standoff with her best friend.

—

Lily looked kind of puffy, was Ana's first thought when they all met up that afternoon in front of the White Barn Inn.

"Hi!" Lily said, going to all of them.

Ana wasn't used to it feeling stilted, the three of them together: Margot fussing over Lily performatively, Lily clearly uncomfortable in her own skin, which wasn't something Ana had seen before. Ana let the other girls fill in for the closeness the three of them were used to. Zoe could gush over Lily's hair. Let Emily flirt with all the guys.

They rehearsed, practiced walking the grassy aisle and standing where the chuppah would be. Lily looked distracted, brushing her hair out of her eyes and forcing smiles, as she stood there across from Jack. Same thing at dinner, during the speech from her brother and the speech from Jack's dad; while they all milled about on the manicured lawn; while they picked at tuna tartare and sipped at white wine. Brushing her hair from her face like a tic, or a security blanket, and it made Ana want to go to Lily and hug her, but instead, she kept a few people between them, scared that if she brushed up against Lily too close, she'd crack.

"This is the thing with Lily, though," Margot said after everyone had peeled off and she and Ana had returned to their shared bed. An olive branch. Even though they still hadn't talked about what had happened in Miami. "She's either in control of everything—"

"Or nothing," Ana finished, offering something back.

"Remember that night abroad?"

Ana did, but it had been years since she'd thought of it. Lily was in Barcelona for the semester, and Ana and Margot had gone to visit her, and Lily had been so glad to see them. She'd been paired with a roommate whom they'd heard only bad things about, but as soon as they met the roommate, they'd both raised their eyebrows in recognition of the fact that the roommate's only flaw was that she didn't care about Lily at all. She was Spanish, and gorgeous, and tan, and effortless in that way that only European women can be. She'd been wearing cargo shorts and a ripped tank top, and she'd been so beautiful, and she'd been on the phone with someone. The roommate had raised her eyebrows at the girls before covering her mouth and giggling into her phone, headed out to the balcony that she and Lily shared, lit a cigarette and smoked it as if they weren't even there.

None of what made Lily relevant at Hawthorne meant anything to this girl, who wore rubber flip-flops and didn't worry about carcinogens. It was the first time that Ana had seen this side of Lily: dejected and out of sorts and self-conscious, twirling her hair and glancing around nervously.

They'd put down their stuff—they were sleeping on the couch and a leaking air mattress—and changed for dinner, grabbed a taxi to a place Lily had chosen. And they'd gotten there, and there'd been a miscommunication or an error and there'd been no table for them, and Lily's eyes filled with tears, and she ran out of the restaurant onto the street, and they went out to her—"Lily," Margot had said, a little annoyed, not at the lack of reservation but at the way Lily had made it a bigger deal than it needed to be, "it's fine, seriously, let's just get drunk or get street hot dogs or something." But Lily had been borderline inconsolable, and Ana had realized how important it was to Lily to be seen for the person she'd worked so hard to become. That three months of this—being invisible in a place where none of the ways she was powerful meant anything—had completely undone her.

Ana rolled to face Margot in their bed. "Yeah, no, of course," Ana said. "Remember that beautiful bitchy roommate?"

Margot rolled her eyes. "Did Lily kind of seem like that to you, a little? Tonight?"

Lily, on that curb in Barcelona, her scuffed kitten heels and the tangle of hair on her face. "Yeah," Ana said. "Like, exactly."

"I'm worried," Margot said, propping her head on her hand. "I'm really tired, and I know we have to talk about how I was a bitch to you in Miami, but you were a bitch to me, too, and tomorrow you have to also tell me what's actually going on with Silas. I know he doesn't have a cold."

A wave outside, the buzz of cicadas.

"Yeah, okay, fine," Ana said.

Forty-Seven: Lily

Lily was tucked into a queen-size bed at the White Barn Inn, her poplin pajamas crisp against the sheets.

Her wedding dress hung from a peg on the wall. She watched it like fog over the ocean, palmed the place beneath her rib cage that had grown soft and padded.

She wanted to cry. She wanted to do jumping jacks. She wanted to pull a Crystal Light packet out of her purse and mix it with water and down it and consider throwing up. She wanted to run out of her skin and into the ocean or try on her dress again or scroll on her phone or get drunk. It felt terrible to be in her body.

But she needed her sleep. Tomorrow was the most important day of her life.

—

The next morning, she woke to Margot and Ana climbing into her bed.

"They gave us a key at the front desk," Margot said, shrugging, then wrapping Lily in a hug. "Happy wedding day!"

"Lily! You look gorgeous," Ana said.

She hated that everyone had been taking stock of what she looked like, even though of course they were; it was her rehearsal dinner and she'd been dressed to the nines, a floral Dolce skimming her ankles and pulling at the place where her hips jutted out.

Lily practiced what she learned during the past few weeks: Is this possible or probable? Is this realistic, or am I potentially catastrophizing? Feel the room, make an appointment with herself to worry about it later.

"You nervous?" Ana asked, patting Lily on the hand. They were sipping champagne: Lily and Margot and Ana and Liza and Emily and Jack's sister, Cameron, sitting cross-legged on flimsy little stools and taking their turns with hair and makeup.

"Not at all," Lily lied. It was taking all that she had to maintain a steady flow of oxygen into her lungs and out of her lungs. "But how are *you*?"

"Oh," Ana said. "Fine!"

Lily nodded. "Silas okay?"

"Hmm? Yeah, you know how men are when they're sick."

"Hmm."

"Hold still, please," the makeup artist said.

There were six hours until the wedding.

"The light is really good," said the photographer. "Would you have any interest in slipping on your dress and sitting out here on the deck?"

"Sure," Lily said, grabbed it off a hook, took it into the bathroom so she could come out in a flurry. Why had her upper arms filled out so quickly? They looked completely disproportionate, like limp hot dogs. She heard Bruce's voice in her head: "Identify your thoughts and name them as they come up." She heard Barri's voice, too: "Just because you're thinking something, it doesn't mean it's true."

She closed her eyes. "Can someone actually help me zip this?"

Margot opened the door. "Of course. Ana, here, I'll hold the zipper closed, and you yank it up, yeah?"

"Right," Ana said, materializing.

Lily sucked in, but she knew, even as she pulled her stomach toward her spine, that there was absolutely no way in hell this thing was fitting onto her body in one piece. That she should have let her mom buy the Clara, which had been too big for her, instead of insisting on the original dress, which had been altered to fit her two-weeks-ago body to a T. That when her treatment team said her weight had stayed pretty much consistent, they had definitely been lying, and she shouldn't have trusted them, and she should have tried on the dress more recently than eight days prior, and she never should have trusted them in the first place, actually, because this was what happens. You listen to people who claim they want what's best for you, only to be standing barefoot on argyle tile, too big for a dress that had cost a fortune, and now her eyes were prickling and she was going to ruin the makeup that had taken forty-five minutes to apply and that, if she was honest, made her face look like the surface of a dusty beige carpet.

Margot was trying not to grunt at the effort of holding the zipper closed, and Ana was trying to look casual about her inability to yank it up, but they were each three glasses of champagne in, and it was enough to take the edge off for each of them, even Lily, and she didn't mean to say it out loud, but she did. "I regret all of this," she said under her breath.

"What?" Margot asked, stepping away from Lily like she was going to explode. "What do you regret about it? The dress? It's not a big deal, Lil. The zipper's just stuck. Here, step out, we'll lube it up. It's fine. You're gorgeous."

Ana nodded. "One hundred percent."

"You guys." Her voice felt tight in her throat. She could see through the half-open door that Liza and Emily were picking at cheese cubes on a charcuterie board, staying busy, allowing Lily to have this private moment in the bathroom with Ana and Margot, honoring the sanctity of their freshman-year friendship, and it was kind of beautiful, honestly, all that they'd been through together, and suddenly the tears started to fall. And instead of saying, "Sorry, I don't know why I'm crying, it's just nerves," she said, "It's too tight. I knew it would be too tight, and now it's too tight, and it fit me literally eight days ago."

Margot: "I think I have an idea."

—

Thirty minutes later, Margot was careening Lily's mom's Jaguar toward the Portland exit.

"This is insane," Lily said, checking the time on her phone. "I'm literally getting married in four hours."

"I know," Margot said.

"I think we should not do this," Lily said. "I can just rewear the rehearsal-dinner dress. I'm gonna be late for my own wedding."

"You can't do that," Margot said, merging confidently.

"I don't know if I can handle it," Lily said. "Like, looking at myself in the mirror in another dress and letting some stranger manhandle me."

"Siobhan isn't like that," Margot said. "Trust me, Lil, okay?"

—

Margot knew Siobhan from some agency shoot. She'd been in set design for years, and then she'd left to pursue her passion, opened a small brick-and-mortar in downtown Portland, Maine, filled it with dresses she made herself, in a loft that overlooked the retail space.

"So we have to move fast, I understand," said the woman, ushering them all in. "Margot filled me in. I'm Siobhan, by the way," she said, hugging each of them. "Lily? Who's Lily?"

Siobhan ushered Lily to a rack before she could protest, her blue eyes lighting up as she walked Lily around. "So: real quick. It's not a bridal shop, per se. We have all kinds of event dresses, so don't limit yourself to white, right? I think we have time"—she checked her watch—"for you to try on maybe four? Just see what calls to you. I'll pull a few things I think are right."

"Okay," Lily said, her breath catching in her throat.

Siobhan plucked a dress from a rack, traced the tulle with her finger, put it back. "Just step here, Lily. That dress you're wearing is thin enough, no need to take it off. We have a bunch more sizes, by the way. I hated the way dress shops start in one size and clip you in, it's so demeaning. I had an eating disorder for many years, including around my wedding. So this shop sort of came out of that."

Lily looked at Margot meaningfully—clearly Margot prepped this woman on Lily's whole life story when she'd slipped out to the hallway to "make a quick call" and "fix this really quick"—but Margot just shrugged, as if she'd had no idea at all. Lily chose to believe her.

Lily stood in a corner of the dressing room, clad in only a lacy thong, and let Siobhan help her into a light-blue wrap dress that tied around her waist.

"I know blue isn't what you expected, but I really think it's such a light color, it's practically bridal, and it's so stunning with your coloring. Yeah, it fits you perfectly. I knew it would."

Lily looked in the mirror. Maybe it was the dim lighting in the dressing room, or the way the feathers on its hem distracted from her ankles, which she hated, or perhaps it was just that she was desperate: that nothing could be worse than walking down the aisle in a dress that didn't fit and knowing everyone would notice.

She took a deep breath in: focused on grounding herself, feeling the floor. Were these negative thoughts about her ankles really hers? Or were they internalized, stuff her mom had said about herself countless times throughout Lily's childhood? If she looked at herself objectively—not through a lens of automatic self-doubt, but as if she was someone she loved, Margot or Lily, for example—was it possible that she actually looked sort of healthy and beautiful? Was it possible that the width in her shoulders that she'd always been led by her mom to hate was not an objectively ugly part of her? That even though her mom would probably hate the feathers on the dress's bottom—"You don't like that, do you?"—maybe Lily actually liked them a lot?

She smiled, winked at herself, scoffed, because that was an embarrassing thing to do, even in private. She actually sort of almost liked how she looked.

She emerged, and they cheered. "Lily!" Margot said, clapping her hands to her mouth. "You are gorgeous."

"Thanks," Lily said, only a little self-conscious. "I guess this works."

Forty-Eight: Margot

Margot ushered Ana and Lily out the door, thanked Siobhan again, breathed out a sigh of relief.

Part of her had been bracing for the possibility that she'd lost her touch. That the situation with McQueen was indicative of the way she'd become: that she didn't have it in her to fix things and drive things and go go go the way she always had. She felt alive with her own power. "Let's do Confessions!" she said, a prickle in her chest as they all got back in the car.

"Wow," Ana said. "I almost forgot about Confessions."

"I know," Margot said, forgetting for a second that she and Ana were still kind of in a standoff. "Me, too. Isn't that kind of depressing?"

"I'm not really in the mood," Lily said. "Maybe after you guys go?"

"Fine," Margot said. "I'll start." She was nervous, but she wanted them to understand. "So, I guess I kind of met someone."

"Margot!" Lily said. "You were the one who made the rule: no boys at Confessions."

"That's the thing," Margot said, before she could question if it made sense to make the moments before Lily's wedding about Margot's budding relationship. "It's a she."

A pause that felt like forever.

"Oh!" Ana said. "Yay! Wait, have you been gay this whole time?"

Margot didn't expect her eyes to well. They were two exits from Kennebunkport. There definitely wouldn't be time to touch up her makeup.

"Honestly," Margot said, "I don't know. I mean, maybe yes, and there was a part of me that wasn't ready to fully admit it to myself?"

"Oh my god," Lily said. "The Keith comment! He told us at brunch, after you left. He called something gay? I can't believe you didn't tell us about this girl—" Her voice cracked. "Like, did you really think we would be anything but excited?"

"Oh my god, I did come out to Keith before anyone else in my entire life." She laughed.

"But why?" Ana asked, a little choked up, too. "You could have told us ages ago!"

"I know. Once I said I was maybe gay, do you remember? And you both were like, 'No way, I don't see that for you.' But that's so not the point. It was a different time, first of all, and I wouldn't have gotten there until now anyway, I don't think? And I don't even know what this means for sure, for the record, about my exact identity. It's just—I guess more about my sexual orientation to everything? Like, I was attracted to my job, and she's so *not*, this girl, and it's not that I'm trying to become her. I'm still myself. We haven't even been on an official date." Margot knew she was blushing. "She just makes me think about my priorities, I guess." She couldn't stop thinking about Alix: the way her face lit up when Margot had returned to buy another cabbage, about the freckles that were visible on the left side of her face but nearly indecipherable on the right, until you got up close. What it felt like to sit in a boat and watch buildings but actually kind of watch Alix instead. "She's a cabbage farmer, which is weird. Or, like, helping her farmer friend while she decides what's next. She's an ex-UX designer, to be clear. Not an actual farmer. Sorry. I'm rambling. I'm sorry for leaving Miami early. Honestly, I *was* kind of upset about the Keith comment. And about all the work I put into planning it, and the guys showing up—it sounds so self-involved now. I was just so focused on work—"

"And I'm sorry for giving you a hard time about that," Ana said. "I kinda blacked out. But I know I give you a hard time for prioritizing your work."

"Well," Margot said, "to be honest, you were onto something. I did indeed girlboss a bit too close to the sun." She told them about her forced sabbatical and about the days spent wandering the streets of Chicago, about the aimlessness that had left her bedridden, about the hopelessness that she'd felt deep in her chest. That maybe it had been there all along and she'd been running from it, busying herself with the full-time job of staying occupied.

"Fuck, now I feel even worse," said Ana.

"Don't," Margot said. "And, Lil, I'm really sorry for being a bitch in Miami. Clearly I was going through something, but I shouldn't have taken it out on you." She was speeding. "Sorry. I kind of co-opted this. Someone else go."

Forty-Nine: Ana

Margot took her eyes off the road and glanced at Ana. "Can you tell us what's actually up with Si?"

Ana rolled her eyes. "Fine. Okay. You're right, he's not sick."

"Obviously," Margot interjected.

"It was just—" She grasped at it: What was it? That she'd felt more at home during that weekend she'd stayed with Bryn and Max than she'd felt since moving into the apartment that she thought would solve all her problems? That she'd deluded herself into thinking that the problem with her relationship was her, that if she tried hard enough and wore the right clothes and took tennis lessons over the summer that eventually she'd fit in, that with enough effort everything would eventually feel effortless?

"You know how I was just so used to being this nerd that everyone thought was, like, quirky? Back in high school. And then I met you guys, and you both just treated me like a real person. Not some caricature of a girl who cared about school. You let me be everything I was, all at once: like, this spazzy, horny eighteen-year-old who lived for straight A's and also Comics Club. You showed me that I could take myself seriously. You didn't make fun of me for being exactly who I was. And I guess—maybe that was what I was missing with Silas all along. Like, taking me seriously. For being who I already was? You were right, Margot, that night in Miami. I don't know. He just—"

Margot cut her off. "Do you remember that time you and Silas broke up sophomore year, and I was rushing out the door, and you told me you really needed me?"

Ana did: Margot had been late for some meeting, elections or treasury review or something else that she'd talked about like it was laden with gravity. Ana missed the way things like that used to feel important to them. That had changed, once everything became so heavy.

Silas had done something annoying: forgotten Ana's birthday, maybe, or flirted in front of her—she couldn't even remember. But the point was, Ana had been inconsolable, and she'd watched Lily and Margot exchange meaningful glances, an entire hierarchization of priorities passing between them. Margot had that meeting, and Lily had some test the next morning, and neither of them wanted to leave Ana wallowing and alone, so Margot had ultimately taken one for the team, showed up for Ana when Ana needed her, skipped the meeting and braided Ana's hair, told her a story about a bear and a dog that her dad had told her when she was young. She'd been there for Ana. When push came to shove, that was the kind of friend Margot was.

"Yeah, I remember," Ana said. "You were there for me. I love you to death, Margot, and you've been there for me. Both of you. More than anyone else."

"I could be better, though," Margot said. "That night, after you fell asleep, I snuck out to the meeting. If I was a really good friend, I would have stayed. In case you needed me."

"It's fine," Ana said. "It was ages ago. And it wasn't like I was dying. I was just sad."

They passed the exit for Hawthorne.

"I shouldn't have snapped at you in Miami."

"It's okay," Ana said, and she meant it. She sighed. "I mean, you were right. It was kind of a cop-out to think Alistair could—" She paused. "What if Silas is the best I can ever do?"

"Oh, Ana," Margot said.

"He's the first guy you ever dated," said Lily. "There are so many more out there. Seriously, Ana. He's not as great as you think he is."

"It seems like everyone thinks that," Ana said. "Even my mom. Speaking of which, my mom was in the hospital, so I went home to Wisconsin."

"Jesus," Margot said. "She's okay?"

"Yeah, she's fine." Ana exhaled. "But going home was kind of weird? It's like—you know when you're at a café and everyone is on a laptop, working? My mom and I went out to breakfast one morning, and there was this book club meeting at the café—just a bunch of loud women, chatting like they were in someone's living room."

"That sounds like the kind of thing you'd love, Ana," Margot said.

"Yeah," Ana said. "Honestly, it did seem kind of nice."

"Do you think you'd ever move back to Wisconsin?"

"No—" She paused. "I mean, maybe. The school year's over soon. I thought I maybe wanted to go back to Oakbrook? But now I'm thinking, I don't know. The only reason I'm in San Francisco is because of Silas. Why not consider other options, too?"

"Like Chicago?" Margot said. "With me? You could see your mom more, right?"

"Hmm," Ana said. "It's worth considering, at least."

Fifty: Lily

Lily didn't feel like confessing anything.

"Um," she said. She couldn't believe this was her wedding day. "Well, I guess, in college I always felt this need to know stuff or whatever? Like, I knew a lot of the upperclassman boys from high school and you guys didn't, and I guess I thought you wanted me around because I could be a connector? It's something I've been talking about with Barri."

"I get that, but that's not really a confession," Margot said, taking her hands off the steering wheel for a second to emphasize her point.

She didn't know what to say. That she still hated her body? Or that she felt like a failure for not having a job, one that would give her two weeks off for a honeymoon that wouldn't even be happening because postponing it had been the only way her treatment team had let her take off the extended weekend for her wedding?

"Fine," Lily said. "I'm in treatment. And I tried to tell Margot in Miami—"

"Oh my god," Margot said. "I'm the fucking worst. I mean, I knew something was up when—the dress—and I didn't say anything . . ."

Ana was quiet in the back.

Lily almost told them not to worry, that it was totally fine.

But she really was working on being more honest. And she was kind of mad.

"Honestly, Margot, I tried to tell you in Miami and—I felt abandoned, okay? And you never followed up. And I've been trying to figure out what to do next, career-wise, and there's literally nothing relevant in Boston. And I'm entering marriage as this unemployed tradwife, which was never the goal, and I do want to stay home to raise kids eventually, but not now, and it's just been really hard. And you're both crushing it at work, and I just didn't want to say anything." A pause. "Honestly, I was embarrassed. About both things." Another pause. "And, Ana, I know we already talked about it a little. But the shit you said when you were blackout—you said I never have to worry about money or work, and it's just so not true. I worry about both those things all the time. Work, especially. I feel so aimless, you know? And Margot, you can sometimes make everything about you and your job, and it makes me feel like my work—well, lack thereof—doesn't matter."

A silence settled over them, stretching out like it might last forever. Lily resisted the urge to take it all back.

"Honestly, so valid," Margot said matter-of-factly.

"Are you sure?"

"One hundred percent," Margot said, taking her eyes off the road to look at Lily. "I've been waiting for you to be real with me like that since forever, Lil."

Lily started laughing. "Really?"

"Yeah. Of course. And yeah, Ana, you were kind of a drunk bitch in Miami, no offense."

Ana covered her eyes. "I am so, *so* sorry. Alistair was giving me this kind of attention that Silas had never given me, and—it doesn't matter. I drank too much because I was miserable in my own life. And took it out on you. I really fucked up. Please tell us about treatment. I am so, so sorry."

Lily wanted to tell Margot and Ana that it was hard, in some ways harder than last time, because now it was on her to decide if she actually wanted to get better. Not on her parents to leave her there and set the rules. She wanted to tell them that she didn't know if she really did want to get better at all. That in a twisted kind of way, everything was easier when she was a little bit sick. That it had always been easier to predict what people needed and give it to them than it was to take up the entire space allotted to her as a person on earth.

She wanted to tell Ana that she'd always known she was a million times better than anything Silas could ever hope to be, that their breakup had nothing to do with the thousands of ways that Ana had walked through the world with the knowledge that she was falling short, and everything to do with Silas: the way he could step into his power only when there was someone else there to prove to him that he deserved it. That Silas wielded his power over Ana like it would run out if he didn't practice. Lily had spent two whole therapy sessions unpacking this before her therapist had redirected her: "Lily," she said, "we're working on your tendency to put others' needs before your own, right? Do you think that maybe you're talking about Ana and her life to avoid talking about your own needs?"

"Treatment is okay," Lily tried. "Hard, actually."

"Back to what you said earlier," Ana said. "I'm sorry we let you feel—I mean, that's a big burden. To feel, for so many years, like we were more into what you brought to our lives than we were into *you*. Or that you were in charge of everything, or had to have this all-knowing role or whatever. But, like, it meant a lot to me, just so you know. You were the first person who was serious and who took me seriously. You made me feel like a real person."

"Ana, I didn't do that for you," Lily said. "Those kids in high school were just trying to put you into some childish box that you'd outgrown way before they'd even learned precalc, you know?"

They were nearing the house.

"I'm really glad this isn't Ana and Silas's wedding," Margot said.

Lily braced for Ana's reaction.

"No, for real," Ana said. "Jack is such an unproblematic king. Like, every single thing has been insane, but I've really never wondered about whether or not he was the right guy for you."

"I feel the same way," Lily said, blinking back the start of tears.

"Then let's do this," Margot said.

Lily grabbed the dress, and they ran into the house, together.

Fifty-One: Ana

They raced back to the room where the other girls were milling about, drinking champagne and zipping each other into their dresses.

"Girls!" said Cameron, going to Lily, hands on her shoulders. "We steamed your dresses. How was it? All good?"

Margot pulled Lily's dress out of its bag. "Cameron, steam this, yeah? It's a little creased from the drive. Em," she said, jutting her chin in Emily's direction, "touch up Ana's eyes? She smudged them from crying."

Ana sat, let Emily recurl her eyelashes, her breath cool on Ana's forehead.

"What's Si up to?" Emily asked. "Look up for me?"

"Well," Ana said, feeling lighter after their drive, like maybe her life could exist without him. Like maybe it would actually be a lot better. "We broke up."

"Oh!" Emily said, standing back. "Ana, I'm so sorry! Are you okay? The tears, of course—I'll stop asking!"

"No, no," Ana said. "Actually, they were happy tears, and it's totally fine. I mean, it's still technically a break? But, like, I don't want him back."

Emily cocked her head, told Ana to close her eyes.

It was almost funny, after all this time, all these years of thinking that Silas held the key to the world, that it was easier, freer, to be here without him, somewhere along the way, Ana had grown into herself, and it had been Silas, not Ana, who'd been holding her back.

"Yeah," Emily said, brushing Ana's lashes, "I never really liked that guy."

"You and everyone else," Ana said.

Fifty-Two: Lily

Twenty-two minutes until the wedding.

Lily looked in the mirror. "To be honest, treatment might be working? Like, I don't hate how I look. Which sounds pathetic, but is actually kind of a big deal?"

"Lily, you look really, really beautiful," said Ana. "That doesn't sound pathetic at all." Margot joined them at the mirror, and it was just like freshman year: dancing at their reflections and making grainy videos and taking the rest of their lives for granted.

Margot turned away, and Lily grabbed her, pulled her back. "I just want to look at us for a second," she said.

"God, that's cheesy," Margot said, rolling her eyes but smiling. Lily could tell it meant something to her, too.

Lily was still in the cotton dress she'd worn to the fitting, and Cameron was running a steamer down the new dress once more, while the old dress hung on its hanger. Now she was back, waiting patiently for Cameron to finish.

"Em," Lily said, "can you just undo all this shit the makeup artist did and do me the way you used to?"

Emily had always been the one to get them ready: She'd rubbed Vaseline and tinted pastes on their cheeks back when everyone their age was caked in foundation. She'd filled in their brows when everyone else was waxing them. She'd shown them how to highlight the way they already looked back when everyone else had been contouring their cheeks into submission.

"'Course. Let me see what I can do."

—

She wished she was wearing shapewear underneath her dress. She worried that she'd look stiff in the pictures, that the mirror she'd used earlier was deceiving her, that she'd look at the photos when they came back and feel disgusted at herself for ever even trying with anything.

Ana was single and Margot was exploring something new and Jack was waiting for her and her mom was going to freak out when she saw that her daughter wasn't wearing the dress she'd gone to great lengths and great expense to have customized for her.

But when she closed her eyes and grabbed for Margot's and Ana's hands, she could feel everything. It had been so gradual, the way she'd slipped into numbness: The less she ate, the less she felt, and the less she felt, the less she ate. It had felt, at the beginning, like flying or gliding, like she'd hacked her existence and all she had to do was stay disciplined, fit herself to the mold of what was asked of her, and in exchange, she could avoid disappointing anyone.

And now, she didn't have that. She had a breakfast burrito inside her and it was doing its thing, breaking down in her system and forcing her to be present.

She didn't feel like the prettiest, best, happiest bride-iest version of herself. But at least she could feel.

And maybe this was what milestones were all about: doubting yourself and worrying about everything and walking down the aisle anyway.

Jack was her person. Ana and Margot were her people. Most of life was awkward and hard. But then there were glimmers—crying over

Confessions in the car with your best friends or feeling the familiar breath of your makeup-artist friend or explaining to your husband-to-be why grapes made you cry and then finding him sprawled out on the couch reading a book called *Understanding Anorexia*—when everything kind of made sense.

Fifty-Three: Ana

Ana was first, arm in arm with Alistair, just like they'd practiced yesterday, walking down the grassy aisle toward a chuppah that backed the ocean. The waves broke on the rocky shore, but the guitarist was louder. Everyone was sitting in chairs with bows on their backs, made up and smiling stupidly. Ana wondered what Silas was doing now: probably working on a Saturday or walking the Lyon Street steps with his mom, or missing Ana or not thinking about Ana at all.

Ana held her bouquet to the base of her bra line, just like she'd been told. She matched her stride to Alistair's, stepped carefully in the grass, taking care to not twist her ankle or let her heel sink into the dirt, wondered if they'd hook up later, then pushed the thought away, because that wasn't what this was about. Took her spot at the chuppah, watched Margot and Emily and Liza and Cameron and Zoe and Eileen make their way down the aisle, too, arm in arm with all these men.

And finally, there was Lily, her face natural, her veil in the breeze behind her, light crinkles at her eyes just barely visible from here.

Ana watched the crowd's eyes collectively widen, taking in Lily in blue, their eyes welling up like Lily had been instrumental to them turning into women, too.

And it all made Ana kind of sad. She knew it wasn't about her: She should be happy that her friend was marrying someone so wonderful and caring and kind, who'd made a point of pulling Ana aside and telling her how happy he was that she was there, that he was so sorry about the breakup, that he loved her—he loved her!—and that he was so grateful for her role in Lily's recovery. He was wonderful, mature, and emotionally available. He was an anchor for Lily; Ana saw it in the way Lily placed her palm on his forearm to steady herself, or grabbed at his pinkie when she didn't want to hold his entire hand.

But still. It felt like loss.

Her Lily, careening into the rest of her life. That the three of them were and would continue to grow up and away from each other. That they were the only people who really *knew* Ana, and yet, they'd been turning away from each other for years, anchored by moments like the one in the car, like this one now, but pulled apart by everything else: taking care of parents and one day kids and always themselves. Keeping up with everyone and everything that wasn't each other.

Life was moving on, and they'd always be each other's college friends, that prefix appended. As she stood facing all the guests, as everyone cheered, Ana thought that it was a little unfair: that Ana would always be Lily's best friend *from college*, and that Jack would get to be Lily's husband, full stop.

Ana and Lily and Margot would be friends until they died, but they'd never again open up their minds for the first time in each other's presence, late at night from where each of them lay on their respective beds. Marriage was a good thing. Lily's recovery was a good thing. Margot exploring her sexuality—unequivocally, a good thing. Even Ana's breakup was a good thing.

But still, it made Ana want to melt into the grass. Lily said I do, and Ana's tears were probably ruining her makeup, but so were everyone's.

Cheers, cocktails, speeches, a dinner of salad and lobster and potatoes and corn and cake. More speeches. First dance, Lily twirling and twirling, light as a cloud. Everyone tipsy, cheeks sore from singing.

"Hey," Lily said, running barefoot across the grass to the dance floor, her hair blowing in the wind. She looked young and lithe, and Ana almost cried at the sight of her. She must have disappeared for a bit—it was that part of the night when time became meaningless, and Ana hadn't even noticed. She looked around, realized that all the old people had called it a night and the crowd around her had dwindled to twenty or so—mostly friends of Lily's and Jack's, a smattering of cousins.

"I had an idea," Lily said, her breath hot on Ana's face.

Jack was there, too, a hand on Lily's back. "I told her she's crazy, it's not even warm yet. But I can't talk her out of it."

"Out of what?" Ana asked.

"I want to jump in the ocean," Lily said, pointing to the edge of the field, where the grass turned into rocks that jutted into the Atlantic.

"Did you say 'ocean'?" Margot asked, kicking off her shoes as she ran off the dance floor and toward them. "Done."

Ana looked out at the water warily, then kicked off her shoes, too.

Soon they were all at the water: Ana and Margot and Lily and everyone else their age, boys and girls shivering in various states of undress, plunging into the jet-black cold, treading inky water, their hands and feet like paddles under the ocean's dark surface.

Acknowledgments

Thank you to Rebecca Gradinger and Laurie-Maude Chenard. This book has both of your brilliance on every page; thank you for believing in me, teaching me what plot is, and cheering me on. Your vision, guidance, and attention to detail are deep in each sentence and pretty much run through my blood. I am so lucky. Thank you to Nancy Holmes, who understood the soul of this book immediately, and whose eagle-eyed, visionary edits made this novel a trillion times better. You are a brilliant editor and a steadfast friend, and I'm convinced we were writer/editor in a past life, likely during the Renaissance. Thanks to Ronit Wagman for more stunning edits: Very few writers agree with basically everything their editing team suggests, and I feel very lucky to be among that small group.

Thanks to Lindsey Cherek Waller, whose art graces the cover of this book, and Tree Abraham, whose art direction I have to thank for putting my name on a cover for the first time ever, which is still surreal! The scream I scrumpt when I saw what you two had dreamed up! Lily, Ana, and Margot definitely each have a poster of this cover in their homes and would be your biggest fangirls (as am I).

Thank you to my early and enthusiastic readers, especially Cindy Frank, Dantiel Moniz, Jackie Chalghin, Koby Frank, and Teddy Frank. Then my friends: There would be no *Girls Our Age* without the way you taught me to love and be loved. Very special thanks to Arianna Cameron, Caroline Coles, Charlotte Alimanestianu, Emily Schleier, Emily Serwer,

Emma Beecher, Emma Effinger (great harbinger of writerly knowledge), Hy Khong, Jared Feldman, Matthew Gutschenritter, and Peter Powers (honorary Girls Our Age), Lindsay Picard, Skye Aresty, and Sophie Janes: You've hyped me up and believed in my work, many of you since well before there was anything to believe in. Learning and growing up with you makes life fun and meaningful. And Sophie and Charlotte deserve an extra callout: The gift of boundarylessness that Moore Hall gave us freshman year has shaped so much of what I know about friendship. I could write a whole book on that. So I did!

Thank you to my mom, Nina Frank, for reading countless drafts and catching even more typos, for telling everyone she knows to preorder my book (and she seems to know everyone), for being my earliest and most frequent reader, and for encouraging me to live the life that ultimately made me a writer. I am so lucky. Thanks to my dad, Lee Kranefuss, for the friendly competition as we raced to release our respective books first, and for supporting my love of learning since always. Thanks to Eli and Eva Kranefuss for being my built-in lifelong best friends, and for being smart, thoughtful, and wonderful siblings—I am endlessly lucky to have grown up, and to continuously grow up, with you both. Thank tons to the Thompsons for welcoming and supporting me: I love being part of your family. You are the best.

A million thank-yous to my teachers. Annie Gordon, who encouraged me in fifth grade to keep a notebook to write down my thoughts and ideas, which has stuck with me ever since. To the singular Lynda Barry, who helped me rediscover unbridled creativity. From the Bowdoin English Department: Brock Clarke, who taught me what it means to read and write fiction; Emma Maggie Solberg, who taught me rigor; Marilyn Reizbaum, who taught me to look deeper and try again; Morten Hansen, who taught me to believe in my own ideas; and Tess Chakkalakal, who taught me readerly persistence. And thank you to Barry Mills and Jonathan Goldstein.

To the writers who inspire me most: J. Courtney Sullivan, Jean Hanff Korelitz, Joan Didion, Kiley Reid, Lauren Groff, Meg Wolitzer, and Taffy Brodesser-Akner. Thanks for giving me everything to aspire to.

And thank you, most of all, to my husband, Chase Thompson, for believing in me way before I believed in myself; for encouraging me every step of the way; for building a life with me; for making me a happier, more complete person; and for saying "obviously" each time this book made it the next step toward publication. When we were twenty-five, you taught me about spreadsheets, and ever since, I've been tracking my words per day. And that's a metaphor: You've been the backbone, the rigor, and the consistency to everything good I've done. Thank you for knowing and loving me as deeply as you do. I love you endlessly. I can't wait to be parents with you.

About the Author

Photo © 2024 Sasha Eck

Phoebe Thompson writes about female friendship, mothers and daughters, and money. She studied English literature at Bowdoin College, got her MFA in fiction at the University of Wisconsin–Madison, and runs a marketing agency in Brooklyn, New York. For more information, follow her at @phoebethompsonwrites or visit www.phoebethompsonwrites.com.